Elegy

on

Kinderklavier

Arna Bontemps Hemenway

Sarabande S Books

LOUISVILLE, KENTUCKY

FIRST EDITION

Managing Editor
Sarabande Books, Inc.
2234 Dundee Road, Suite 200
Louisville, KY 40205

Library of Congress Cataloging-in-Publication Data

Hemenway, Arna Bontemps, 1987–
[Short stories. Selections]
Elegy on Kinderklavier : stories / Arna Bontemps Hemenway.—FIRST EDITION.
    pages cm
Includes bibliographical references and index.
ISBN 978-1-936747-76-4 (paperback : acid-free paper)
I. Title.
PS3608.E4735A6 2014
813'.6—dc23

2013031147

Cover and interior layout by Kirkby Gann Tittle.

Manufactured in Canada.

This book is printed on acid-free paper.

Sarabande Books is a nonprofit literary organization.

This project is supported in part by an award from the National Endowment for the Arts.

The Kentucky Arts Council, the state arts agency, supports Sarabande Books with state tax dollars and federal funding from the National Endowment for the Arts.

As always, for George—

Contents

Elegy on Kinderklavier

The Fugue

Wild Turkey wakes up. It's the last day of June, and an early summer thunderhead has marched across the peripheral Kansas plain (the lights of town giving out to the solid pitch of farmland) while Wild Turkey slept. He knew it was coming, the lightning spidering forth behind and then above him last night as he walked, the air promising the rain that is now, as he blinks in the thin blue morning, making the rural highway overpass above his head drone, a room of sound below.

Wild Turkey lifts himself out from the body-shaped concrete depression that nestles just under the eaves of the overpass—that word too big for the little nexus; really it's just one lonely county road overlapping another. He knew to sleep here last night because of the rain and because he saw the overpass was old enough to have this body-shaped concavity, a "tornado bed" they used to call it, and now he reaches up into the dark of the girder's angle and feels around until he finds the ancient survival box for those erstwhile endangered motorists: a flashlight that doesn't work, a rusted weather radio, and—yes—a bottle of water, thick with dust, but Wild Turkey is thirsty and doesn't care. He stands and stretches on the sloped

concrete bank, against the theater of the rain. He was right about the long night-walk out along the country road being good for coming down, the darkness being good for discouraging one of his fits, but wrong about being able to make it to the school before morning.

He makes it to the school now, in the rain, sopping wet. The school is, as it ever was, more or less in the middle of a cornfield, and the thick leaves and stalks cough in the rain as Wild Turkey comes once again upon the old buildings. He rounds the tiny campus in the storm as if he is still in junior high, still traipsing from class to class in the cloying polo and khaki uniform. Now, as then, he does not fail to think of the strangeness of time when he sees the buildings—themselves somehow eternal-feeling, always but only half in ruin. Even in use (back then, as an ad hoc Episcopalian school, and now, apparently repurposed as a childcare center) the moldering white portables and darkly aging main brick building sit in situ, oblivious.

Standing on the concrete path alongside the portables and trying to look into the darkened window of an abandoned room, Wild Turkey has one of his little gyres in time—a brief one, only sending his mind back to those moments when he just an hour ago woke under the little bridge—and he realizes he woke thinking of Mrs. Budnitz, his second-grade teacher, specifically of the rank, slightly fetid scent that would occasionally waft subtly from somewhere inside her gingham dress on a tendril of air in the last weeks of school before summer—though the scent or smell itself wasn't subtle at all but sharp, rich, pungent, even vaguely sweet, like the smell of human shit anywhere outside a bathroom. Nor was it really a smell so much as an *emanation*, or at least that's how it'd seemed to Wild Turkey, sitting on the carpet in the middle of the room, transfixed by this sense delivered to him on the wavering bough of the window fan's breeze.

They did not have air conditioning installed in their classroom yet, and the heat and consequent sweat, secreted beneath Mrs.

Budnitz's plain, sturdy dresses and folds of fat and thigh, probably amplified the smell. It was only noticeable every ninth or tenth breath and so not really something Wild Turkey ever felt he could speak or complain about. But it was distinctly sexual, or carnal in its fleshy, mildly lurid bodiliness—in its intimate note of vaginal musk, though, of course, this particular understanding would only come later, the experience at the time being importantly a momentary one. The scent refused to linger, and so existed for Wild Turkey mostly in the wince of shame at his own interest, in the same way he sometimes at that age lingered for just a few seconds too long in the school's bathroom over the shit-stained toilet paper in his hand before flushing it, feeling a rush of something he didn't understand. It was oddly comforting, in the end.

And why this smell now, or rather, then, upon waking—why does it chase him? Maybe this school harkens his mind back to that other classroom, Wild Turkey thinks. Though really it's the feeling of it as he drifted on the carpet in Mrs. Budnitz's classroom during nap time, the confluence of those two sensations—drifting helplessly into a tired, sweaty sleep; drifting helplessly into that intriguing, somewhat disgusting scent. It was a kind of surrender, a voiding of the mind; a reversion to some preinfantile state of abandon. He's been finding the declensions of that experience in his life ever since, often as he falls asleep, or which he wakes into: the stagnant air of soiled women's bed linen and spilt chamber pot in the small house in Ramadi; the attenuated scent of the bare bed after he and Merry Darwani had anal sex for the first time; the closeness of the rain-soured, coppery metal of the small bridge's girding. Wild Turkey is used to his life proceeding this way: this or that detail of his day stepping down out of some first world of previous, essential experience. These sensate allusions are always only whiffs or pale imitations of the original, in the same way that the rainy, pallid light now breaking

from the clouds as the morning regains its heat is cousin to the small fist of bright fire over the limbs of the girl in the courtyard in Ramadi, or the rhythmic flash of the tactical grenade's phosphorous strobe, and all three are mere shavings of the pure white lightning of one of Wild Turkey's fits.

He turns away from the window. There is nothing to see here. It was stupid to come. He begins the long walk back.

•

Wild Turkey wakes up. He's eight years old, on his back in the middle of the wheat field that has sprung up by chance in the sprawling park behind his parents' subdivision. He does not know why he's on his back, does not remember how he got there. Strangely, however, he does remember what happened just before he woke up, which is that he had his first fit (though he doesn't know to call it that yet, knows only the image lingering spectacularly in his retinas, in the theater of his mind). He'd been running through the field, feeling the itchy stalks resist his stomping feet, and then he'd been standing in the field, caught up by something in the air, by a small flash in the sky, and then he was looking and looking and seeing only the beauty of the high afternoon sun on the blurry tips of the wheat as it rose and fell on the invisible currents of wind. Like on a seafloor, he thought, just before the brightening in the sky, before it turned in a flash into an overwhelming field of white lightning, so much and so close that he remembers nothing else.

Later, he will not tell the Marine recruiters or doctors about the fits, but will have one anyway on the first night of initiation, before he even gets to boot camp proper. He will be among the guys at the long tables in the gym of the local armory building: the recruits being

kept awake all night, forced to keep their hands flat out in front of them, hovering four inches above the tabletop. They are not allowed to move, or to move their hands, or to let their hands touch the tabletop. Then, the lightning.

"Why did you let me stay?" he will ask later, toward the end of actual boot camp, and the instructors will explain (allowing their voices to dilate a little with respect) how he'd looked, sitting there seizing, his hands the only part of him held perfectly still, four inches above the table. Though Wild Turkey will suspect the truthfulness of this, seeing as how he woke up in the wetness of the ditch outside the armory building, his white shirt stained with blood from the tips of the chain-link fence he hopped (he guesses) to escape, the faces of the instructors pale moons in their huddle above him. Eventually he will get medicine for his fits, but the medicine will make him spacey, drowsy—the medicine itself, in effect, simulating the aftereffects of the fits—and so Wild Turkey will be unable to parse his waking. It will never be clear to him whether he is waking from a lacunal fit, the medicine, or a memory, as if all three are essentially the same thing.

•

Wild Turkey wakes up, but Jeannie has already left the bed. Wild Turkey can see her, if he hangs off the side of the mattress, down the narrow hallway: the bathroom door ajar, the bathroom light golden and warm in the cool, cesious fall morning. They're at his place, the duplex right on top of the train tracks, across the street from the college. Jeannie is doing her hair, naked, still overheated from the shower. She stands in front of the mirror quietly, getting ready for class or work, he can't remember which she has today. He's been home from his deployment for two weeks now and he still can't get a

hold of time. In the afternoons he gets in the shower, wastes no minutes, gets out to find it's two hours later.

Last night Wild Turkey took Jeannie out to the old school buildings, overgrown as they are, stilled between their days as the school he and Jeannie went to together and its current incarnation as some daycare's repurposed space. This was something they did in high school too, back when Jeannie still had her green Mustang convertible; late October nights they'd drive out there with sleeping bags and put the top down and park in the middle of the erstwhile baseball field, already half-reclaimed by brush, and look at the stars. The buildings were abandoned even back then, or between abandonments; Wild Turkey and Jeannie having decamped for the public high school, the original private school having finally amassed enough nonscholarship families to fund a new building (itself a repurposed old country club) inside city limits.

Later still last night, after they'd gotten too cold and come back to his duplex, Wild Turkey had lain down naked with Jeannie on his mattress, which was on the floor, and curled his body around her in-turning fetal position and called out, "Jeannie in a bottle!" which was one of their old jokes, and she'd laughed, sounding half-annoyed at her own easy nostalgic amusement, but then Wild Turkey had repeated it and repeated it, "Jeannie in a bottle! Jeannie in a bottle! Jeannie in a bottle! Jeannie in a bottle! Jeannie in a bottle! Jeannie in a bottle! Jeannie in a bottle! Jeannie in a bottle! Jeannie in a bottle! Jeannie in a bottle! Jeannie in a bottle! Jeannie in a bottle! Jeannie in a bottle! Jeannie in a bottle! Jeannie in a bottle! Jeannie in a bottle! Jeannie in a bottle! Jeannie in a bottle! Jeannie in a bottle! Jeannie in a bottle!" over and over, with just enough slight vocal modulation and wavering emphasis as to keep it from seeming like a glitch, repeating and repeating, which he did helplessly, "Jeannie in a bottle! Jeannie in a bottle! Jeannie in a bottle! Jeannie in a bottle! Jeannie in a bottle! Jeannie in a bottle! Jeannie

in a bottle! Jeannie in a bottle! Jeannie in a bottle! Jeannie in a bottle! Jeannie in a bottle! Jeannie in a bottle! Jeannie in a bottle! Jeannie in a bottle! Jeannie in a bottle! Jeannie in a bottle! Jeannie in a bottle! Jeannie in a bottle! Jeannie in a bottle! Jeannie in a bottle! Jeannie in a bottle! Jeannie in a bottle!" on and on until the sound became extenuated, then lost all tone, then resolved briefly into song before crumbling into over-articulation, each alien phoneme distinct and meaningless. Eventually he'd stopped. Jeannie lay there very quiet, very still, stiffened as she had been from somewhere around the twentieth or twenty-fifth repetition. Then, in the silence after Wild Turkey's voice had ceased, when it was clear he had really stopped, when he finally released her, she very carefully unfolded herself up from the bed and walked silently to the bathroom. Though Wild Turkey knows at some point she must've returned to bed (did she? or did she sleep on the couch?), her presence now in the bathroom seems contiguous to her presence there last night, which makes it hard for Wild Turkey to tell how much time has passed, if any has passed at all.

She finishes doing her hair and makeup and gets dressed in silence. She does not avoid looking at Wild Turkey; she holds his eyes as she pulls on her jeans one leg at a time before turning and letting herself out, her expression level, empty of anger, empty of assessment. When she gets back, if she comes back to the duplex instead of her own apartment, Wild Turkey will be there or he won't, she's already used to that.

•

Wild Turkey wakes up, the voices of the other men in the unit insistent. They're all in the dining area of the forward operating base, talking to the doctors from the casualty attachment, which

is something the other guys on the team get a kick out of, Wild Turkey's never known why. It's Pizza Hut night, which is why the team is all out here in the base's main area, the only real chance for the team and the doctors both to see each other, before the former, their day just beginning now that it's nightfall, slouch back into the restricted access staging area and ready themselves for their next operation.

Someone is telling the story of how Wild Turkey got his name. Wild Turkey can't see who is speaking, but it doesn't really matter as the story is now collective, accessed by anyone on the team, each small contortion of detail sponsored by the men's own willingness.

It was back in Carolina, before the team was strictly assembled, when they were all still loosely gathered at the base waiting to be repurposed. It was the day before Thanksgiving and the commander in charge of the base had a vaguely sadistic obsession with getting the men prepared for the Suck, high concern over the lack of regulatory discipline etcetera, and so had ordered for the men no Thanksgiving meal, and had replaced that order with several shipments of turkey and mashed potato and cranberry sauce MREs, which were dried out, reconstituted, ready-to-eat, etcetera etcetera, and so Wild Turkey (though he wasn't called that yet) had gone prowling during one of the exercises in the golden leaves of the fall woods, and gotten God's Grace to go with him.

God's Grace was Bob Grace, a gentle-faced, soft-spoken man from Tennessee, eventually included on the team mostly for his perfect marksmanship. He was religious, though very passive about it, and ended up being God's Grace because he often said "God's grace" in a kind of summarizing way when he saw something that made him feel like speaking. Later, Wild Turkey would see God's Grace get shot through the neck while their vehicle was stalled in traffic at an intersection in Tikrit. This day, though, God's Grace

stood calmly at the tree line as Wild Turkey crawled forward slowly over the rural highway, which they weren't supposed to cross.

"So Wild Turkey's out there, doing this dumbass crab-crawl across the highway because just on the other side what has he seen but three fat old birds, turkeys, wild turkeys, rooting around there in the ditch on the other side of the road and this is a no-discharge drill and Wild Turkey's got long underwear on beneath his gear and hasn't brought his knife, so he's going to do god knows what—wring their necks, or whatever, but only if he can get close enough to grab one of them. Anyway, good old Wild Turkey hears a sound and must be real hungry or maybe just a pussy because he spooks and takes off sprinting at the birds, who of course just completely lose their fucking shit. We're watching this all on the helmet cam back at the comms camp, laughing our fucking asses off."

"So what happens?" one of the doctors, a bald little man with glasses, asks.

"They fucking scatter, is what happens, because Wild Turkey's a fucking idiot. You can't chase down a turkey. And so we're all on the line in his earpiece giving him all this shit about it and what happens just at that exact moment but a semi comes tearing around the corner of this bumfuck nowhere little road and almost kills Wild Turkey, who dives out of the way, only to find, when he gets up, that the fucking semi has taken three of the birds' heads clean off."

There'd been blood all over the highway. Wild Turkey had lain there in the ditch, shaking. In the concussive silence after the semi's blasting passage, Wild Turkey heard God's Grace shift in the leaves behind him. He'd retrieved the headless birds, was holding them out to Wild Turkey.

"God's grace," God's Grace had said.

Mostly they call Wild Turkey "Wild Turkey," the full name. Sometimes one or two of the black guys call him Jive Ass Turkey,

with an unknown level of aggressive irony. Once, after the courtyard in Ramadi, Wild Turkey heard one of the newer guys ask someone in the bunks about him, heard whoever it was readjust their head on the stiff cot before answering, "That's Wild, man, that's just Wild," in that ambiguous way that seemed to mean both the adjective and the proper noun. Ever since Bob Grace got killed, when they mention Bob at all they just smile and call him Gracie, like he was one of their lovers from back in the world that accidentally found himself there with them in the desert.

Wild Turkey has always been mesmerized by their language, the team's utilitarian military patois always morphing what they said just enough to approximate some slightly more surreal world, a language somehow better suited to the world they are actually confronted with. Often the unthinking word or slight lingual shift ends up being eerily or confusingly apt, in the way that Wild Turkey's friend the TOW missile gunner whom they call Tow Head really does resemble a "towheaded boy" (the phrase surfacing in Wild Turkey's mind from some old novel read in a high school English class), or in the way that Wild Turkey will end up buying fifths of Wild Turkey to take the edge off his highs back at home. The Shit, meaning the desert, the war, Iraq, becomes the Suck becomes the Fuck becomes the Fug becomes the Fugue, finally meaning just everything.

•

Wild Turkey wakes up. He's sitting in the rear corner of his brother's large backyard patio, the snow having fallen so gently and quietly while he slept that he is now covered with its soft, undisturbed angles. Wild Turkey wakes to the sound of his brother carefully closing the patio door behind him so as not to wake Wild Turkey's sister-

in-law; wakes to the click of the motion-sensor light, which his brother has forgotten to turn off, tripping on. His brother approaches the wrought-iron patio table that Wild Turkey sits at, and sets down the familiar foil-wrapped plate. It is very late, and very cold, but the snow has quieted everything.

Wild Turkey's brother is an associate minister or junior minister, Wild Turkey can't remember the exact title, at one of the local churches. Few people in the town know they're brothers. They only grew up together until the age of thirteen, when their mother died and they went to the group home and Wild Turkey couldn't bear to go along to the better group home, the one that required adoption by the church or some family in the church. There'd been something so disgusting to Wild Turkey about the idea that they (the potentially adopted boys) should see their adoption and transport as "God's grace," which is what the man who came to talk to the two brothers said they should think of it as. He just couldn't bring himself to do it and so his brother got out of the state home and he didn't. They got along, though, after that, understood each other in some basic way; the brutality of that state group home (at least for those two months when they'd been fresh meat) a kind of dark night of the soul for both of them, forcing each to make his own manner of unfeeling calculation as to down which road salvation, etcetera, he guesses.

Now Wild Turkey's brother sits down heavily in the snowy chair across from Wild Turkey. He sighs, rests the side of his face in his hand. He's tired, equanimously perplexed by Wild Turkey, by his continued presence here these occasional nights.

The first time Wild Turkey came to his brother's house it was for the same reason as this time: he needed to eat. This is one thing Wild Turkey knows his brother's wife hates about him: she sees him as needlessly homeless, and as what she calls in her unselfconsciously

cute little way a "drughead." Both of these assessments are more or less fair, insofar as Wild Turkey does technically have a home back at the duplex (he was officially evicted when he stopped paying rent, but then the building was foreclosed upon and Wild Turkey has just kept living there, the color of the notices on his front door changing every few weeks, but nobody really bothering him about it) and yet he sleeps under bridges sometimes, or on the street, or in the fields, or spends all night walking around high or low on the pills he ingests. Paradoxically, Wild Turkey's sister-in-law doesn't count the duplex as a home, mostly, Wild Turkey guesses, due to the fact that three of the walls now have huge gaping holes, covered only by minimally effective plastic tarp, from where the landlord removed the windows to sell before the bank could take them. Though, in his own defense, it's also true that Wild Turkey doesn't have any money: he gave almost all of it to Jeannie, minus some he gave to Merry Darwani for her broken jaw and some he gave to Tow Head for his new gun. Wild Turkey doesn't want the money. He brought back from Iraq enough pills to stay in Dexedrine for as long as he wants, and so doesn't really need any money. Sometimes he eats with Jeannie. Sometimes he eats at the shelter. Sometimes he doesn't eat.

Wild Turkey's brother watches him unwrap the plate of leftovers and begin to eat. Neither says anything.

The first time he came to his brother's to eat, Wild Turkey stood in the dining room afterward and listened to his brother help his wife with the dishes in the kitchen. The house was quiet and oddly peaceful in the nighttime lull. Wild Turkey knew his brother and sister-in-law wanted children but had none. His brother's wife had been silent all through dinner. Wild Turkey's brother had talked about his ministry.

Standing there that first time, Wild Turkey heard his brother in the kitchen apologize, his wife sigh.

"It's like with a dog," she said. "If you feed him, he'll just keep coming back."

The look on his brother's face, when Wild Turkey had then risen and peered into the dim kitchen through the half-open door, was exquisitely pained: torn, it seemed to Wild Turkey, between his love for this woman and his real feeling of charity, of grace. His face, upon his return to the dining room (had Wild Turkey stayed around to see it, he's sure), full of resignation at this discrepancy between the practical and theoretical theologies of love, or charity, or whatever.

Now his brother is very still, watching him eat. He does this each time. Wild Turkey doesn't know if the irony of the arrangement—of him now being actually fed like a stray dog: secretly, guiltily, on the back porch, with the implied hope that he *will* keep coming back— is lost on his brother's wife, who tacitly allows it. He doesn't blame her. Wild Turkey knows she was friends with a man in a Bible study group in her old hometown who'd gone on an outreach mission early on in the supposedly safer Kurdish north and been kidnapped and was now missing, presumably beheaded. He knows she has, at some level of consciousness, transferred her anger and grief onto Wild Turkey himself, whom she is convinced committed his own atrocities in Iraq.

"I am the least of you," Wild Turkey's brother says now, in a kind of bored wonderment, and Wild Turkey isn't sure if he's quoting scripture or paraphrasing scripture or if he has hit, in his unintentional summary of several of Jesus' sentiments, an ambiguous middleground in which he can just say something and mean it, or want very much to mean it. Neither speaks. The motion sensor light trips back off, and they are thrown again into darkness.

•

Wild Turkey wakes up in the desert. He's in a slight, body-shaped depression at the base of a mud wall, over the edge of which sits the fake village. This is a training exercise, the last preparation for the grab team before they go over to the Shit. They are in Arizona. Wild Turkey lies still, listening to the grumbling of the other guys on the team, and watches the mud ruins (fake? real?) seep with the grays and blue of the thin winter sunset.

Sometime before zero dark, Wild Turkey stands paused in his position in the team's tactical column, lined up against the exterior wall of one of the village houses. Inside he can hear the muted noise of a radio. In a minute, at the first man's signal (two consecutive blips of static on the radio earpiece) the men will go into their suite of motion, so practiced and efficient and many-parted as to seem almost balletic. Wild Turkey, who is the Defense Intelligence Agency officer attached to the team (which really just means he is responsible for the confirmed identification of team extraction targets), breathes in the quiet, in the dark. He closes his eyes and thinks through what is about to happen, the steps so familiar, mechanical, though less in the way of machines than of soul-hollowing boredom. This is why these men were chosen for the grab team, Wild Turkey has often reflected in these moments: because they will do this with perfect disinterest, not keyed-up, not even eager in the way of the adrenalized Army kids.

But what Wild Turkey thinks of now in the eternal moments before the twin blips throw the night into action is where he is standing, is the fake village, meant to be a simulation but really more of a simulacrum, a psychological agent at play in the men's imaginations. It's all an effort, really, at making their imagination of what they will soon face in Iraq "more real," if such a thing makes sense, Wild Turkey thinks. As if anything could be more or less real than anything else, as if all reality isn't contained in every instance of it, this

desert being very apropos of all this in that it really is indistinguishable from the Iraqi desert (though Wild Turkey will only confirm this later) and so contains that other reality, or is contiguous to that other reality. The real desert and the village and the specific house that this one is meant to represent are actually just a double, a repetition. He's had a lot of time to think about it.

Wild Turkey has often been overcome by this sense during their operations in the fake village—this feeling that the real Iraqi village/desert/target house is actually very close by, maybe over the next ridge, and that it is or will be the exact twin of this village. The feeling has spread until Wild Turkey hears two sounds in every one fake mortar explosion or real explosion of blank assault rifle rounds: the exercise's sound and, somewhere behind it, the real one. In a way, this should serve the military's purpose in making the fake village seem more "real" but has instead only emphasized the surrealism of the entire exercise. He wonders when they are actually there, if it will seem finally real. This is what he thinks about, in all the time they have to hurry up and wait, and think.

This is all made worse by the tasks they've been assigned so far in their time in the fake village here in the desert in Arizona. It's a full exercise, meaning as close an acting-out of real operating procedure as they can possibly undertake without actually being in the Shit. The unit was dropped off kilometers from the village. They approached by night. For a week they've been calmly doing reconnaissance on the fake village, on its real inhabitants. Wild Turkey has watched through special optics fat middle-aged men take their tea, slurping it from saucers, has logged the arrival and departure from the water source (a nearby well) of women in flowing fabrics that are given form by the wind. He's listened on his headset to conversations within the crumbling walls of the low houses, his half-learned Arabic lagging behind, keying into family names, locations, etcetera. It's all very authentic.

It's these people that get to him, as Wild Turkey now shifts uncomfortably against the wall, waiting for the signal. The crushing irony of their physical existence here: they are real Iraqi villagers paid to play Iraqi villagers in America; immigrants from Iraq given asylum and money to come to this other desert and this other village and play themselves. They are given whole complicated psychological profiles to enact, Wild Turkey knows; they each have a role and a set of actions or conversations to complete at predetermined points. They each will behave differently when threatened. They are paid for the performance of reality, for the performance of their identities rather than for their identities themselves. It is all very thorough.

Two nights ago, Wild Turkey watched two of the younger subjects, masked by red kaffiyehs, drag one of the "local politicians" out into the square and videotape themselves staging an execution. The grab team received this video on their digital comms link the next morning, though it wasn't the same video as the one taken below, in the fake village, Wild Turkey could tell. He doesn't know if he was supposed to notice this or not, and has decided now it was a real video of a real execution, something scrounged from a dark corner of the Internet.

The whole thing has worked by approximation, which Wild Turkey will especially think later, after Ramadi. Later, actual reality (Wild Turkey crouched in the tactical column outside the actual house in actual Ramadi) will seem also like an approximation of experience somehow, the distance between what happens (as Wild Turkey hears the two blips and rises into action, then later, as the tactical phosphorous strobe breaks the night and the vision of the house's interior into its discrete pulses of scene) and the "real" experience (even then, something slightly Else or Other, as if there is yet another house, the real target, just over the next rise in Ramadi) making his own feelings seem like an exercise too.

Now, however, on this night, with this crowning exercise, something real will occur, Wild Turkey thinks. Someone really will get identified, then grabbed, then extracted. Wild Turkey has spent the entire week identifying the target, going over the tactical plan. He wonders if, when the team does penetrate the building, when they've cleared the rooms and assembled the members of the family (a wife, a young teenaged daughter, a middle-aged man and the "cousin" they are housing, who is really the courier for a local "militant faction") if they'll show real fear, if, taken by surprise by the timing if not the nature of the event, they will revert to their natural human reaction, to terror. Though it occurs to Wild Turkey now (as the tactical column remains paused) that the family members must've had their dreams exploded into violent light and sound many times before as unit after unit was trained here, and Wild Turkey wonders if it must be frustrating to them (especially the teenaged girl) that they still feel scared when it happens, that it's still actually terrifying, when they should sort of know it's coming. And it will occur to Wild Turkey later, when he remembers this night's exercise, that this thought was probably the seed of that later, momentary feeling, when he will be standing in the rear bedroom in Ramadi, looking down at the partially collapsed head of the teenaged girl: that flush of stupid anger at her for not somehow knowing what would happen.

In his ear, Wild Turkey hears the two blasts of static.

•

Wild Turkey wakes up. Tow Head is driving, drumming his fingers on the wheel, staring straight ahead and humming something that is not the song playing tinnily on the radio as the ancient pickup jounces around on the country road. It is January and so cold the

air is almost completely thinned out, knife-edged in Wild Turkey's nostrils and mouth. Tow Head picked him up from the crumbling duplex very early this morning, before first light, and Wild Turkey is coming down, the brutal sobriety of the air helping out.

Tow Head is excited to go shooting at the unofficial range they are now bouncing and fishtailing toward. He's excited about his new gun, the reissued, remade World War II rifle that, in its combination of antique design and modern mechanics, is a sort of simulation of itself, giving Tow Head both of the experiences he seems to want: the struggle of a marksman in Normandy in 1944 and the smooth riflery of all the advances made since.

Tow Head is Wild Turkey's friend, and he isn't doing too well, Wild Turkey thinks, though he's never really been doing too well. He has a big, robust head and brow, but very small shoulders and a wilting torso that makes his whole appearance vaguely downcast and disconcerting to Wild Turkey, like his body has failed the promise of his martial features. This gives Tow Head a puzzled, frustrated mien. He's a good guy, really, always says just what he means, which is why Wild Turkey has agreed to go shooting in the freezing cold even though it's the last thing he really wants to do.

Beside him, Tow Head bops and twitches in his seat. He's like this here in the States, Wild Turkey knows, always a little nervous, never quite holding still or maintaining visual focus on any one thing. He talks very fast (he's talking now, Wild Turkey realizes) and pauses only occasionally to acknowledge the conversant, though not in a way that requires any response. He always has a lot of conversational energy, and jumps from one subject to another according to his inscrutably associative thought. In Iraq he wasn't like this, at least not while Wild Turkey knew him there. When they first met, and Tow Head realized they were both from Kansas, from even adjacent tiny towns, he looked as happy as a small boy. It's this

look that Wild Turkey had kept in mind, when he was giving away all his military pay and set aside the amount for this rifle, which Tow Head, in their previous conversations, always circled back to the subject of.

Wild Turkey hadn't heard from Tow Head for some time when he saw the flyer at the library for the Wounded Hero Arts Share event. This was two weeks ago. The reading was held in one of the public library's anonymous meeting rooms, plastic chairs set up in solemn rows facing a podium. Tow Head was the featured reader. Wild Turkey went by himself and sat far to one side, where there was a chance Tow Head might not see him, beside a covered piano.

Wild Turkey didn't know that Tow Head liked to write, and spent the time while several middle-aged women went through the introductions wondering if this was actually supposed to be some kind of effort at therapy, or if this was a preexisting interest of Tow Head's, or, if it wasn't, if Tow Head could possibly parse his own answer to that question now. Finally Tow Head got up and took the podium and began to read in a deep, affectless voice.

It was a story, sort of, though really it was just a long description of a man making a wooden guitar amplifier from scratch in his garage, which eventually disintegrated into a sort of list of instructions, but in the third person. As Tow Head's voice settled further into its low timbre and the instructions became repetitive, the sum effect became markedly sinister, almost sexual in its fixated self-surety, until the description of the main character's coating and recoating and recoating again of lacquer on the amplifier's wooden exterior seemed distinctly violent. Before he began, Tow Head had mentioned that the story was about a veteran home from Iraq. Or maybe Wild Turkey only thought he'd said this when really he hadn't.

This was more or less a true story, Wild Turkey knew; Tow Head had told him about fabricating from scratch a wooden electric guitar

amplifier in his garage in Kansas, or attempting to fabricate one—now in the library, as in the original recitation, Tow Head reached the point where he fucks up the interior wiring—though Tow Head had begun the reading (this Wild Turkey does remember) by stating the story was fiction. In his uncomfortable plastic chair Wild Turkey wondered at this strange disavowal of the experience, wondered if it really was fiction or if he'd just said it was, or if, ultimately, Tow Head even knew anymore. This experience of the wooden amplifier had presumably happened at least three times, Wild Turkey realized: once in actuality, once in Tow Head's recitation of the story to Wild Turkey in Baghdad, and once in the re-creation of this, his fiction writing—like a matryoshka doll of experience, understandably involuted, confused.

In fact, sitting in that little meeting room in the public library, Wild Turkey was having a very similar experience of confusion due to the particular arrangement of chairs. These same chairs, in this very same formation, were used in the fake/real base near the fake village in Arizona, in the fake (real?) chapel area for the fake/simulated funeral service that they were all required to attend during the exercise. Presumably this was held in order to prepare the men for attending the same thing in reality, in the Shit. They'd been very thorough, Wild Turkey remembered, with a chaplain and soldiers speaking and eulogies that managed to work in vague references to the details of the casualty.

But Wild Turkey had later found, after Googling the name on the fake funeral program, that the service was in fact held for a real soldier, for a real person who'd been killed in Iraq (IED), which made the fake funeral not so much a simulation of a memorial service (as the officers insisted) but a reenactment of it, a doubling, technically a recurrence. It was unclear if the ranking organizers (let

alone the chaplain and the volunteer eulogizers) of the fake/real base near the fake village even knew that it was a real person they were memorializing: the fact that the biographical information on the fake funeral program didn't match what Wild Turkey could find about the real soldier killed in action suggested that they didn't know. This also brought up the possibility of sheer coincidence, of the chance that the master designers of the fake Iraq experience had chosen by accident the name of a victim of the real Iraq experience in order to simulate the loss of a real person. The whole thing was very similar, Wild Turkey felt, to the real video of the execution they'd received on their comms link that was supposedly of the fake execution he'd watched through the night optics the night before.

In the library Tow Head finished up, getting to the point that functioned as the end of the story, where the main character finally completes the wooden electric guitar amplifier only to realize that he does not, in fact, own an electric guitar, or even know how to play. In the applause afterward, Tow Head had caught sight of Wild Turkey and waved, compelling Wild Turkey to stay for the reception, where Tow Head hatched the shooting range plan.

Now they're parked at the edge of the wide field that serves as the range, and Wild Turkey is leaning against the side of the truck, watching Tow Head carefully reload the rifle, bobbing his head to the pulsing techno music coming from the huge boom box he's set up by his feet on the little shooting platform. This is really a skeet range, and Tow Head has insisted that Wild Turkey sling the clay pigeons out into the white plane of the snowed-over field and washed-out winter sky. They only have one of the cheap plastic hand-throwers so for an hour now Wild Turkey has made the strange sidearmed motion, skipping the bright orange clay disks out onto the currents of air. Tow Head is an excellent shot. He's hit each one, the disks

wobbling or splitting cleanly in half, their flight turned to mere gravity. He seems to be enjoying himself.

The landscape does in fact resemble Normandy in winter, which is fitting for the rifle, though since Wild Turkey has never actually seen Normandy in winter he supposes it really just resembles what he thinks it would look like. He wants it to look like Normandy in the snow for Tow Head, though, even if it did, Tow Head wouldn't know it.

Tow Head is ready again and Wild Turkey flicks away his cigarette and steps forward. "Ready," Tow Head says, then, "Pull!" and Wild Turkey whips his arm, sending the clay disk high into the air. Tow Head fires, missing, but at the sound of the rifle's report a raft of geese rise into the air from some hidden tufts in the field, their winged shapes very dark against the air. Wild Turkey realizes Tow Head is screaming before he realizes that Tow Head is firing, though the two actions are concurrent. But Tow Head is screaming and Tow Head is firing, and firing, and firing, until Wild Turkey hears the small metallic clink of the ammunition cartridge going empty and there are no more birds in the air. Then Tow Head is running out into the field, slipping, falling down, getting up, still running, still yelling, though now laughing too, the techno music throbbing very loudly, and finally Tow Head reaches the area of bloodied snow where he has expertly dropped what must be at least ten birds, and Wild Turkey can see him lifting the rifle, holding it at either end above his head like he's wading a river, and Tow Head is dancing and laughing wildly, the sound rising and rising in joy, and Wild Turkey, watching, loves him, loves him, loves him.

This is six months before Tow Head, who has this day refrained from his usual running obsession with the possibility that he suffered an undiagnosed Traumatic Brain Injury at some forgotten

point during his deployment, will use the replica rifle to shoot himself through his cheekbone, perhaps purposefully making his theory impossible to ever disprove or confirm.

•

Wild Turkey jars awake. He's in his position, last in the tactical column, crouched against a low mud wall in a residential compound in Ramadi. The target, Wild Turkey knows (the drone's heat-imaging burned into the inside of his eyelids), is sleeping in the small house just ahead. The team pads forward quietly in its line. They pause, waiting for the radio signal.

Inside the house, Wild Turkey mentally recites, there will be two civilians (a middle-aged male and a female, presumably his wife) and the target, whom they've previously claimed is a cousin but who is actually a low-level messenger between militias. All are asleep. The operational information has been confirmed, according to the radio clearance an hour earlier, presumably by more drone imaging.

In his ear, Wild Turkey hears the two blasts of static.

There is the sound of the steel ram battering the door open, the loud flash of the tactical stun grenade, the shadowy flow of the bodies in front of Wild Turkey funneling into the house, the shouted commands for the occupants to lie flat on the ground. From all corners of the house, from its four separate rooms, Wild Turkey hears the voices of the team confirming that the rooms are clear. "One female in northwest bedroom," Wild Turkey hears someone tell him either over the radio or the night air. "Holding."

There are several things that are wrong, Wild Turkey thinks as he stares at the lone male lying face down in front of him on the carpets of the main room. One is that this male is clearly not either of the

males (not the target, and not the middle-aged man) from the assignment profile. Wild Turkey will have to go through the standard pro-
cedures to confirm this, but he can see, even in the dark, that the
man in front of him is very, very old. The extraction clock in Wild
Turkey's head is ticking, ticking. The rest of the team stands, idly
tensed, adjusting their equipment. Wild Turkey tells them he needs
to go see about the female.

In the back bedroom, Specialist Freidel is standing inside the
doorway, watching a teenaged girl, who is naked, cower in the far
corner.

"What the fuck?" Wild Turkey says.

Freidel shrugs. The girl in her crouch seems almost feral, eyes
flashing. Wild Turkey, in his real-time catalogue of the operation,
struggles to age her, distracted by the combination of her child's face,
her dirty thighs and half-hidden, adolescent breasts.

"Did two men leave this house tonight?" Wild Turkey asks in
half-hearted Arabic. "Where is your mother? Where is your father?
Was there a houseguest tonight? Did he leave?"

The girl doesn't answer, but winces sharply at Wild Turkey's
voice, showing her teeth.

"Bring her into the main room," Wild Turkey says, frustrated.
Freidel steps forward and grabs the naked girl by the upper arm. He
begins to drag her, but then she stands up, still resisting.

"I think they gave us the wrong fucking house," Wild Turkey
says (to whom?), and Freidel turns, or starts to turn, starts to say to
Wild Turkey, "What?" when the naked girl rears back, sending one
hand with its nails arcing over, digging into Freidel's neck.

"Goddamnit," Freidel says, or starts to say, as he turns and
brings his weapon's thick stock up and around possibly more swiftly
than he means to, and there is a single sound, something like a crack,
and the naked girl is on the floor at both Freidel and Wild Turkey's

feet. Her head is unmade: the upper left quadrant of her skull collapsed, blood very dark on the floor, a jagged-edged concavity with a fleck of white bone just visible in Wild Turkey's flashlight here and there, the wound tangling with her hair.

"Fuck!" Freidel says.

"Fuck," Wild Turkey says.

Wild Turkey helps drag the girl's body out into the dirt-floored courtyard, thinking maybe he can radio for a medical addition to the extraction, once he gets clear just what the fuck is going on, but Wild Turkey can see—the girl's complete limpness, eyes lolling with the dragging motion between whites and wide, black, fixed pupils; the lack of any rising or falling of the small breasts, now bared where she lies on her back in the pitch of the night and the dirt—that she is gone.

"What do we do with this?" Freidel says, voice taut with desperation, and Wild Turkey can feel the stares of the rest of the team, gathered near the doorway out to the courtyard.

Wild Turkey is not afraid. He can write the report exactly as it really happened, he knows, and it will more than likely simply be forgotten, lost, after a brief bureaucratic murmur, to the labyrinth of operational After Action Reports. They'd be more interested in how the team was given the wrong house, the wrong info from the drone, more interested in the failure to extract the messenger man than anything else. Even if the report caught the eye of some officer worried about exposure, all that would happen would probably be that Wild Turkey would be rotated back home, though he didn't want to go back home. Wild Turkey knows all this, looking down at the naked girl with the ruined head, knows that he can report it or not report it, but he can't leave the body as it is. Not to be found, and photographed. Not to be seen. This is when he says it, when he raises his eyes to Freidel's and the others.

"Burn it," he says.

"Burn it," he says.

"Burn it," he says.

He helps them prepare the body. He gets the jug of kerosene from the house's tiny kitchen. He has Freidel get the bed sheets from the room they found her in. The sheets are stained with the blood that has spread on the floor. Freidel deposits them next to the body, which Wild Turkey is pouring the kerosene over. Wild Turkey straightens up. He's holding the tactical phosphorous strobe grenade in his hand.

And does Wild Turkey smell, cut by the fumes of the kerosene, that rank, fetid waft from the girl's bed sheets? Does he feel himself falling for just a second into that complex of faintly vaginal, excretory musk—does it seem familiar to him? And the girl's naked body, shining with the wetness of the kerosene there on the ground before him—what is it that strikes him as so oddly sexual about it? Is it what he saw Freidel doing as Wild Turkey entered the room? Did he see Freidel wrestling with the girl—in what, an effort to restrain her? Did he hear him laughing?

Wild Turkey has the team clear the courtyard and prepare for egress to the extraction point. He will experience this night twice, have two simultaneous nights: the one that now occurs and the one that occurs on paper. He will be honest in his report, but in his honesty he will be no more able to separate what actually happened, for the most part, from the false implantation of memory, of narrative memory, which was coeval with the experience itself. And so the truth of the night will forever feel to Wild Turkey somewhere in between the fragmentation of experience and what he remembers: he will have both seen and not seen what he saw, what he smelled. All of this with one lone exception: the moment when the phosphorous strobe, nestled underneath the naked girl's back and buried beneath

the shroud of the soiled bedclothes, ignites, and shatters the night into pulses of pure white light, and the absence of it.

And already, as Wild Turkey watches (though the strobe cannot be watched, though "watching" the strobe would render him temporarily blind, as is the tactical strobe's function), the team, and Wild Turkey along with it, is leaving, clearing the buildings in the neighboring compound just in case, only to discover empty room after empty room of desks, of broken chalkboards (the mistaken compound a school, apparently). Already they are clear of Ramadi's outskirts and jogging into the field where the helicopter will briefly land and collect them; already they are back at the operations base, going to sleep; already Wild Turkey is waking in mid-fuck with Jeannie; waking in the invigorated air of Merry's room after a punch; already he is waking to the town's lights buzzing with the edge of his pills. He wakes outside the courthouse with Jeannie even though his heart's not really in it; he wakes on his second tour in Iraq, on a pile of rubble in Fallujah, the roar of heavy metal being pumped at the insurgents, a roaring room of sound all around him, as he closes his eyes again and falls back into the city air's approximation of Mrs. Budnitz's rankness; he wakes on the adolescent night he loses his virginity to a sweet-faced girl named Helen, who, out of fear of it hurting too much, gets him off manually and only then, as Wild Turkey drifts on the edge of sleep, mounts him unexpectedly; he wakes in the overgrown baseball field outside the country school, remembering the spring afternoon he woke in the outfield years ago in the middle of a game, the air heavy and perfect with the rumor of rain; in the desert, in the lightning, in his crumbling duplex, in the field, in the many rooms of night, Wild Turkey wakes up, he wakes up, he wakes up.

The Half Moon Martyrs' Brigade of New Jerusalem, Kansas

Because our town was so small, the Army recruiter, Family Affairs Liaison, and Casualty Affairs Officer were all just one man, who went by the name of Douglas Reeter. This became a problem that winter, after the real fighting started and people had to stop and crane their necks whenever they saw Doug drifting down the half-plowed streets in his ancient Buick, everyone trying to get a good look in order to see by his uniform in which capacity, exactly, he was making his visit. It didn't take long after the first few casualties for people to let the "t" in his last name slip into the "p" it already seemed to be sliding toward. This was how soft-spoken, dark-haired Doug Reeter became sober, bitter Doug the Reaper, whom no one ever wanted around much, even in off-duty hours. When I lay in bed at night that year of the deployment, I used to imagine what he'd look like in the morning if it was a bad day coming, and I'd dream him up in my room's half-light, Doug standing before his little mirror in his Class A uniform, the thin manila envelope pale in his pocket.

Everyone could recite those first few by heart. Daniel Willis's father (helicopter crash); P.J. Holdeman's brother (bullet through the neck while taking a piss); Jackson Kepley's dad (grenade dropped in

his path out of nowhere during a neighborhood patrol). And everybody had their own private reels too, the confused images drifting
across our minds in spare moments—the pause in a teacher's endless afternoon grammar lesson, the wait while our mothers filled the
car up at Bone's One Stop. Suddenly the air would be full with the
concussion of a listing helicopter's blades, or the unhurried spurt of
an artery bleeding out in seconds, or the path of light made by the
tops of high alley walls as someone looked up at the sound of something falling. But those were the early days, before any of us knew
the Arabic word for "stop" or that you couldn't shake on anything
because the Iraqis supposedly used one of their own bare hands for
toilet paper (though none of us could agree as to which hand). It is
true, in all eventual fairness, that those first few dead and their stories did briefly hold our imaginations, back when the men of our
town were still dying exotic deaths, deaths with details and accounts,
before the casualty announcements just became a series of thick letter-
codes that didn't mean anything, really; before the long paper list
posted behind the scuffed glass at the armory just read KIA, and
IED, IED, IED.

·

This is where we lived: New Jerusalem, Kansas. I always liked to
imagine the well-meaning if already disillusioned ladies and gen-
tlemen of the New England Emigrant Aid Society cresting Doak's
Ridge way back when and looking down upon the endless plains and
the river and the space of mud where they would make their new city
of God, really believing (as was their great gift) that it would become
something grand. Though they soon enough packed up their wag-
ons and lit out, as they say, for further territories, I also like to think

some of that pure hopeful spirit has hunkered down in the low places around here and stayed, however improbably, like the fog does on some familiar summer mornings. Their pluck certainly has, anyway.

Back around the time of the first war in the sand, a representative from the state tourism board convinced all four members of the New Jerusalem city council that our town could be a minor draw on the endless straight-shot of highway that filleted our state. At the town hall meeting he kept saying the word "synergy" and told everyone we needed to use what we had, which was, as of the year before, no longer the chemical plant. All we had was our name by then. So came into being The Old City at New Jerusalem, a replica of the heart of that other Jerusalem, but right here on the plains. This was also how the funds for the new church sanctuary were raised (via a questionable state grant) and a pale brick and mortar Church of the Holy Sepulcher (of the One True Congregation of the Savior and Nazarene) was built, scaled down seriously in size, on the main street off the highway. Besides the church and the "Temple Mount" building (a would-be community meeting space), everything else in the New Old City was a life-size cutout front, like on a movie set. Even our school got into the act. The New Jerusalem Knights became the New Jerusalem Crusaders ("Lest anyone think we were the bad kind," Samuel Lincoln deadpanned later) and people painted squiggles for imitation Arabic on the signs marking the fake bazaar, which was actually the flea market. Little kids climbed the piled quarry slag of the Wailing Wall and spit down neon soda pop when their friends tried to follow.

Years later, by the time the most recent war had come and the men of our town deployed, the undersized green plaster dome atop the corner of the empty Temple Mount building was faded and chipped, like an obstacle on a putt-putt course. The Temple Mount building itself had been overtaken and commandeered as the church's

fellowship hall, and so it was where the women met, twice a week, for their "Army Wives" support group, even though half of them were really mothers, or sisters, or girlfriends of indeterminate commitment. Those first few meetings, while our fathers and brothers and cousins were still just sitting on some base in the middle of the nowhere-desert (unassigned as yet, somehow still unnecessary), the voices of the women and girls were very serious, telling each other over and over the latest they'd heard or read about the war or Iraq or army lingo or Arab peoples. But soon after, when word sent from the base became either dull repetition of what we all already knew or petered out completely, the meetings took on a different tone. Nobody knew what to say. The support meetings became potlucks and people brought even the youngest kids, who ran around wildly while their mothers stood, staring blankly at the big maps they'd tacked to the wall next to the Useful Bible Verses display, and chewed their macaroni.

When the men of our town were eventually given a mission and guided into the budding nightmare that was still just an unsettling dream in Fallujah, the women brought videotapes they'd made of the news reports, and in the Temple Mount they took turns watching the grainy footage or taping up computer printouts of wire articles. Once, some kind of regional administrative officer visited. He wore the strange cubic fatigues they all wore stateside and stood before us and asked if anybody had any questions. Faced with the sudden opportunity, the sudden presence of the one whose absence the wives had taken to bemoaning, everyone was startled into silence. After a while someone in the back asked in a small voice if the officer knew anything about when the men would be coming home, though we all knew he wouldn't. At the next meeting the mothers parceled up care packages full of chewing tobacco and magazines and made lists of the things they'd ask next time, if they ever saw the man again.

All of which is to say that nobody—not the adults who worked the booths in the New Old City for the tourists, not the older kids, who had mysterious things to do that involved drinking and summer jobs, and certainly not the mothers—much wanted us around for the long summer months, and so didn't mind one bit our annual, prolonged stay of boarding and verse lessons at the Hope and Grace Bible Camp (formerly a rickety collection of wooden vacation cabins) on Galilee Lake (formerly Baldwin's Pond).

•

There was no baseball diamond in the entire city of New Jerusalem. The story went that the community of Fundamental Christians ("*We're* Fundamental Christians," Samuel Lincoln explained. "Back then all Christians were fundamental, so you didn't have to say it") that founded New Jerusalem did so largely in protest of the burgeoning mining and railway town to the east called Pittsburg, and principal in their complaints (after the brothel for the railroad men and the multiple purveyors of card games and spirits) was the Louis P. Stilton Municipal Ballpark, home of the rough-and-tumble Pittsburg Pickers, apparent corrupters of many a young Christian girl from the nearby Kansas State Teachers College. Whether or not this was the actual explanation for the continued absence of baseball from the town of New Jerusalem, it was at least true that it had never occurred to the powers that were of our New Jerusalem Christian Day School to build a baseball diamond or field a team, the only member of the Southeastern Kansas Independent and Home School Athletic Conference not to do so.

Strictly speaking, there was no baseball diamond at the Hope and Grace Bible Camp either. There was, however, the Dust Bowl:

our space of cloddy soil and four honest-to-god bases and a six-foot-tall homerun wall of corn, kindly provided by the next field over, which had yet to be harvested. The previous summer's Bible Camp had been full of near disasters (the crowning jewel of which involved an older boy named Calvin Jenks being discovered not only smoking marijuana, but doing so alone with a girl, herself apparently in what Elder Peters called a "near-Eve state of clothedness"), and it was perhaps because of this that we arrived that summer nine months after our fathers' deployment to find that the church had miraculously invested in both a renovation of our mostly theoretical ball field *and* an official team manager, who turned out to be Brother Douglas Reeter himself. "IT'S THE DIVINE GRACE OF GOD COME INCARNATE," big, jolly, slow-brained Hilton Hedis, who had no other volume than ear-blasting shout, said in awe that first day when we saw the field.

The Elders had turned two of the less trustworthy picnic tables on their sides twenty feet or so behind home plate, making a backstop. They'd taken what looked to be several fishing nets and strung them together, hanging them down from the high tree limbs that cast their shade onto the batter's box. They'd also taken twenty or so bags of gardening soil and emptied them unceremoniously about forty feet from home plate, making a very messy pitcher's mound. And finally, in the most incredible of all their additions, the Elders had built, via the stacking of many cinderblocks and two well-placed corrugated metal sheets, a pair of real dugouts.

That first day we found Brother Reeter, as Elder Peters instructed us to call him, with several nails in his mouth, standing in foul territory and pounding away at an arrangement of two-by-fours gathered at wild angles.

"I guess the carpenter's our coach," Samuel said, hugging his leather glove and spitting.

Ralph spat too and said leave it to the Elders to go out and get us a coach only to fix us with some grade-A Jesus luck, which is what we called luck that was likely to get you killed, like being picked to walk point on a security patrol, or being the Son of God, or having a dumb hick carpenter whom everybody hated for a coach.

"I DON'T KNOW," Hilton blared, looking to Brother Reeter and then back at us, his eyebrows working, which meant he was thinking. "JESUS WAS A CARPENTER AND HE COULD DO SOME OTHER STUFF PRETTY GOOD TOO."

Where was I during all this? I was on the top plank of the newly carpentered set of wooden bleachers, which none of the boys kicking dirt around home plate had yet caught on Doug the Reaper was crafting a mate for. I don't think it's true that my father wanted a boy. He was a kind, wilting, educated man who was taken to long moods of quiet melancholy and wistfulness. I had a better chance moving him to expression with an idea about a book I was reading than by making my throws pop into his glove in the warm evenings when he came home from work. If he minded much that I'd come out a girl, he never did let me see it, though it's true that he taught me a mean sinking fastball. He used to play catch with my mother, before she died when I was eight, before she'd even had me, when they were just young married kids. I still have a picture of them as they stood lined up in the yard, my father crouched, squinting at something behind the camera, my mother scowling, the ball held trickily behind her back, ready to go into a windup. And it only occurred to me a couple years ago, once I had a house of my own, that it might've been her pitch that he taught me, that fastball with the slight downward movement. But anyway.

I was really mostly allowed as a de facto member of the ball team because my father was the commanding officer of our town's Army company and, when his reserve unit wasn't being called up to go to

war, he worked as the floor manager in the pet food plant two towns over, which still employs most of the people around here. Everyone in New Jerusalem liked him because they thought he was fair. I was allowed more or less free range by the Elders, and the people in the town. The boys on the diamond (which is also to say, the boys in all my classes, the boys who were my friends) let me along with them in most things because both my legs were bound up in painful, complicated orthopedic braces and because when my dad was at home he was the boss of half of their fathers, until the reserves got called up to go to Iraq, and he became the boss of all of them.

•

What do I remember?

The sun burning high and hazy in the sky above the green sea of the corn past the outfield, but not yet high enough to burn the color out of everything. It was maybe two weeks before the summer ball season started. The boys were one by one coming in from the field at the end of their morning practice, gathering on the other set of wooden bleachers. I had my braces off and was lying across the highest plank of my own bleachers. Two planks lower, Marly was lying with a forearm draped over her eyes, her cotton shorts and T-shirt scrunched up in a way that had caused a good number of fielding errors already.

I've been holding off on Marly, saving her for as long as possible, but Marly never was one to be held off, even in memory, and I can no longer neglect her presence, her glorious body: thin, tan, her rounded chest, her impossibly blond hair. She was twenty-two I think, seven years older than me, and I counted her as my friend. Her and Doug the Reaper rented the little falling-down house on the rear

of my father's land, and she spent a lot of time that year in our house, especially when my aunt, who was supposed to be my caretaker, was gone to Stillwater to see her friends. Marly was quiet and beautiful wafting around the rooms of our house. People said she'd run around on Doug during the first seven months of our fathers' deployment, before Doug came back to do his three-fold job in town, and it seems possible, just because she was always so supremely bored, but I don't like to believe it. Douglas Reeter was the only one of the men allowed to come back before their tour was done.

Finally all the boys were back in, splayed out in the bleachers, and we were listening to Brother Reeter, having finished his pep talk, settle in to one of his stories.

•

Pat Lincoln, John Hedis, and Peter Powers are walking alongside the Humvee, which rolls along in the caravan across the dirt road out in the desert. Along one side of the road is a kind of olive orchard, the men think. The trees are not much taller than they are, and scraggly. Along the other side of the road stretches an open, undulating green field. You can never tell what Iraq is going to look like, the men think. Sometimes it looks like this, sometimes something else entirely. Hard to know which is the real country. It is very hot. This is the road that runs behind the orchard of olive trees; on the other side, somewhere through the trees, is the main, paved road that the coalition supply caravans keep getting attacked on. The insurgents are using the olive orchard as cover, the officers think. So now the men are pushing along the back road, trying to flush the insurgents out.

Are there shadows between the layers of slender trunks? Does the sandy soil shift in the breeze, as the loose end of a scarf masking

a face would shift? A stray goat idles in the roadside ditch. Scott Holdeman, who is all of eighteen years old, is up in the vehicle's turret, slowly swiveling the machine gun back and forth. Doug Reeter is driving the Humvee behind them, watching. His windshield is like a video screen when the explosion goes off. The spray of dirt against the thick glass is unexpectedly gentle in the space after the great sundering, like rain against a house's window.

Then they are all out of the vehicles, someone is shouting IED, IED, half of the men are flat on their stomachs taking cover in the ditch, which is now a chaotic landscape of dirt. Is anyone down, is anyone down, someone screams. Reeter is out of the vehicle now, staring at the road in front of them. The road is gone, just a big crater, but placed in it, spanning it actually, like a toy car some giant child has put there, is the Humvee, and the men who were in it are tumbling out, coughing but OK. Reeter, along with everyone else, looks wildly around for the men who were walking alongside it. John Hedis and Peter Powers have fallen together, their limbs tangled, into the opposite ditch, which they are crawling out of, stunned, maybe concussed, but whole. Reeter looks again at the crater. People start screaming Pat Lincoln's name.

They can't find him. They don't see him. The thought is there in the back of everyone's minds; they've heard about the larger IEDs, guys on patrol being partially or wholly vaporized by the force, especially if they were the ones who triggered it. Then a figure appears across the field, three hundred yards (swear to god) away, and the men on the road almost open fire.

"Fuck, no, shit that's him, that's him," someone yells, waving his arms. The figure staggers, but waves back. There's no helmet but they can make out the uniform. He starts to jog toward them in the thick soil, and they can see it is him, it is Pat Lincoln, unharmed. The men stand there, stilled on the road, and stare in amazement.

Just at that moment there is a heavy, loud, close, wet sound, and they all fall down again in panic, only to realize that the wild goat's head, apparently airborne this entire time, has landed on the hood of the stalled vehicle.

Brother Reeter sat back on the bleacher plank, as if in disbelief at his own story.

"I mean, can you imagine the trajectory?" he said, reverently, and it was unclear whether he meant the goat's head or Pat Lincoln's flying body.

•

Later the next day, Samuel Lincoln sat up on my bed to go. We were there in our underwear, my upper-floor bedroom dry and hot in the afternoon sun, the window open, blinds lazily bowing in the occasional puffs of breeze. Samuel was a sweet boy then; he always carefully took off my braces and blew for a long time on the red marks they left, his breath cool on my skin. He liked kissing the freckle that sat catty-corner to my bellybutton before he kissed anything else, and I generally let him do what he wanted after that, my palm prickling warm against the muscles of his tan back as he moved above me.

We'd been done for a while, not speaking, just lying there together before we'd have to go to get back to our cabins at the camp. This was Saturday afternoon, which we had free from Bible study, and which most of us used to go home and see our families. That morning Douglas Reeter, Casualty Affairs Officer, had visited the Powers household, and Gary (Peter Powers' son) wasn't in morning worship, and so we'd all come to know that his dad had become the sixth man from New Jerusalem, Kansas to be killed in

Iraq. I was thinking about Doug Reeter, Doug the Reaper, wondering what it was he said to Gary's mother.

"Listen," Samuel said, not looking at me. He sounded unsure, so I stayed quiet. "You know the well-marker shack, out in the third field over, behind the Dust Bowl?"

"Listen," he said, looking at me now, having decided something. "You got a watch and a flashlight?"

As he climbed out of my window and crab-crawled across the roof of the porch before dropping down into the sideyard, I leaned against the sill. Standing there I saw Marly in her front yard, beside the fluttering white shapes of her wash hung out to dry. She was watching me, one hand on her hip, the other shielding her eyes.

•

I still have the tapes, of course. Though I've only watched them once since I made them, on a rainy spring afternoon a couple years ago after I found out Hilton Hedis had been killed in an accident at the grain elevator. I was missing those boys, then, and I realized I didn't have any pictures of them, only the tapes.

What is not on that first miniature videotape: the faces of the boys, barely legible in the dark of the shack. It was not a big space, that shack, and they were arranged around the squared U-shape of the well-pipe coming out of the ground. Also not on the tape: the long walk out there: the cool air and imperfect dark of one forty-five in the morning; the cabins asleep behind me; only the small plastic and metal sound of my gait, the seething of the cicadas, the fog drifting between the trees, out of the crops.

In the shack, P.J. Holdeman shoved the video camera at me and I took it and looked up at them. Samuel nodded and watched me, see-

ing what I would do. The other boys met my gaze, then looked away.

What is on the tape: the image jolts on and we are outside the shack, the camera's night vision picking up the ambient glow of the night sky. There is the sound of a struggle as Truman Renolds and Ralph Simonsen materialize out of the stalks of the field, dragging a hooded figure between them that I know is Gary Powers.

The boys are all outside now, a clump of dark bodies. The five whose houses Doug the Reaper has already visited begin to wrap cloths that I can't quite make out around their faces: checked red tablecloths, indistinguishable from what we knew were called kaffi-yehs. Those five: Ralph Simonsen (roadside IED), Truman Renolds (Vehicle Borne IED), P.J. Holdeman (his brother shot through the jugular while urinating on the base of a tree), Jackson Kepley (his father riddled with shrapnel from the grenade dropped down onto the street at his feet), and Daniel Willis (his dad knocked uncon-scious, then burned alive in a helicopter crash). Those five, masked now, open the door to the shack and disappear inside. I feel Samuel's hand push roughly at my back. On the tape, his voice says, "Go on," faintly, almost gently, but I don't remember that.

There's a limit to what you can be surprised by, I guess. And hadn't I already seen first Daniel's face, then P.J.'s, then Jackson's after we'd found out about their dead—bruised, eyes swollen like pastries, lips split, empurpled? I remember it making sense, in a way, when I saw them like that; it was how I imagined it must feel privately, just externalized. But I didn't think about it, not really, and when I saw them in the shack, tying Gary Powers awkwardly to the pipe, it was no revelation. I'm sure I was surprised. I'm sure the whole thing was vaguely terrifying to me. I was fifteen years old, after all, and not one of them, not really. But I stood there in silence and pointed the handheld video camera where they wanted, and there has to be a rea-son why I did not leave.

I was more startled by the violence of the movement on the video-tape, on my little TV screen, watching it that day after Hilton passed than I was standing there at the time, watching them beat Gary over the top of the little pop-out viewfinder. In person, it felt like one person hitting him (the hood now off his head) at a time, which is, in fact, how it was, each one of the boys taking turns with their fists, but on the tape it looks more like a close mob, a gang, a group beating, unfair. The tape, unlike my memory, has not been granted the small mercy of silence, either, and when I watched it alone in my living room, years later on that rainy afternoon, I winced at the solid, wet impact of the awkward punches, at Gary's whimpering, more panicked than I remember it being.

One thing that's not on the tape, but that I do remember clearly, is watching Gary three days later during Bible class. Samuel told me much later about how it was his duty to take Gary to the camp nurse afterward, because he was good at stories. But what I remember, sitting there that morning in Bible study, is Gary Powers' face, the bruises already turning their muted, sickly colors, half of his upper lip so swollen that it almost succeeded in obscuring his goofy smile at the boys who had abducted him.

•

The 27th season of the Four State Christian Summer Baseball League started off for us about how you would expect. The only thing the members of the One True Congregation of the Savior and Nazarene who ran the Hope and Grace Bible Camp actually paid for were our hats, which were maroon with a gold cross above the bill. We did have uniforms (embroidered by the generous Sisters during a marathon Army Wives meeting in the Temple Mount). They only

had two words on them, both on the front: HOPE on the right side of the buttons and GRACE on the left, and each set of letters was situated too high up, almost in line with the collarbone. The effect was to make the words seem like labels for our arms (a detail not missed by our opponents' bench, who guffawed every time Hilton's GRACE rocketed the ball to center field while trying to catch a runner stealing second, or Truman's HOPE sent a batter in the on-deck circle sprawling to the dirt). Four games in, all of which we lost, the league donated some batting helmets so we could stop borrowing the other team's, and the day before the best prospect for our first win Brother Reeter brought a collection of his old Babe Ruth League bats from when he was a kid, which cheered us all up, even though they were the old fashioned kind ("Wood was good enough to see to Christ's demise, it'll work fine for yours," he grouched). It was also around that time that the other teams started calling us the Martyrs.

I can still see our starting lineup. Everyone's positions seemed almost preordained, fated in a way. Gary Powers, for instance, whom everyone called You Too after the day Sister Brooks told us about his namesake in history class, was small and wiry and played a rangy shortstop. Hilton Hedis, of course, played catcher ("Just to give the ump some protection," Brother Reeter said, only half joking). Samuel Lincoln was our star pitcher, but when he wasn't pitching he wiled away his time bored in the outfield, making comments to himself about the opposing team's batters that only Ralph Simonsen, whom he split the outfield with, and P.J. Holdeman, who played second base, could hear. Third base was covered by Truman Renolds, a tiny, quiet kid who heckled the batters with surprising meanness and who occasionally, when we were already down by a lot and sometimes when we weren't, missed incoming throws on purpose, letting the balls fly into the opposing team's bench and sending them diving. To round out the infield, our first baseman was a slightly older

kid named Honor Riley who wanted to be an Elder when he grew up, who we had to convince to be on the team so that we could field an almost full roster. Our only options after Samuel got exhausted on the mound was to end the game watching Truman throw his angry fastballs in the very general direction of the batters, or to watch Ralph loop the one pitch he knew how to throw (a fat curve) over and over again until Brother Reeter stormed out to the mound and told him that if he kept pitching like that even the apparition of Jesus Christ himself wouldn't be able to save his arm.

●

What do I remember?

John Hedis is lost on patrol. He hasn't meant to get lost, but there he is, in the alleyways and the narrow streets (that are indistinguishable, in parts, from alleyways), and he is lost. Only Reeter is there with him. Reeter—against the wishes of the unit, which is holed up in a building while they try to figure out where in the hell they lost Hedis along the way—has broken off on his own, because he thinks he knows where Hedis vanished from the group. He is sure that he saw that towering hulk of John Hedis's body wandering, his big, dumb face distracted, slightly off route as they went through the big open square where the villagers were having their bazaar. Reeter is pretty sure John Hedis got flustered when that kid came up to him and tried to sell him the lighters with the picture of the planes crashing into the towers on them, and when John Hedis looked up, the line of his squad were nowhere to be seen.

It's not really John Hedis's fault. Things have gotten pretty relaxed with their new assignment (not yet in Fallujah): just a small village, in the middle of nowhere, no real history of insurgent activity.

This feels closer to what they were really qualified to do, as reserves: that is, to walk around with their weapons on safety and nod and smile at the Iraqis.

But then there is the chattering teeth of small arms fire, at once distant and close, and both Reeter and Hedis are now apart from the unit—a major screwup in standard operating procedure—and Reeter begins to run. He rounds the corner and there is John Hedis looking, bewildered, up at the towering wall of an apartment block above him. And there is more small arms fire, and then the muffled concussion of a grenade going off, somewhere back in the direction where the rest of the men are.

Reeter grabs Hedis by the equipment harness and pulls him into the nearest doorway. They collapse to the floor behind some tables and as the dim light resolves, they see they are in, of all places, a bakery. Flour hangs in the air, coats their faces, their arms. Reeter does not think it is a good idea to go back to where the other men are engaged with the insurgents, by the sound of it. The back-and-forth reports go on and on. How terrified they are, in the bakery listening to the destruction outside, half-expecting the walls to come crashing down on them. Afternoon stretches into dusk, then evening, then night.

Reeter wakes Hedis up by shaking him, whispers that it's time to go. Together, they make their way slowly through the streets back toward the building the unit was holed up in, hoping they are still there. The village has become a zone of intense battle, by the look of it. They pass three buildings in a row on fire, not a person in sight. The air is searing hot as they pass, but they cannot get away from it, only hurry through.

Then they are back at the building, and the men are still inside, and the man on guard, Pat Lincoln, stands up from his crouch and stares at them. What? Reeter says. What? Hedis says. Lincoln approaches and begins to pick at their skin. Reeter feels something breaking off and Lincoln holds it up for him to see. The flour had mixed with their

sweat as they lay. When they walked by the fire, the heat baked it: thin lines of bread, right there on their skin.

But Samuel isn't even really listening anymore. The boys in the bleachers after practice look about half-impressed, half in wonder, except for Samuel. Big Hilton Hedis looks so happy he might cry. Reeter won't look anyone in the face.

•

On the mound I remember Samuel's great unthinking. There's lots of space on a baseball diamond, and even with his cleats sinking into the potting-soil mound I could see there was a sort of rapture in the lonely field. Around about four innings in it would suddenly feel like he was a great distance away from the other players, Brother Reeter leaning back into the shadows of the dugout, the handful of curious Bible counselors or little kids in the stands fading into an unfocused blend of color and light, and he would—there was no other way of saying it—more or less forget what he was doing out there. He still threw, sending the ball hissing through the air where he knew no batter from St. Pius X or Veritas Academy could hit it, and he still felt the ball appear back in the smooth leather of his glove after Hilton's mindless throws, but he thought a lot about the desert, what it must look like to the insurgents, perched high in his imagination on rock outcroppings, as they watched a speeding convoy pass, kicking up a dust cloud below, as they whispered into a handheld radio.

He cycled his pitches, gripping the seams, letting the ball slide off his fingers as necessary; the other team would eventually figure out what was coming, but it didn't matter. He always finished on his curve, what Hilton called his cliff ball for the way it dropped, seeing as the ball left his hand what the terrorists must be seeing: the convoy stopped below,

his father getting out of the lead vehicle, the unseen man crouched above, raising his rifle just as the pitch, which had first appeared to the frightened batter to be coming right at his face, dropped into Hilton's glove in the center of the strike zone, the innocent kid looking up into the ump's growling face as if hurt by the idea of a world where a projectile could change so quickly. Then the inning would be over and Samuel would be blinking as Hilton flipped the ump the ball and jogged toward the dugout, laughing his big loon laugh, saying, "WOE BE TO HIM WHO CALLS A STRIKE A BALL AND A BALL A STRIKE."

I'm imagining this, of course, how it was for him. He certainly never talked about it, then or later, and so there is now a kind of truth to what I think it must've been like, as I seem to be the only person who still thinks about that season at all. It really was something to behold, him up there on the mound, which had begun to look like a dark wound on the dirt. Is there anything more full of the bumbling divine grace, anything further from what life will make of a person, than a fifteen-year-old boy in summer?

That is how the days more or less passed, anyway, Samuel pitching in his trance until he couldn't anymore, then us losing as I watched from the bleachers, the late afternoon quiet ringing in my ears. But then, on the seventh Saturday of the summer, Hilton Hedis's father stepped on an improvised explosive device wired to three pounds of plastic explosive, and we took the tail end of a doubleheader against the Good Harvest Baptists for our very first win of the season.

·

Hilton's tape is particularly hard to watch, because he keeps looking up at the boys after each punch like he's sorry, like he doesn't understand, and he cries and cries.

•

At some point I sat with Samuel in the airless little town library on a Saturday afternoon so he could use the free Internet. He was showing me videos of IEDs going off in Baghdad, pictures of Kalashnikovs. He pulled up a long list of names, and pointed to one.

"This is the one they're fighting in Fallujah," he said, pointing to a line that read: The Badr Brigade.

"What does that mean?" I said. "The badr brigade? What's a badr?"

Samuel leaned back.

"In Arabic it means 'full moon,' apparently," Samuel said. He laughed. "We're like knockoffs," he said. "We're like the half-moon brigade. We're the half-moon martyrs' brigade," he said again, distantly.

Later that day, or maybe the next Saturday, Marly put down her fork at dinner and leaned forward, steepling her hands, her elbows on the table.

"Where have you ever even been?" she said to me. "Have you ever thought about that?"

At some point, by some miracle, we won enough games to get the last spot in the regional playoffs.

•

The game was on a Sunday, and church that morning was packed with double the usual crowd; the families and fans of the Athens' First Baptist Blasters looking slightly uncomfortable in our Church of the Holy Sepulcher (of the One True Congregation of the Savior

and Nazarene). Brother Reeter was supposed to give the special blessing at the end of services that day, in honor of the game, but he was missing the whole morning. Instead, Elder Peters had to get up and extemporize with some well-meaning verses. He seemed cheered by it, his voice rising as he went on about being the "shepherds of all that flies in the field" and avoiding "the errors that let our objects pass by our hands in distraction."

Brother Reeter didn't show at warm-ups either, though we didn't talk about it. None of us were talking much by then.

There are times in Kansas at the end of the summer when the land offers itself like an upturned palm, when the green and the air seem somehow elevated, overwhelming, and the late afternoon of that play-off game was like that. Both makeshift stands were full, and people had brought out lots of lawn chairs and large glass jugs of lemonade that they shared as they fanned themselves. They must have cheered at times during those first four innings, but mostly I just remember the quiet, heavy and flat, that seemed to have come over everything.

Samuel was pitching solidly, the ball cracking into Hilton's glove, sometimes the Athens' Bible batters visibly flinching at the sound. Seven innings in and he was throwing a perfect game: no hits, no walks, almost all strikes too.

Samuel didn't want to drift into the place he was used to going. He tried to focus on the particular details of each batter before he threw, tried to keep his mind there—he was tired of the desert, of ghosting behind the insurgents as they moved according, even in his head, to some mysterious design.

By the bottom of the seventh inning it was still tied, and all the uninitiated in the stands had by this time had it explained to them what a no-hitter was, what a perfect game meant in its spectacular rarity.

There were two outs and Samuel had run up a full count on the batter he was facing when he saw him. He threw a fastball and the

kid in the batter's box meekly presented his bat and by sheer luck the ball nicked the barrel and glanced off high, popping up straight down the third-base line.

I don't know why Samuel didn't look. He just stayed facing forward, while everyone in the crowd rose to their feet as one, craning to see if the ball would stay fair and ruin his perfect performance or drop safely into foul territory. Once he realized what was going on Reeter must've waited, hanging back, not wanting to show himself, not wanting to ruin at least this small thing for Samuel. But Reeter couldn't help it when that ball went up and the game was in the balance, and he took a small step to lean out around the corner of the stands he'd been standing behind and the dark green of his Casualty Affairs uniform gave him away.

His hands were clasped in an official-looking manner in front of him. The black of his military beret and his carefully polished shoes seemed very dark against the trees and the grass. As the ball fell safely foul and everyone relaxed, regaining their seats, most of the crowd looked at Samuel to see his reaction, his perfect game saved. Brother Reeter did too, by reflex, his body already moving back to where he'd been hidden. But he saw that Samuel was looking at him, saw that Samuel had seen him, and I watched a small cloud of frustration pass over Reeter's face before it went blank and he looked down and away and I knew that he had the manila envelope, and that he was waiting there for Samuel, for Samuel's mother, to be done.

Samuel Lincoln only paused a moment. Then he threw a blistering fastball that the batter fanned at hopelessly and the inning was over. While we were at bat in the eighth, the people in the stands must've realized that Brother Reeter was there and seen his uniform, because a kind of quiet swept over them. We kept on playing but nobody cheered. Around me in the stands, nobody said anything.

Samuel threw and threw, his breath hard and flat. He didn't wait

for Hilton's signals: it was all straight fastballs anyway. Around him the sky drew itself up for dusk, the air going watery and bluish, shadows gathering themselves in the corn and under the trees. Tiny birds played in the grass of the outfield, occasionally rising in a shifting, hovering form, as if to a soundless call. In the distance, behind the stands, the waters of Galilee Lake winked in the long sun.

The eighth inning passed, and the ninth, and the tenth. Brother Reeter had solemnly stepped out into full view after I'd seen him, and he stood now, watching silently. There was some discussion among the Athens coaches after the tenth inning, as if they didn't want to let the game go any further, like it was cruel now, but Samuel was already back on the mound, not even waiting for the batters, slamming the ball to Hilton again and again. When the first batter stepped up, it barely broke his rhythm.

In the top of the eleventh, Hilton floated a long fly ball over the corn for a home run. In the bottom Samuel struck out the three batters he faced in a row. The game was over and people began to get up from their seats, but Samuel hadn't stopped throwing. Hilton obediently stayed in place. Everyone was quiet. He just kept throwing. After about ten pitches, the batter who would've been next stepped up to the plate. Then the next. As each one struck out the next stepped up, the whole Athens team cycling quietly through again and again. After a while the majority of the crowd got up and petered away, averting their eyes as they went. A while later the rest of our team trotted slowly in from the field, then sat down on the bench to watch. They were followed by the umpire, who wordlessly stripped his gear. Samuel didn't look at anyone.

The Athens batters kept going, their coaches standing silently, their arms crossed. I don't know how long this went on. Samuel was doing something else by then, the pitching steps raveled into a suite of movement, a semaphore for nothing.

Finally one of their bigger batters swung hard and made contact. Everyone who was left watched as the ball sailed high and straight. It seemed to stay in the air for a long time before finally disappearing into the corn. Samuel turned around and breathed in the near dark. His teammates were all standing still, looking at him. Hilton had taken off his catcher's mask and now stood, glancing back and forth between Samuel and the bench. Brother Reeter was the only one left in the stands, and he stood. Samuel let his glove drop to the mound, and went to face him. We forfeited the next game, and just like that, summer was over.

●

They did not ask me to tape Samuel's turn in the shed. By then there were so many hands, so many punches to take. What I do know is that he had to go to the ER afterward, and that he sputtered blood all over the nurse's uniform trying to explain that he'd started the fight, that it was his fault, really.

●

We didn't find out that Douglas Reeter had been lying until late September, when my father and what was left of the unit came back. I told him at dinner all the stories Brother Reeter had told the team. I didn't even ask if they were true, but my father just got this long look in his face and stared over at the window for a while and said, "Honey, Douglas Reeter sat at a desk in Kuwait the entire time before coming back here. It was a reward for his typing skills. We didn't even see him."

It seems impossible that none of us had asked our fathers, in all those emails or calls, about Brother Reeter's stories, but I only remember the boys leaning across those rows of bleachers, looking off up into the sky or trees or grass, listening and listening. There was a news story once the men of our town that could come back did come back. We were briefly the town with the highest casualty rate of all the places in America that had sent men to the war. It only lasted a few months, though.

•

In the fall cold at midnight, the group of dark bodies standing back in the fallow field that fronted my house had a specter of frozen breath hovering over it. There was Samuel's face at my window. I followed him out without speaking.

Three of the boys were carrying their father's shotguns. Samuel already had his farm license, and we sat in the back of his truck, Douglas Reeter lying face down, hooded, gagged, hands bound behind his back with plastic zip-ties, between us.

In the shack, on the tape, his eyes are wild when the boys pull off the hood, when he sees the gun. They don't hit him. For some reason, this tape is the hardest of all of them to watch. He looks, his eyes so wide, at the shotgun that Samuel holds up to his face, but it's not that. There is the sharp, ammoniac scent of urine. Then, the part I can never get over: you see his shoulders soften, his eyes go dull—like he's accepting it. He closes his eyes. Samuel Lincoln pulls the trigger and there is only a click. Someone undoes Reeter's hands, and the boys file out, leave him there. They do not beat him. They do not really even touch him.

The tape follows the boys out, catches their faces where they stand together out in the cold, exhilarated. There is the faint sound of Reeter weeping, back in the shack.

And I remember them there well, I remember their faces, lit by the glow of the cigarette they pass around on the tape. Truman, who will accidentally kill his girlfriend driving around after prom, when he will take a hill on a gravel road too fast and the car will flip and roll, crushing her to death but sparing him perfectly, without even a scratch. P.J., Gary, and Ralph, who will move away after graduating, getting as far as Oklahoma City, St. Louis, and Omaha, respectively; all three mechanics, if you can believe it. Hilton Hedis, who will become an overweight student football manager for the University of Kansas, before getting fired after being arrested for breaking three bones in his girlfriend's face after a drunken fight, and finally end up with the job at the grain elevator in Cloud County. In the end only I will stay in New Jerusalem. Only I will be left around to remember.

•

The Old City at New Jerusalem still stands, more or less, though it's been closed to tourists ever since a wooden cutout of a minaret fell over on a kid from Kansas City, causing him a head injury. The well-marker shack and all of the old vacation cabins at the old Hope and Grace Bible Camp were pushed down a few years ago so the church could sell the land.

Samuel Lincoln and I dated all the way through high school, and we tried to keep it together in college—me at Pittsburg State, him at Missouri Southern—but Samuel eventually dropped out to go roughneck on an oil derrick outside Wichita Falls, though not before getting me pregnant with my beautiful daughter, who is five years old

now. I don't feel badly toward Samuel, in the end. As he got older he got eaten up by an anger even he didn't fully understand, I don't think. He sent along what I think must've been nearly the entirety of his paycheck, all the way up until the day he fell from some rigging and hit his head on a girder and died three days later in a hospital in Dallas.

Douglas Reeter and Marly ended up buying that old house on my father's property, and getting married. Three months after their wedding I was at college, and so I wasn't there at my window to see Marly steal away, leaving him as he slept. Nor was I there four weeks after that, when Douglas Reeter took himself off into the woods, making sure to get clear of my father's land, and put a bullet through the roof of his mouth.

Nobody really knows where Marly went, how far away she got. None of us have ever heard from her again, not a single word. I'll confess that sometimes, when the house is quiet and the light long and blue, I'll fantasize about the phone ringing, about me picking it up to hear nothing but a familiar breathing on the other end of the line. I want to ask her where she made it to, where she ended up going, what she ended up doing. I want to ask her if she made it all the way to the real Jerusalem, what it's like there. And I also want to tell her to come here and sit in my living room and dream up those dead boys with me again, Reeter and all. But I don't know what story I could tell her about how things went to convince her. I don't know what story there is that could bring her back.

The IED

1.

What is he looking at? The maze of light made by the high mud-brick walls of the narrow alley that the line of men, generously spaced, are navigating. It is the early part of late afternoon, the heat subdued into a smoldering focus by a low ceiling of clouds, everything very dry. The dust from the passage of something or someone—recently? hours ago?—floats through the diffuse angle of light at the intersection of two alleyways, giving the air there a sort of grain, causing it to briefly coruscate. But that is only at the border of what Abrams is looking at as he feels the strange texture under his boot, the slight resistance of the rectangular metal contact plate.

Though it's not a maze of light he can really see, not completely, at the moment, just one he imagines. The part he can see is, he supposes (or was supposing in the microseconds before registering the change under his foot), only one corridor. Farther along, he can also see the beginnings of a perpendicular corridor, another alley. Together they make one small corner of the maze.

It is enough: the narrow, dirt-floored alley, cast partially into cool shadow by the obstruction of the high walls on either side. It is

almost pleasant, the quiet at the end of their patrol, the stillness of the village around them, the genial fatigue of the men, which is a kind of gladness, Abrams has always thought. And it is this moment of mindfulness—when Abrams looked up from the ground in front of his feet and noticed the alley half in shadow and the slump of the shoulders of the men in front of him at their delicate distance—which caused Abrams to look farther upward, to allow his face to continue on its vertical pivot enough to take in the sky, the light, the unparsable complex of sky and light framed in that curious way by the tops of the walls into a kind of maze. And it was exactly then that he felt the slight slip, the sudden ease of friction beneath his right boot afforded by the metal contact plate.

Though that's not quite right either because it implies a false parade of events, when what it is surely more accurate to say—accuracy being meaningful to Abrams—is that there was a sensory-cognition master-fade type situation going on somewhere in his cortex, the phrase *maze of light* fading out even as *contact plate* or, more simply, *IED* faded in. That is to say that even as *maze of light* was dawning on Abrams (seeming, in fact, to fall down out of the vision in order to describe it) *IED* was beginning its scaled march into attention, so much so that the two thoughts may be said to have been coeval.

Neither is the irony lost on Abrams that it was a moment of actual mindfulness (and not distraction or carelessness) which possibly led him to place his foot on the small stretch of shallow dirt that hides the contact plate. He can still hear the instructor during the lengthy predeployment training exercises in the real alleys of the fake village in the Arizona desert. Specifically, that in order to *never ever* be *caught unawares* by the presence of an improvised explosive device while on patrol in the Shit, they needed to first and foremost learn how to *cultivate a state of extreme mindfulness* in which each of them could stare at the ground, the dirt in front of their feet (carefully stepping

only in the compressed boot shapes of dust left by the man ahead), for hours and not become *zombified* or otherwise rendered senseless to the small hints of micro-terrestrial disturbance that would signal the presence of a device.

Abrams had thus far handled the weeks of their patrol assignment by allowing himself to focus so hard he lost all sense of scale. In his vision the miniature landscapes of alley dirt became actual landscapes; the ridges and mounds, the troughs, the swales, all began to loom, began to feel like life-sized features of an entire sprawling world.

No, what Abrams and the other men actually needed was a sort of mind*less*ness, an absence of thought that would allow them to stare at unremarkable stretches of dust and dirt for hours at a time without developing an acute awareness of the moment, or the light, or the other men, or any of the marginalia of actual experience that is *mindfulness*. It now seems a strange irony that such a human moment—the maze of light, the pleasant preprandial lull of the village, the alley wearing its stole of shadow, the pleasant cutting scent of the other men's sweat—has possibly led to Abrams' imminent cranial evacuation by way of shrapnel moving through the tissues of his face at unimaginable speeds.

Unbidden, the flash of memory: Mrs. Clowney (sharp-faced, gently obese English 9 teacher). She is repeating, somewhat smugly, the *true definition* of irony. *Irony is when the audience is aware of something that the player on stage is himself unaware of.*

Unbidden, also, the related memory of Mrs. Packard, Abrams' third-grade teacher, trying, for some reason, to impress upon the class the unthinkable speed of light. She is standing at the classroom's light switch, flipping it on and off, which sets off tremors of giggles. Abrams raises his hand (the teacher's face falling at another of his questions) and asks which is faster, then, the time it takes the

electricity to go from the switch to the light, or the time it takes the light from the light bulb to reach their eyeballs, or the time it takes the students themselves to know that the lights are on? For a moment, Mrs. Packard, in her sturdy floral dress, goes silent, her face bled of its pride at her lesson. She clasps her hands in front of her in a way that Abrams understands on some level as a sign of vulnerability, of being hurt in some way by this child, which makes him feel really bad the rest of the day every time he looks at her, though, of course, he can't explain why.

Later, when he learned about it in college, Abrams couldn't believe how slowly perceptions and conscious sensations move into our attention, outpaced often (always?) by even our own reptilian subsystems. Also in college, Abrams, long suspicious of Mrs. Clowney, ended up looking up the definition of irony, finding its root to be in εἰρωνεία, meaning "dissimulation" or "feigned ignorance," which Abrams thought sounded more like it. His body (specifically his foot) knows before he does, but cannot bear to short-circuit his mind's self-myth of mastery, and so must feign ignorance, must wait until the phrase *IED* finishes its patient fade into Abrams' mind, *maze of light* still echoing in some synaptic hallway.

2.

But does his foot know? Is it reacting? The extraordinary efficiency of the human sole cannot be denied. Think of the things it is capable of—eloquent distribution and redistribution of weight, shifting phalangeal deployment, a notable ability to take the changing physical demands of a normal day (sprinting toward a bus stop in wooden-soled business shoes) in stride. That Abrams has become aware of the contact plate at all is in fact proof of his foot's intelligence.

And yet. And yet his right foot, encased in its boot, is not stop-ping, is not pausing in its rolling heel-then-arch-then-toe impression into the dirt. The heel strikes—it has no reason to pause. Even when the mid-sole falls, is pressed into the dirt—still no cause for hesi-tation. But then, finally, the ball. The hinge of the cuneiform bone (beautiful term) extending into the gentle metatarsal has predeter-mined Abrams' fate. The application to the ground of the plantar fas-cia (horrible term) may not be stopped. And so the ball of the foot, the ball of the boot's outsole, falls, and Abrams' weight begins to shift onto its pad, and the strange texture beneath.

But already Abrams' heel is rising (has risen) from the location of its initial strike, separating itself from the dirt, and the cuneiform bone is pulling at the local terminus of the metatarsal, taking it along in its launch back into the air and light.

This moment Abrams does truly grasp, understanding pluming up through all levels of processing—he can feel it in the arch of mus-cle between his shoulders. It is a kind of resignation—bodily, men-tally—intuitive, but encompassing in its intuition. It is the feeling of helplessness at time passing, of the loss of experience even as it occurs.

Abrams has been aware of various declensions of this moment his whole life—one scene which now cloud-shadows its way across his interior vision.

He stands in an abandoned lakeside dairy, which has been repur-posed for the night into an event space for his best friend's wed-ding reception. He stands at the edge of the high room, a cuneiform alphabet of pipes still decorating the walls and ceiling; he stands there with Sarah, his girlfriend, who they do not know yet is sick, taking in at once the writhing organism of the dance floor, the large glass windows of what was once (he guesses) a loading bay. Beyond: train tracks, the black expanse of the lake, only a field of absence in

the dark. It has been a wonderful wedding, held out of doors in the uncharacteristically brisk late August day, on a grassy knoll outside of a relative's cabin. Beyond the pastor on the little platform there was the lake, its waters lacerated by the small, sharp edges of wind. And now: the night in the abandoned dairy, the reception. Earlier, someone passed out toy kazoos before the bride and groom arrived and when they finally entered everyone played "A Bicycle Built for Two." Those without kazoos had sung. And now here Abrams is, standing very still. Sarah is exhausted, draped over a chair beside him. They do not know she is sick yet.

He can feel the mass of experiential detail swelling, as he stands there, a sundae in a Styrofoam bowl from the make-your-own sundae buffet melting in his right hand. He's waiting for the train. It has come through once, not slowing, very early in the event, right after he and Sarah arrived. The tracks, once laid for easy loading from the dairy, pass within feet of what is now the wall of glass. It is fiercely loud, piercing in its intensity. It is truly a *blast* of motion, so near and pervasive that one's body seems a participant in its very direction, to the point where the explosion of dark metal (and sound) seems to be emanating from the atoms of one's own body. For a few seconds, while your consciousness is still catching up (slow, so slow), you are the train, barreling into the nothingness of the night by some propulsion that is beyond will or intention. The waiting has become excruciating.

The waiting has become torturous, less due to anticipation than the nagging sense that Abrams has understood the experience too late, that it is even now slipping from the grasping electricities of his memory. He will never be in this abandoned dairy again, he knows. There can be only tragic falling-offs from the first world of this night, from the train's transcendent passage. The passage he is now waiting for, if in fact it ever comes, will be over almost even as it begins,

exactly because Abrams has become aware of its singularity. It feels ridiculous to be made panicky by something so abstract and common as the passage of time, but the simple fact of it—Abrams understanding it on a muscular level—deflates the experience for Abrams even as the train does arrive, and the dancers are shattered into fear and surprise, and Abrams tries and fails to itemize his perceptions and observations and the ironies of the moment so extensively as to slow time to the point of cessation. Of course he fails, he *must* fail, and the rest of the night feels like a letdown, had already felt like a letdown, even before the train noise recurred.

But Abrams' sense of anticipatory nostalgic loss is not altogether unpleasant, in its way. He doesn't know when he developed it, how young he was when he first understood. The relaxation that he experiences in the moment of his knowing about the contact plate beneath the ball of his right foot and that same foot's continued motion, is—it must be said—distinctly pleasurable. Another cloud-shadow of memory darkening the screen of his mind: the sweltering parking lot in Minneapolis, some forgotten road trip with his poor, nervous mother.

He is standing outside one of those old-fashioned Dairy Queen stands, this one planted in the middle of a gray concrete parking lot that seems to Abrams as vast as the sea. He is a little boy, and the stand, with its antiquated retro neon signage, looms above him spectacularly. His mother has let him order for himself, and in something like a fit of pleasure Abrams speaks up and asks wildly for the combination he's noticed on the menu board, the synthesis of two of his favorite treats—a vanilla ice cream Blizzard, with (the electric quiver of joy) Nerds in it. "Nerds" being the sour, granular candy popular at the time, which came in unexpected marriages of colors, a small mountain spread in the palm of one's hand turning into a pointillist residual portrait on one's skin. A great deal of the pleasure for

little Abrams is to be had simply in the breathless idea of such a thing: the play of the possible visual alone (the sharp, glossed color of the Nerds, implanted delicately in the creamscape of the vanilla ice cream) making his skin tingle. But also the taste—previously unthinkable—the contrast at once of the milky, cold, sweet vanilla against the eye-squintingly sour acid of the Nerds: an oral chiaroscuro never before conceived of by the staff of all other Dairy Queens Abrams has ever visited. This all not to mention the texture, the queer graininess of the ice cream with its hard secret of Nerds, the sensation carrying with it the unmistakable sense of transgression, as if eating rocks and dirt. And all of this present just in the thought, the galaxy of delight expanding rapidly, anticipatorily in Abrams' mind and nerve centers as he orders—nervously, having to repeat it again louder for the visored teenager at the till. Abrams speaks his order again anxiously, as if a jealous deity might perhaps strike him down for requesting of the world such a thing as a Nerd-filled Blizzard, offered almost clandestinely by only this particular Dairy Queen.

And so Abrams stands there on the concrete sea, in the sweltering heat, and looks down at his narrow cup, the red spoon stabbed into the blank territory of pleasure. Abrams feels the anxiety of the first bite spreading over his body like a very tiny horse race across his epidermis, Abrams tracing its progress from the environs of his anus up into the space below his belly button and then across the plain of his chest. He can feel his intestines spasm. He looks down into the cup and uses the spoon with its garish red to swirl the already melting contents. Shockingly, something Abrams has not foreseen: the color-coating of the Nerds, enveloped by the ice cream, has begun to bleed into the pure bed of ecru. Each individual Nerd leaves an arcing trail of hue, dissipating in intensity and, worst of all, revealing at its core a heart of whiteness, which all collectively sit on the field of ice cream like teeth thrown across an unwashed linen sheet.

Abrams supposes that this feeling, this loosening from between his shoulders through his core and reaching finally his sphincter, is what makes men, particularly soldiers, defecate in the process of their deaths. It is a kind of peacefulness, it is true. There's nothing particularly special or original about the pleasure of abandon, Abrams knows. Perhaps there lies within the sensation of knowing, of (literally) striding forth into the moment of his fate, some sort of masochistic desire, a sense in which Abrams' appreciation of the maze of light and the calm fall of shadow was in fact beckoning the violence of the thing in the dirt which he cannot see. A death wish. Perhaps this is what—underneath all the paroxysms of memory—he's really wanted. Why else can he not stop his foot, really?

Just as he cannot stop now the memory of Lara Fugelsang, the tall, severe-faced, blonde lesbian in the philosophy seminar he'd taken back in graduate school.

Abrams had assumed Lara was a lesbian mostly because she had a girlfriend, and a face that featured prominent, martial cheekbones. She was writing her thesis on some inherently boring, ultraspecific example of gender politics in government language usage, and her comments in seminar were always throbbing with disgust and carefully curated anger. Abrams hated her. He hated her comments. He hated gender politics in general, and especially her diluted third-wave, recherché feminism which was really, he'd always suspected, just a collection of exceedingly normal personal anxieties. He had no idea what Lara was really like, or where she'd come from. He only really knew that she'd gone to Brown.

Abrams spent a lot of time staring at Lara in that seminar. And it was this that he hated the most about her: that the sight of her made Abrams wonder if, really, deep down, he hated women. He worried about this a lot. He did not feel that he hated women. He supported feminism, when it was not being annoyingly espoused in seminars,

and generally shared the reasoning of many girls and women he'd known who hated men. He was, by all accounts, a conscientious, generous, and democratic lover. But there was the blowjob thing, which was undeniable.

What he would eventually begin to do, every single time the seminar met, was to look at the female members of the class and imagine, especially when they began to talk, forcing his penis into each of their mouths. He needed no extended barstool monologue from Lara (though he'd heard her give a very good one on the subject) to understand the inherent misogynistic issues involved in the act of oral sex itself, let alone what it might mean about Abrams that he sat there and imagined what he did about the women in the seminar, not all of whom he hated. He didn't hate all of them, but the exercise was especially exciting, he squirmingly admitted to himself, when it was someone he did hate, when it was Lara herself. He was consistently taken aback, somewhat horrified in the midst of his helpless reverie, by the violence implied in this carnality. He often even felt victimized by it himself. He did not want to be the kind of man who sat there and imagined—with asinine pleasure—this act. And yet he was that kind of man, apparently. Which made him think he secretly—unbeknownst even to himself—bore some vast reservoir of hatred for women. Which made him hate Lara—Lara in the specific, he defended to himself, who *happened* to be a woman—even more.

But then the computer lab. The first deposits of their theses were due the next day, and Abrams and Lara were the only ones left at their workstations at 2:47 in the morning. Abrams had been reviewing leaked U.S. Government memos for his own thesis (*False Narrative Constructions in Intelligence Reporting, 1976–2001*), which would eventually get him the enlistment appointment with the Defense Intelligence Agency, and which in turn would lead to his job at the Combat Review Repository in Tucson (which itself would

eventually lead to his attachment to this unit, in Iraq, in the dusty alley where the device of his fate awaited him). He didn't know what Lara was working on.

What he did know was that they were both printing off large amounts of material, and had been taking awkward turns getting up from their seats and going to the boxy printer to retrieve their documents. As the hour grew later and later, however, their papers became mixed, and they kept getting in each other's way during simultaneous fetchings. Abrams was pretty sure Lara had twice now taken a stack of documents that belonged to her and purposefully included in her grab the documents he'd printed off, then thrown them away on the other side of the lab. He retaliated by doing the same to a packet of hers at the back of his own pile. The next three times they got up, Lara became more physical, elbowing him out of the way. On the fourth time, when she went to elbow him, Abrams shouldered into her, which she responded to by hip-checking him sideways with surprising strength, sending him caroming painfully into the corner of the table the printer stood on and then to the ground. Abrams got up quickly, the blood in his face pounding, and pushed her.

By some tangoing struggle, Abrams ended up standing against her from behind, and pressed up against each other like that, they each suddenly and simultaneously became aware of his erection.

Abrams was so tired and supremely confused by the erection, and the situation that gave rise to it, that he took a small step backward, his face falling, feeling both ashen and humiliated.

"Listen, I—" he started to choke out. He was going to apologize. Lara did not turn around.

What Lara did was bend slowly forward, bracing herself against the table, which motion reclosed the space between her ass (its shape Abrams had noticed watching her go to and from the printer, covered thinly by her light dress and tights) and the taut front of Abrams'

slacks. She looked back over her shoulder at him, her eyes flashing, almost angry, but sincere.

"Oh, just do it already," she said, and without really thinking Abrams undid his pants and let them drop and pushed up the soft material of her dress and pulled down her tights—she wore nothing underneath—and commenced intercourse with her, just like that.

Even as he was doing it he was aware of the queasiness of it, the problematic nature of what was happening. There were so many things at once: Abrams had never had sex in public before; he was terrified that he was enacting some surely misogynistic male proto-fantasy about "turning" a lesbian by phallic force; he was also concerned that he was raping her, and he stopped cold at the thought, looking at his hands lightly grasping Lara's narrow hips, trying to scan an objective description of the situation for any signs of resistance (was she being sarcastic? were her verbalizations now ones of pleasure or horror? was he in any way manhandling her?) but she only moved back against him more forcefully. And overlaid on everything was the childish surprise: he'd thought Lara hated him; he'd thought he hated Lara. With a shudder, and a sound from Lara, he ejaculated, and was done. They were still for a few long seconds, his heart beating wildly.

Abrams knows, if their seminar that semester had encountered this scene in a novel, the women of the class would have had a field day tearing it down as a completely unbelievable, pathetic projection of the author's openly misogynistic domination fantasy, and moreover would point out that it was irresponsible to put it to paper under the aegis of fiction, that it took advantage of the faux-displacement of responsibility for the scene onto the (flawed, sexist) character, and also that it was just totally unbelievable—and Abrams would've agreed with all of that. But it happened! It really happened, just that way! This was part of the irony of it, he supposes, remembering how

he'd backed away, softening out of her, the air in the computer lab suddenly licking at his slickened penis like cold fire. Lara had gathered herself silently, with effortless dignity, and excused herself to go to the bathroom. She'd left the building from the bathroom, and never said a word about what happened to Abrams. The ultimate irony being that even if he'd wanted to (which he did not), he could never have told anyone what had actually happened, because nobody would ever believe him. Thank god she had not performed the sex act he'd spent so many long hours imagining in seminar, Abrams thought, or there was no way he'd be able to live with himself.

The uncomfortable but honest point of all this being that, in those moments when everything began to happen—when she'd leaned back into him, and Abrams' mind leapt forward, already thrusting away at her pale skin—he'd been possessed by the purest instance of joy he'd ever felt. His whole body became light and airy. This seems to Abrams on some fundamental level pretty unfair to the more meaningful and substantive things in his life that he has experienced before and since, but it is, nonetheless, true.

When it came time for them to peer-review each other's theses, her notes were, oddly, both harsh and funny, a somewhat disturbing combination that over the years became even more so due to its tendency to inexplicably recur in other contexts around him.

3.

Abrams was so delighted by the last of these phrases, he didn't even mind that it came back to him in the middle of a document dismantling (in methodical, phosphorescently intelligent terms) his first Combat Action Sustainability Tactic (or CAST) report at the DIA center in Tucson. *Unrepentant lily-gilding*, Abrams thought. If that's not a perfect synecdoche for the joy to be had in life, there isn't one.

The evaluation was written by Brockton L. Albright, technically Abrams' only colleague in the CAST report pod. Abrams
was pretty sure the DIA had picked up Brockton on waivers from
the CIA, mostly because he simply couldn't imagine Brockton—
who had the dark brown ringlets and vaguely mournful mien of an
Eastern hagiological icon—ever willfully enlisting in any wing of the
military. Brockton, whose interface review setup was just across the
pod, spoke very, very little. Sometimes Abrams would see him coming into the cavernous space of the hangar that housed the twin geo-
desic domes of the interfaces, as Abrams paused behind the small
organ of super-servers humming diastolically to one side. Abrams
would watch him move over the polished concrete floors of the heavily air-conditioned hangar soundlessly, as if gliding.

Abrams' assignment was to prepare and submit CAST analy-
ses of raw media from the field, which he displayed on the 3D view-
ing screens arranged in an angled cascade of triptychs around and
over the desk in his interface office. Specifically, this was data focusing on the temporal environs of any American casualty that occurred
in Iraq, as gathered by the many unblinking electronic eyes that the
DIA and the Defense Advanced Research Projects Agency might
bring to bear.

The most helpful of these technologies was by far the improbably named Gorgon Stare Platform (basically: a hovering bundle
of very high-performing, very expensive video cameras and sen-
sors, which sits static high above an Iraqi town when U.S. forces
are operating in the area), especially when used in conjunction with
the somewhat more aptly christened ARGUS system, though it was
unclear if anyone at DARPA was aware of that namesake's ultimate
fate. ARGUS, that is, being the Autonomous Real-time Ground
Ubiquitous Surveillance system, the overall objective of which was
"to increase situational awareness and understanding enabling an

ability [sic] to find and fix critical events in a large area in enough time [sic] to influence events." What these two utilities meant for Abrams was that, once he'd booted up the Casualty Data Packet for that week, he could start, stall, restart, and otherwise retard diegetic time, all while remotely controlling the focus, zoom, and direction of three-dimensional vision in order to examine any person, face, gaze, biometrical reading or sight-line in the town when someone was killed. It was such an advanced and acute technology, and was played out in 3D for so many hours on the towering, enveloping screens, that Abrams always ended up with the feeling of *actually being there* as the casualty event happened, over and over and over.

What a CAST analysis or report really was, according to Brockton, who spent three weeks of painful vocal communication and social company training Abrams, was a *narrativization of combat casualty data*. They were to place a special emphasis on *creative conjecture* with the ultimate goal of using all this literally fantastic technology and data to render a written narrative of the casualty's *subjective experience of the pertinent combat event*. The precipitated narrative was, presumably, to be even more telling, accurate, and useful, from a procedural standpoint, than the soldier's actual subjective experience, were he alive to describe it. Brockton, whose reports Abrams also peer-reviewed, was very good at it. He had the right kind of obsessive attention and (much rarer) eidetic imagination for the job, and, moreover, he seemed to be well enough acquainted with the kind of quiet, continuous inner suffering necessary to become each casualty, to know both the soldier's mind and the technology's omniscience at once. Abrams was not so well suited to the task, he thought. What Brockton made Abrams feel about himself, basically, was that he simply wasn't intelligent enough to be in the pod at all.

This wasn't Brockton's fault. Each day, Abrams and Brockton ate lunch together at a picnic table outside of the hangar, in the falsely

natural landscaping of the empty civilian industrial park. Each day they made polite if burdened conversation, and Abrams always felt like his pathetic eagerness, his desire just to listen to Brockton speak—about anything really—was writ large on their awkwardly syncopated conversational silences.

What Abrams really wanted to do, though, in those long hours of watching Brockton's thin fingers expertly disassembling his daily orange, was to ask him about his childhood, what he'd been like as a kid; if his father (as was Abrams' suspicion) had died when he was young; if, a little older, he'd had a girlfriend, and what that had been like, what the girl had been like, and had they ever had sex, and if so, how, and etcetera etcetera etcetera. It was a kind of aggression, Abrams understood, his desire to know—information being a kind of domination, a kind of ownership, when it came to another person's life. And it was probably also a more or less understandable overspill from the task they paused each day for lunch; the delving into personnel files, the scans of letters home, but also the imagining, the conjecturing. *What you're really trying to do,* Brockton had explained to Abrams, in a rare moment of fluster during those weeks of training, *is not just explain why the subject died but what it was about the subject's very being—i.e., the subject's life, training, attention—that led to the casualty event.*

The report that inspired the delightful formulation *unrepentant lily-gilding* was one Abrams wrote about the death of Pfc. Ferrero Rodriguez in the gentle elbow of the Tigris. Abrams doesn't know what it was about that particular Casualty Data Packet that got to him. Maybe it was the dumb nature of the casualty, pretty much an accident, a tank parked in an inopportune place. Or maybe it was the data from the operator-facing control-board combat camera, the way Ferrero had just been sitting there at his station, how he looked around at the first strange sucking sound, then tried to brace himself

at the initial shift, the tank's sudden, listing angle. Confused, a blank-faced teenager (Was this a prank? Ferrero was thinking. Or did the tread fall off or something? Did the navigator Ash-Dog steer them into another pothole, the idiot?). Then that data-stream cutting out as the tank made its slow topple into the river.

Or maybe it was the overhead view from the satellite, the pastoral beauty of the picture: the angle held wide, the waters of the Tigris a brilliant emerald snake in the sun. Or was it the maudlin thing, the scan of his last letter home, which they'd stopped: just a list of things he needed his mom to send him, that he couldn't or was too afraid to ask for from the other guys: underwear, chapstick, something called Boudreaux's Butt Paste. Well. It didn't really matter what it was that made Abrams say screw it, basically, and write what he wanted to write.

He gave Pfc. Ferrero Rodriguez a good life, a better life than he'd actually had. And he used the last half of the report to describe, in increasingly florid, turgid, self-consciously rococo language, the kid's last moments. In his report the eternity of the tank's dorsal rotation into the water stretched on and on, creating a sort of zero-gravity type situation where Ferrero Rodriguez could watch the grease pencils and loose snacks and dirt and strands of chewing tobacco float, weightless, in the air around him, and wonder, and reflect. And so, of course, Brockton's lightly caustic evaluation of the report had been accurate, and fair, and had happened to include the phrase *unrepentant lily-gilding*. *This is not the truth*, he'd also written. *This is you being desperate for some kind of validation*. But the truth was that Pfc. Ferrero Rodriguez drowned in the Tigris when the bank under his parked tank collapsed, drowned slowly, drowned knowing he was going to drown, drowned clawing desperately at the sharp metal of the blocked hatch that was now beneath his feet, drowned defecating all over himself in utter terror. And Abrams just couldn't write that.

What is Brockton Albright doing now, this moment of Abrams' foot's fateful lifting progress? After they'd both left the pod assignment (Abrams reassigned to actual unit attachment, Brockton having finished his contract), Albright began a very successful career as an academic and a public intellectual. He's now in residence at the Sorbonne, Abrams believes. And Abrams thinks of him now in some Latin Quarter square, almost dusk, his thin fingers lost in his lap, his tiny cup of tea forgotten on its saucer before him. Oh, what Abrams could've been in life, if he'd only tried a little harder.

But Abrams' favorite thing to remember from his time in the pod with Brockton in Tucson is actually the rare instance of Brockton's smile. Such a saccharine thing to willfully remember, but it holds the same relation to Abrams' happiness (even now) as Lara Fugelsang's smirking sneer does to Abrams' shame. Brockton was an unexpectedly funny guy, Abrams remembers, though he never smiled at or after his own deadpan, absurdist one-liners. Abrams can't actually remember what made Brockton smile those few times—surprise seemed to have something to do with it, and being unobserved—but Abrams can remember very clearly what it looked like. Brockton's whole face changed, opening up, brow for once relaxing, lifting, spreading—and the impression of vulnerability flashing then across his features was so startling as to make Abrams look away. For just a second Brockton seemed just like a little boy, granted a pulse of pure, unmediated feeling.

"Momentary joy" was the phrase that always stuck in Abrams' mind when he thought of it. A blooming. What a thing to have seen.

The principal legacy of the CAST pod assignment, though, these years later, now that Abrams has been attached to an actual unit in the actual Shit, is the ghosting awareness of being on the other end of the CAST technologies' flow—of being in the midst of all the "data" that is really just the world, the village, the late afternoon, the alley. It's stopped

Abrams cold each time he's allowed his mind to wince itself across the thought. What CAST data operator, sitting in what American hangar, was watching him now, displaced in time? That, of course, was the very worst part of that assignment: the nebulized awareness, as he worked, that the subject was being kept alive there before him for only the exact duration of Abrams' close attention, and that, at some point—a point Abrams could feel dawning even as he opened for the first time each new Casualty Data Packet—Abrams would grow bored, and tired, and inured to the human life which he held in the circuitry of the control board before him—in the circuitry of his mind—and would allow it, finally, to expire. What finite expansion of memory and experience would he grant himself, if he found his own CDP loaded up on the screens, the cursor ticking away? And the irony, even in this moment of abandon, of there now actually being created, at this very moment, a CDP for this purpose, is not lost on Abrams, though he knows it's not irony, really, just the remediated sadness of knowing.

4.

The contact plate itself is suspended, the tiny metal ridge on the underside of the plate now loosed from its delicate restraints by the pressure of Abram's foot. Its destination—the small metal tab which will complete the electric circuit, thereby triggering the small deto- nation charge, which, in turn, will trigger the primary explosive (in this case, Abrams knows, probably an unexploded landmine sal- vaged from the Iran–Iraq war)—awaits, patiently. The contact plate has thus far been stilled in that motionless nadir of its spring-loaded inverted arc of travel but, as Abrams' foot helplessly begins its lift (the pressure of his weight on the contact plate lessening every microsec- ond), the charged metal surface is now rising, heading toward its kis- met of electronal reunion.

The alley's stole of shadow moves again, Abrams thinks. The alley is attempting to shrug it off, it seems. The reverse inertia of what is about to happen is lightening the alley before him, it seems.

IED is really a terrible term for the device, for what this device that is agent of Abrams' fate really is. There's nothing "improvised" about it, first of all. There's nothing spontaneous, extemporaneous, or accomplished without preparation there in its careful circuitry, its repurposed materiel. "Explosive" is a little better, but also fails to capture the true quantum entanglement of possibility in this alley-deposited incendiary: that is, that it could fail to go off, could not be explosive at all, ultimately. It is a *possibly* explosive thing, a probable explosive. This is a relatively unforgivable lingual oversight given the defiance of experience—of life itself.

"Device," though, is the telltale heart of the term. It marries in its etymology the essences of its Middle English, Old French, and Latin ancestors, pulling through the original sense of "desire" into "will" and even "last will," and bringing the word to its dark end of signal with "means of division." The IED is fate itself. Abrams was always moving toward it. It was created (he imagines some nameless scarred ghost of an insurgent bent over the basement table in perfect silence, with no morbid élan, even) for no other death than his. Time has existed in his life for no other purpose than to draw him through it, to guide him into this particular stride.

What has he imagined he'd think of, in this moment? All that most indulgent memory of private beauty, the jetsam of his thirty years blinking in the sunlight of this planet.

Abrams at twelve years old, on a trip to London, lost in the deserted financial district, when the clock hits noon exactly and suddenly the buildings burst with people, and he looks up, and all around him are men all wearing (thrilling, the coincidence) pastel shirts and ties, a shifting, towering forest of brightly-colored

thoraces, Abrams overwhelmed with pleasure. Also as a boy, his mother calling him ABCD, instead of Abrams, for no good reason. Approaching a county fair's carnival from a far field, the loopy, maniac music of the rides, the rich smell of funnel cake, it all reaching him before he can see anything but a sort of macula of light on the horizon. When he is older, a tour guide's funny voice echoing around his visit of Pompeii. The grassy mountaintop campus in Sewanee, Tennessee. The shirt (long-sleeved, striped with a Creamsicle orange color) that his first girlfriend kept on the first time he ever had sex. Going to a local café late at night after a different girl's volleyball games and drinking overly rich hot chocolate while eating artisanal pizza and pretending to be in Paris, or Rome, talking to each other about all the great sites they pretended to have seen that day. But also, the only perfect date he's ever been on, much later, in Athens. They'd had gyros (the woman's hair still wet from the shower) at a small corner restaurant in a very quiet neighborhood square, the dark face of the church at the square's other end somber and still. Then they'd gone to an anonymous building, gone up the stairs to the top of it, to a rooftop showing of a terribly dubbed American movie on a screen just beside which, in the near distance, was the Acropolis, set ablaze in the sunset. At the intermission, they'd both bought strawberry-and-ices, and sipped them silently together back in their seats, in the warm night.

5.

What is he looking at? The maze of light made overhead by the high, mud-brick walls of the alley system. The aimless whorl of dust motes on the thick, slanted bar of brighter light in the intersection ahead. The synclinal area of darkened cloth at the back of the next man's uniform, below the deeply umber, slickened skin of his neck.

And there in the very last glancing collision of thought in his mind's eye, the realization: while the sole of his boot was there on the ground, a small system of trapped spaces must've formed in there between the rubberized nubbins and blocks, closed off by the sudden floor of earth beneath the boot. Closed off, a labyrinth with no entrance or middle or exit: a lightless maze. It is piercing to think of this miniature, lightless maze, enclosed by the fateful fall of his foot; a maze of darkness made of the once grand miniature landscape of Abrams' obsessive attention, itself set within the momentary beauty of the maze of light made by the high walls of the alley. But just as soon as the image (or anti-image, as it were) is formed in Abrams' awareness comes the hounding truth, the stomach-pit feeling of the truth: that the perfect maze of darkness within the maze of light only existed for the brief moment of the boot's full contact; that Abrams himself has ruined it with his boot's lifting progress; that it was ruined from that first moment of rising heel, which let in the light; that he has realized the truth about the maze within a maze just slightly too late to truly wonder at it; that it is all, in fact, already gone.

A Life

The man's body was floating face down, slowly drifting counter-clockwise in the clear water of the natural pool, his dark skin glistening as if newly splashed, like he might at any moment raise his face out of the water. Sambul and Soren perched on the low stone wall, watching his lazy circling and the deeper shimmer of green light as a turtle made its sudden glide from rock to rock beneath. Sambul watched Soren, the pool's reflection filling the white man's overlarge sunglasses as he crouched, kneading one hand with the other, and everyone waited for him to say what they should do.

Sambulru Moekena hadn't been the one to discover the drowned man; instead, it had been Benny, one of the trackers, knocking nervously on Sambul's door before first light, talking quickly about the thing he'd seen, or thought he'd seen, in the spring's small reservoir. Sambul had asked Benny no questions, instead only waiting calmly until the sun was fully risen before going to see for himself. Standing there with nervous Benny beside him, the fog still swirling low in the brush, there hadn't seemed to be any way Sambul could avoid going, upon his return to the compound, up to the great house and interrupting Soren at his breakfast. Soren, for his part, had

seemed curious, almost excited by the prospect of such an anomaly, but now that they were there, in the presence of the body, Sambul recognized the old frustration in Soren's posture: Soren's annoyance with Sambul, the guides, and the world in general for presenting a problem that could not simply resolve itself.

Soren squatted on the lip of the crumbling wall surrounding the pool. He was looking up at the distant hills whence an errant British mortar shell had arced fifty years before, landing in this spot and leaving in its crater the revelation of the spring and its cool, pooling waters. Soren told Sambul once, in a jovial mood as they drove around the grounds of the preserve, that he'd always imagined the soldiers, far from home and country, had been drinking and suffered a crisis of faith when ordered to volley a last round into the native village below, turning their artillery instead to this vast stretch of flat red dirt and brush. Sambul could remember how they had laughed together, briefly, at the thought. It had now been a long time, though, since Soren had been in such a talkative mood. As if making up his mind, Soren sighed and dropped his gaze back to the body, speaking without turning to one of the guides.

"Can you bring him out?" he said, sounding very tired. "I need to see his hands."

●

Sambul's earliest memory of Soren Wheeler always began with the puzzle of light pieced above his head by the overlapping leaves of tea bushes as he ran crazily down the tunnels of their rows. Sambul was small enough—still no more than nine years old—to fit into the darkened miniature corridors formed by the hidden spaces between the rows of trunks, their dense tops, when viewed from the road,

fitting seamlessly together in a carpet of waxy green. Running the
rows was Sambul's—and every other child's on the tea concern—
favorite thing to do, hilariously escaping the overanxious thrall of
Mama Potol, the panicky woman assigned to look after the children
while their mothers worked in the fields or the warehouse. The game
was to slip off into the rows and race and race, exploding finally onto
the dirt road that divided the fields, preferably when a group of people (sometimes foreigners, tourists or investors, but always white)
was just passing by, giving them a scare before jetting across into the
opposing row, howling with laughter at the pale gourds of their faces.
It had been in the midst of this exact activity, in fact, that Sambul first
encountered Soren Wheeler, when Sambul leapt from the rows, surprising a small family of white people, and Soren, himself only seven
or eight, but taller, tried to follow as Sambul made his escape.

Though, of course, Sambul, now separated from the day by many
long years, knew this was not really the *first* time he had encountered Soren, knew it could not have been, for when had Sambul ever
seen such a thing as the impossibly white-blond hair trailing away
from the other boy's face as he gave chase—when had Sambul ever
before even seen a white person so small? Yet his memory of watching (winded and perched in a tree at the far edge of the field) the very
top of the boy's blond head crashing through the row toward him
was not one of surprise, or fear.

Sambul instead believed that what set this memory perma-
nently in his mind was the sight of his own mother, scrambling, falling, running toward him down the hill of tea rows behind the tree,
her picking bag slurring a trail of leaves into the high, brilliant sunlight around her. It was the only time Sambul ever saw anyone stop
working during their shift, and that feeling—his slow realization
that he'd done something wrong, that her eyes, wide with fear, were
turned not toward Sambul but to the blond bobber of hair coming

fast through the rows and beyond it the figures (Sambul only now thinking to look) of the white man and woman, standing frozen back on the road—was the same feeling that Sambul would associate with Soren's presence all the way until they were teenagers: a small, tense knot of queasy excitement and shame.

As far as Sambul could later reconstruct, this incident must have taken place shortly before Soren's father, concerned over his young American child's loneliness on a new continent, doubled Sambul's mother's pension and paid it eight years early in exchange for her allowing the Wheelers to take Sambul to live with them "for the season" at the family estate, a full day's journey inland by car from the tea grounds. And if this was true then it could only have been a few months later that Soren's mother, Martha Wheeler, sat Sambul down on one of the estate's stiff living room couches and told him that his mother, retired in the small town near the tea concern, had died of untreated malaria. This was Sambul's second memory of being a boy with Soren: Soren's hand rubbing small circles on his back as Sambul lay on his bed and cried; Soren trying his best, saying, "Well, you're too tall now to run the rows anyway, at least."

They'd lived in those years on the grounds of what Soren's father, Danforth Wheeler, called "the lodge" and everyone else, including the Kikuyu servants and Soren's mother, called "the estate." The estate was a compound of buildings arranged around a great house originally built by one of the Wheelers' forbears as an American hunting lodge and meant to rival the opulent British ones of African lore. Soren's father had preserved the hunting and guide business, relocating and updating it into a circle of semiluxury tents and communal showers. The idea was to offer all paying guests an authentic safari experience while still allowing them to avail themselves of the estate's well-tended grounds and the emphatically blue waters of the modern swimming pool. Beyond the compound's electrified strands

of fencing lay many square miles of bush, populated by the boun-
tiful descendants of the wild game that had over the years drifted
onto the land or been purchased from other preserves. As boys,
Soren and Sambul watched Danforth Wheeler entertain groups of
American hunters, watched Soren's father bagging almost insouci-
antly the many kinds of impala and eland that roamed the bush and
that regarded the men who had come to kill them with stolid stares.
Many years later, by the time Sambul had been promoted to manager
of the entire estate, Soren would ban any hunting from the land and
instruct the guides to freely discharge their rifles only at the sight of
poachers.

For the first years of his life with the Wheelers though, Sambul
slept in a small, narrow room exactly halfway between the cavernous lounges of the estate and the small bundle of shacks that the servants and guides occupied. Beyond the shacks were the pool and the
big safari tents and, beyond that, the wilderness. Often, walking up
to the great house for dinner, Sambul would encounter a particularly
intrepid bush deer stilled perfectly in the middle of the path and the
two would stand there in the near silence of the dusk, watching each
other, Sambul thinking of the meandering route the animal must
have taken after jumping the fence, of the way it must have walked
so quietly along the pool and past the tents and shacks, just to arrive
there, at Sambul's feet.

In Sambul's adult memory, the subsequent years he'd spent at
the estate condensed themselves mostly into the passage of several
long afternoons with Soren, full of their desperate attempts to fight
the heat and boredom. When later pressed by the braver and more
curious of the servants, Sambul found himself capable of recalling
for them other details. Sambul could remember taking his school
lessons from Martha Wheeler in the mornings, for instance, in the
company of Soren, a handful of the servants' young children, and

an old woman from the local village. These sessions were held in what Soren called the "solarium," and when Sambul thought about it he found himself struck again by the way the morning light came in through the windows, backlighting the many fly-aways of Martha Wheeler's hair into a gentle, messy corona.

There were other things too, that came floating back: Sambul walking slowly around the rooms of the estate when the Wheelers took their annual trip to the States for the holidays, trailing his fingertips along every wall of the house; Martha returning from Nairobi every season with new athletic clothes for both Soren and Sambul, each of whom complained bitterly about the way they matched. But these things only returned to Sambul's mind when one of the servants—their disbelieving, almost painfully curious faces raised to him late at night—gathered the nerve to ask if it was true about how he had been raised as family to the Wheelers when he was a boy. The rest of the time, watching as Soren talked animatedly to one of the tourist chaperones or trying not to watch as Soren quietly attempted to eat dinner as he sweated through his shirt with fever, Sambul thought only of those afternoons.

The boys would begin each day around two o'clock, after lunch and after Sambul had finished his job helping the maids clean the tourist tents, picking up the cigarette butts, laundering the towels, and beating the beds for scorpions. They usually met in Sambul's room, lying on their backs, shirtless, against the cool tile floor and staring up at the posters of the various football stars Martha brought Sambul by request from the city. They talked idly of football sides and tactics or the various strange and amusing characters that had appeared in the most recent bunch of tourists. Once in a while, if Martha had returned from a shopping trip recently, the boys had a new tape of music to listen to. When this happened, they would listen together to the best song of the album on repeat until they both

knew every word. Then Sambul would goad Soren into performing
for him—the tall, thin, blond boy standing atop Sambul's bed and
crooning with exaggerated earnestness into an invisible microphone.
Sambul liked it best when Soren would make some motion—running
his hand slowly back through his hair, for instance, while tracing the
long trajectory of a single, wavering note. Eventually it would cool off
enough to go outside and one or the other boy would slowly stand
up and stretch, fake yawning, hamming it up, before bolting out the
door and calling out names of the things the other was slower than.

The running became a feeling in itself; the late afternoon breeze
pushed over their torsos and faces as they sweated, cooling them
as the light got long and reddish over the brush and the dirt roads.
They were allowed out of the compound as long as it was still light
and they stayed together, and their jogs traced long, erratic laps of the
relevant geography: the place where the road dove into the river that
would cover it in winter and reveal it again in summer; the small bluff
from which the tourists in their jeeps were taken to watch the hippos
and elephants loll around a mud hole; the circling path around a tree
where small tribes of monkeys scolded them, occasionally tossing
down fruit cores at the boys' heads. When bored or winded Sambul
and Soren would stop, dallying along the main road that led away
from the Wheelers' land or lazily following one of the women from
the village as she herded her goats back toward the cluster of improvised shanties in the distance.

They played a game sometimes when all else failed to entertain them. They called it keepy-uppy, and it consisted of each taking off their shoes and socks and venturing a few rows into the small
field that the Wheelers allowed the servants to keep behind their
quarters. It was never clear to Sambul, even later, why Soren and
he had felt the need to do this, to draw the veil of tall green corn
stalks behind them, but it is what they did, wordlessly, when one

or the other wanted to play. The game was this: Sambul would lie down on his back in the cool, soft dirt between the rows and Soren would carefully step up until he was standing on Sambul's chest, the soles of his feet roughly in the area of Sambul's pectoral muscles. Soren would then see, counting in a whisper (here another mystery to Sambul in his middle age), how long Sambul could bear it, could keep Soren up. Eventually, lungs bursting, Sambul would roll, sending Soren flying off, laughing, and then the boys would switch positions. Sometimes to make it more interesting, one or the other would tease the one on the ground by balancing on one foot and placing the other sole ever so lightly against the prone boy's face, nibbling the cheek with his toes. Even at the time Sambul sensed the intimacy of this—the smooth hold of the corn's husks, the weak yellow sun wavering behind Soren's listing head suddenly infused with a sense of nervous joy. This is how the memory would continue to feel, anyway, even many years later, when Sambul could recognize neither boy in his and Soren's tired faces.

This arrangement lasted until sometime after Soren's thirteenth birthday, when, on their holiday trip back to the States, Martha Wheeler was killed in an automobile accident and died, leaving Soren and his father to return to the estate alone and defeated, as if all the words had gone out of both of them. That fall, Mr. Wheeler announced that he was sending both Soren and Sambul off to boarding schools in Nairobi for the remainder of their education. Soren was sent to a preparatory academy mostly filled with the children of European diplomats, while Sambul arrived on his first day at a Catholic school on the outskirts of the city that specialized in native children who had been identified (by the foreign businessmen in the city who employed their families) as showing some amount of promise. For a year the two boys saw each other only at the training sessions and matches of the Massey Insurance Juniors, a local football

club that both boys played for and that Danforth Wheeler owned a controlling stake in. That was only for the one season, however. By the next time Sambul and Soren found themselves alone in the fields together, Soren would be returned to the continent with an American degree, Sambul would be head manager of the Wheeler estate and safari business, and Soren would be dying.

•

Soren waited until all the guides, redeployed for the day as messengers, had returned from the villages before ordering Sambul and Benny to wrap up the body and put it on the rear board of one of the jeeps. No one was missing, and there were no reports of an unfamiliar man in the area. Soren was quiet as they drove back to the compound. He made them go very slowly, and allowed no one else besides Sambul and Benny in the vehicle, as if to limit the number of people forced to have contact with the nameless man's corpse, sheathed as it was in a way that looked both ridiculous and ceremonial. Benny had returned to the spring with several rounds of old, yellowed muslin. Standing there before the body, laid out in the dirt between Soren and Sambul, Benny had turned his round, pitted face up to them, only then recognizing the inadequacy of the cloth.

Now, riding in the back seat of the open-topped vehicle, Sambul had one hand over the swaddled form tied to the luggage board. Beneath his fingers the man's body felt neither cold nor warm, only hardened. The deep tone of the man's skin could not be masked by the thin muslin and its deeper hue shone through in an ill-defined way. As they entered the gates and slowly trolled up through the safari camp, a few guests leaned out the front flaps of their big tents or stood on the porches of packed earth and watched them pass.

Sambul knew it was not a good solution, but thought it was the only one. Soren for some reason hadn't even wanted to move the body, other than to remove it from the water, as if to preserve the basic facts of the story that might be told to any family member the guides might bring back.

Sambul had squatted beside Soren and, quietly pointing with a pinky finger, suggested that the yellowed flesh of the calluses Soren was looking for did in fact pad the man's palms, forming a ridge at the top of the ball of the right hand. Sambul knew that Soren knew that all the men had been thinking the same thing since first seeing the body: that this man was just another of the migrant workers who wandered undocumented over the border, that they'd find no name, no family, and no story.

"He doesn't have anything with him for travel, though," Soren had argued, looking up at the other guides, who watched from a small distance away, leaning against the vehicles and spitting.

"And there're no wounds, no immediate cause for death," Sambul added helpfully, without knowing why. The guides squinted at Sambul for a moment then shrugged and readjusted their feet. Soren had looked at Sambul for a minute, blank-faced, before sighing and turning away.

By the time all the guides returned, it was too late in the day for anyone leaving the estate in one of the Land Rovers to make it to town and the municipal morgue before nightfall, when control of the highway reverted to the rural gangs who financed the rebels with robbery and beheadings. There was also the matter of the party that had been planned for that night, for the twenty-five or so guests currently in residence at the safari camp. So Sambul eventually had to say it, because Soren seemed to need him to, had to suggest the walk-in freezer in the great house's basement kitchen.

When he, Benny, and Soren reached the house, Sambul helped

them carry the body into the frigid space, each hefting it under his right arm.

The party was held for each group of guests on the last night of their stay. The camp hosted guests on ten-day rotations and Sambul, overseeing the safari outings, had this summer become familiar with how Soren would appear about three days in, whipping one of the vehicles at high speed up to where the guests in their open-topped jeeps would be taking their break after the morning game drive, and hopping dramatically out of his car. This was how he began, Sambul knew, how Soren started his process. By the day before the party the guests inevitably felt that he had become one of them, and were excited by the presence of the master of the estate right beside them in the lounge chairs of the pool in the early afternoon's clear sunlight.

Sambul always wondered at Soren's ability to recognize the urge in one or another of these guests, and at these other men's ability to recognize and respond to it in Soren, all without any doublespeak or sidelong look—without any sign, as far as Sambul could tell, at all. It was as if they were speaking a mental language encoded in the very facts of each other's bodies: in things like the effortless order of Soren's combed hair, of course, but also in the high cheekbones and dark stubble of one particular guest's face, in the litheness of another's body, the lack of resistance in his shoulders. Sambul was witness to these exchanges, could tell clearly when an understanding between Soren and one of the guests—usually a young, single professional on this trip with a large group of other young, single professionals from the same company—had been reached, but what bothered Sambul was how *at ease* each of these chosen guests was with the situation, the way after dark they walked up the path for their personal audience with Soren without shame but also without flippant striding.

In these last weeks of summer, the estate had been hosting mostly long strings of high school and college tour groups, led by huffing geography teachers from the middle of America and spouse-chaperones along for the ride. Accordingly, Soren's taste had gotten startlingly younger; Sambul watching in disgust as Soren flirted openly with the thin, tan boys who did knifing dives into the pool, skimming along its bottom, their half-developed muscles rippling in the water before surfacing, the air filled with their surprised, buoyant laughter. *Is this what Soren wanted?* Sambul found himself thinking, watching the display. *This idiotic lightness?*

Soren's interest in these youths (the exact ages neither Sambul nor Soren were ever certain of, though what did it matter when they all looked to have been stalled in some vague prepubescence, their only body hair a delicate blond undercoat that served merely to bring the curve of their tanned lower backs or stomachs into further defini-tion) was made even more unsettling given Soren's changing appear-ance. As Soren's lovers had gotten younger Soren himself, or at least his body, had begun to age considerably. He was back to losing weight again, helplessly—the bedclothes that Sambul had the maids change every morning sopping with sweat, the full plates of food pushed away in defeat. To the men and boys who stayed at the safari camp, however, this only accentuated Soren's natural good looks, his face even more angular and sly. His small shoulders kept his fleshless torso from appearing skeletal, and his entire body only got even more out of the way of the unexpected pale green eyes that, as a boy, had flashed but that now gave him a calm, distanced air.

Soren had prepared Sambul and some of the servants for this yo-yoing health that would eventually just never rewind itself, but when Soren's first descent into sickness had started no one had been ready for the racking coughs, the inability to eat, the wandering, tem-porary dementia giving way finally to the immobility, the weakness so

great that Soren could barely even move his cracked lips to request the water that Sambul had to drip into his mouth. How had that not been the end? What was that, if not the end of Soren's life? But it wasn't: he'd more than recovered, everything happening in reverse, abilities one by one regained and remastered. And this robust infection of good health hadn't stopped there, but continued until Soren was more hale and lively than he had been upon his adult return to the country. "Har har, just kidding," Soren had joked to the servants after this recovery, without smiling.

So everyone at the estate knew that the plateau of good health would end, knew that what they were doing was waiting. That had been a year ago, though. Then this summer had come with the boys and simultaneously, as if mocking their youth, the stirrings of the weight loss, the shaking hands at dinner as he tried to eat his soup.

Soren was doing fine for the moment, though, with the body safely away in the freezer and him free to return his attentions to the young Indian man from somewhere back in Britain. Soren had seated himself beside the Indian and kept leaning slightly over to deliver his punch lines so that their shoulders touched lightly, though this was the only contact they had. The man, impossibly young-looking, with rounded cheeks, a shock of black hair and big, earnest eyes, had already agreed, Sambul could see. He was smiling, happy to be taken in by Soren's older, comforting grace. When the dinner petered out and the other guests took their big bottles of beer to the pool, Soren quietly got up and made his way back to the great house. A few minutes later the boy got up and followed. When it was possible, Sambul left too, walking the long way up before taking his usual position.

Technically, Sambul used the small room off of Soren's quarters when Soren was sick, or when someone needed to keep a vigil over him as he slept. In healthier times it was used as a sort of all-purpose

folding room by the maids who kept up the great house, with the understanding that they quietly slip out the door that led to the back stairs whenever Soren entered his quarters. There was no door between Soren's living room and this small space; instead, a long, gauzy curtain hung in the doorway that was generally respected as if it were solid.

Sambul thought of what he did in these situations in a vaguely proprietary way. Soren might need something, for instance, might get sick, with no one there to help him but his clueless young men. But Sambul also knew it went beyond that, felt that Soren somehow needed him to see, to witness, in the same way that he had no compunction in calling Sambul to his quarters when he'd lost controls of his bowels in the night.

Sambul could see them now, through the narrow space between the curtain and the doorframe. The young man was standing, Soren kneeling in front of him, head bobbing, reduced in his disease to this exercise, this pleasuring of the other. There seemed something off to Sambul about this setup, something wrong about the young man being the one experiencing this feeling, his eyes closed, his body stiff. When he was done Soren slowly stood and said something to the boy. They each moved around each other awkwardly, actors ignorant of the scene's proper blocking, until the boy was bent, kneeling forward on an ottoman facing the other wall and Soren was behind him, arm working at himself, head looking down at the boy's full buttocks, where Sambul knew Soren was not even touching him, masturbating instead into a doubled condom. Sambul sat like this for a long time, unfolding the linens and then refolding them, looking up after each one to check that Soren was still there, to see that there was still the fact of his body: naked, pathetically curved into itself, his diminutive, shallow buttocks very pale and cupped in the effort. Sambul watched him begin to shake weakly, and waited for the famil-

iar moment, the climax that would not come, that would be replaced with the strangely banal sound of Soren's infirm weeping.

•

Soren Wheeler left the country for an East Coast American university in 1986, failing to stick around or even visit to bear witness to the gradual decline of Danforth Wheeler's business empire-in-miniature. Besides the estate, the crown jewel of his father's holdings was Hotel Sporting Nairobi, a towering hotel for businessmen, diplomats, and foreigners, full of curving white architectural lines and glass. This was where Sambul had spent his solitary breaks from the Catholic school, wandering the lonely corridors, convincing a friendly barman to slip him weak drinks, not knowing where Soren went for his holidays. Sambul had taught himself French during his last years of high school and, a year after Soren left for college in the States, had won a scholarship to study humanities at the Université Cheikh Anta Diop in Senegal, which he did until his program ran out of money and he was forced to finish at the University of Nairobi in a lowly mechanical faculty. After that he'd gone to work for the aging Wheeler as a handyman in the same tea concern town where his mother, almost twenty years before, had died. Sambul eventually worked his way up through the ranks to a position at the lodge's flagging safari business, and made a comfortable home for himself among the servants' quarters of the estate.

By the time Soren returned, all that was left of the Wheelers' Hotel Sporting Nairobi was one wing of high business offices in the commercial development that had taken over its floors. Danforth had died a year earlier, and the workers in their mourning had been given security in the interim until his estate could be sorted out. When it

seemed that he had exhausted all options other than to run the company himself or sell it off, Soren had arrived again in Nairobi.

As his first order of business, he'd summoned Sambul to the high, corporate office and informed him firstly that he was to be promoted to head manager of the entire lodge and estate business and secondly that Soren himself was sick, that he was dying.

Soren said this in a tired, matter-of-fact way, and Sambul had sat back in his leather chair. The office was dim, the day brooding outside, overcast and rainy in the floor-length windows behind Soren's desk. Soren put the cap back on his pen, sighed, smiled in a gentle, sad way and stood, turning away from Sambul. He looked down and out the big windows as he spoke, as he narrated the disease's probable progression, the secondary infections, cancers, pneumonias, organ failures. As he explained about a new drug system, something called Highly Active Anti-Retroviral Therapy that had just been introduced in the States and nonetheless featured extremely low chances of helping his particular situation, Sambul rose and stood beside him at the windows. He wanted to put his hand on Soren's back, to press his palm gently into the flat space of gray suit-coat material that draped so smoothly away from his shoulders, but he didn't. Soren's hands were in his pockets and he was quiet for a few minutes. After a while he pointed down at a gray oval on the neighboring block encircling a deeply green space.

"We used to play there," he said. "The Massey Juniors, remember?"

"Though it wasn't there, exactly," he added after a minute. "They've torn the old city place down. This one is much nicer."

Sambul had nodded and not known what to say.

Perhaps it was because of this strange comment's reference that Sambul later could remember this meeting only in the context of his great theory about the true source of Soren's disease. Sambul had

missed Soren over the years of his absence, had missed him so much and for so long that by the time he'd entered the office—Soren rising and smiling sheepishly, raising his arms a little in the suggestion of a hug—it felt exactly the same as not missing him. Later, remember-ing again and again the exchange, the medical words, Sambul only felt confused and angry. Soren had finally returned, just to be dying? And why was this happening (here, in Sambul's aging consideration of this late development in Soren's life, the seed of his great theory) other than because he'd been reckless—utterly, mysteriously, and unforgivably reckless—in all things since Danforth Wheeler had sent them apart and away?

And so the memory of the afternoon that Sambul learned of Soren's disease ended up always reaching back to include that season of the Massey Insurance Juniors, Sambul a solid defensive midfielder who rode the bench, Soren a mercurial starting striker, the last year that they'd seen each other as boys, their last year together. Sambul always remembered the dangerous, angry way Soren charged around the pitch, his sharp elbows swinging or his spikes turned up maliciously as he went to ground for an ill-advised tackle. It had been wild and relentless, the way he'd thrown himself against and into the other players, scoring occasionally but fouling nastily. Soren never lasted more than thirty minutes before getting injured or sent off, thus creating a necessary substitution, sending Sambul in. It was like he meant to do it this way, relaxing only as he passed Sambul on his trek past the bench, always giving him a quick, conciliatory look. They hadn't really spoken much in training sessions, either, which had only been one more disappointment. Everything had been taken from them that season. Sambul remembered the first day of training, his heartbreak and embarrassment at discovering that the name of their game, "keepy-uppy," was really just a little kids' term for juggling the ball. After that, the two boys could barely even look at each other.

As far as Sambul's great theory held, Soren's reckless behavior only continued at his American college. Sambul pieced together scenes from his endless Nairobi University dorm-room daydreams of Soren's campus (its students laughing, calling out to each other across the college green) and the small bits of stories he'd overheard from others, Sambul concocting a thousand different stupid acts and men that could have put the disease in Soren's body. And to Sambul's mind, the recklessness thesis was given proof positive by the arrival on the estate, soon after Soren's return, of Peter Oprong.

Sambul never really knew Peter Oprong in his brief tenure at the estate, but he could remember clearly the man's skin: black but mixed with some other mysterious, dusky race until his coloration was a cloudy, almost Indian hue, which suited particularly well his face, with its high Portuguese nose. He lived in a slum outside Lodwar, and apparently worked as an assistant to a Mozambican carved-trinket importer, which was how Soren met him. Sambul only became aware of Peter Oprong's presence when Peter moved to Amdin, the little town about an hour's drive from the estate. During the months that the safari camp was shut down while the servants renovated it to Soren's new business standards, Peter Oprong spent long stretches at the estate, during which he and Soren were inseparable. Sambul was kept busy in his job overseeing the rebuilding and retraining, and only ran into the two men glancingly, though their happiness infected the other servants, who smiled at the ever-polite Peter whenever he was around.

Sambul himself now, years after the episode, remembered being taken by the two men's joy only twice. Once had been in late afternoon, as Sambul took a break from rethatching the roof of one of the "authentic" huts, when he heard their voices, each on the verge of laughter, carrying across the air as they stripped off their clothes on the riverbank and dived in. That time Sambul had been struck

how, even at a distance, he could see the solidness of Peter Oprong's body: his legs rippling up into his full, rounded gluteus muscles as he dove, his body disappearing into the muddy water. The other time, Sambul had discovered them together one night in the wide group tent that was the servants' bar. Someone had turned on loud music from a hidden radio, and Peter, his long, curly hair gathered back in a woman's wrap, was dancing in place, clapping his hands and singing in his clear, deep voice, much to the delight of the servants and guides who laughed and cheered him on. But what Sambul remembered most about this last encounter was Soren, sitting in his own seat and glancing back and forth happily from the cheering crowd to Peter, Soren clapping and calling, bobbing his head and trying to get into it with the rest of them, his nervous pride childlike and obvious.

It was the courier man who ran errands for the estate who told Sambul, on the day that it happened. The man had been every week assigned to deliver the gifts that Soren sent to Peter in the days after one of his long stays; this was the man instructed to drive to the square in Amdin and find the tall building that Peter Oprong shared with several other men like him, and so it was this courier who was the first one from the estate to see the pillar of smoke, and the remains. A group of frenzied villagers had gathered in the middle of the night and engulfed the building in flames. When the men inside had come running out (stumbling, coughing, and collapsing into the square) the crowd had taken rebar rods salvaged from a nearby construction site (some of which had been held in the fire) and beat the men to death, stripping and piling their bodies in the middle of the square and leaving them there for anyone to see.

Sambul spent all morning at the scene. In his anger at Soren, Sambul (listening to the chain of requests on the messenger's CB radio) had not told anyone to stop Soren from taking one of the Land Rovers, had not stepped in to stop the courier from guiding Soren's

frantic driving to the proper square. Sambul's feeling only broke as he saw the vehicle pull in at the far end of the square and stop, as he watched the tall, lone figure of Soren jumping out, unsure of whether or not to hurry, still in shock—only then did Sambul run over to step in front of him, to do him the mercy of blocking his view.

Reckless, Sambul had decided, and stupid. As if the estate were the world. Sambul had been shocked more than anything at the swiftness of it all: three months, start to finish, from the day the man had come into their lives to the day he'd gone out. The one time Sambul found himself alone with Soren in those months of the remodel, Sambul still thinking about the conversation in the office, he'd shifted in the jeep's seat, and said without looking at Soren, "Why—why are you trying so hard with the new guest?" And Soren had only smiled and sighed and looked at Sambul and, after a while, said, "It's alright to still have, you know, a life." To which Sambul had said nothing, only shook his head slightly, thinking, *A life? Can you imagine? A life?*

•

Now Sambul found Soren curled halfway into a fetal position on the carpet where the Indian had left him. Sambul had not waited to hear the sounds of the boy leaving the room, had instead slipped down the back stairs and outside for a cigarette. Upon his return, Sambul glanced through the space between the curtain and the doorframe and saw a sliver of Soren's prone body, like someone had laid him there. Thinking he'd collapsed, Sambul rushed to him, only realizing once he was standing over him that Soren was still crying softly, dryly, a tiny wet spot of saliva staining the carpet near his mouth. It was as if his arms and torso had wanted to assume the inward-

curled posture but his long, thin legs could not be convinced, and were splayed awkwardly, like two bent sticks. A small breeze sighed through the window. The wrapper from the condom skittered across the wooden floor in the next room.

Sambul spent the entire week shut up in Soren's quarters with him. He slept when Soren did, which was extremely little, and the combination of the fatigue and the drawn curtains and shutters (Soren cried and recoiled at the intensity of even weak daylight) made the entire period seem like one never-ending day to Sambul. Soren allowed no one else inside. Sambul started off trying to keep him in bed, but the diarrhea (Soren too weak and the waste too watery for it to be controlled), combined with his retching, full-throated coughing made this impossible, and eventually they gave up and set up shop in the large bathroom itself, Soren lolling weakly in his fevers over the cool tile of the floor.

Because this stage of the sickness had happened in a very similar way the first time Soren had regressed after his return to the country, Sambul found himself watching what was happening with an uneasy detachment. His confusion the first time turned now to identification, his helpless noticing replaced by idle reflection. Here were Soren's lips impossibly pale and bled of color. Here was the actual pool of liquid, of sweat, left beneath his fevered body when Sambul helped him up from the floor to the toilet. Here was the barking cough, the cough that seemed to come almost from Soren's stomach, repeating and repeating but never producing anything except shallow wheezing, which itself soon gave way to the crazed, rapid breathing, like his lungs had suddenly shrunk to a child's size. Certain areas around his mouth and feet and hands turned a graying blue so vivid during these episodes that it almost felt like a hallucination on Sambul's part. There was not much Sambul could do except watch, except manhandle Soren's body

into the positions he needed to be in but could not ask for, except notice the invisible struggle that seemed to be playing itself out in the body before him. When Soren vomited it was a dark brown color, its acidic tang wafting, filling the entire bathroom. When his bowels evacuated, Soren was not even strong enough to hold himself upright on the toilet, and folded himself instead forward, arms wrapped under his knees.

Sambul had been trained by a nurse in Nairobi to carefully administer a simple IV of fluids, which he did, holding the bag high above Soren as he moved, trying to help him keep his arm straight so the needle would hurt less. Sambul also fetched when he could the steroidal medicine Soren had been given the first time this happened, retrieving it from the cabinet beside the small minifridge where they kept the more expensive medicine for his disease that had to be flown in.

This latter was the medicine that had been left unused, untaken, in the months after Peter Oprong died. First, Soren had returned to the country, installed the minifridge, and brought a doctor out from the American hospital in Nairobi to explain to Sambul the careful administration of the drug therapy. Then had come the renovations and Peter Oprong's long visits. In the months after Sambul had guided Soren away from the grisly site in the square, Soren had seemed to give up. He became dramatic. In his grief he was reticent, staying away from the tour groups and instructing Sambul to stop counting out the pills from the containers in the minifridge. Once during this time, Soren made Sambul stop on a drive to a nearby town so that Soren could walk out and lie down in a field of soybeans as the wind pirouetted through their leaves. Another time Sambul witnessed Soren strip down, wade into the river, and float on his back for almost a mile, drifting serenely very close past the dangerous shapes of a family of hippos, a few small crocodiles twitching

into the water in fear as he passed, the guides screaming at each other as he emerged, unscathed.

That time, in the pall after Peter Oprong's death, when he'd stopped taking the medicine and gotten sick, it made some amount of sense. *This is the end*, Sambul had thought numbly, watching him sweat and fight for breath. But it hadn't been. Against his will, Soren had gotten better. When he finally started taking the special drug therapy again, it was in resignation. For a while after that, Sambul had felt like they were living out some poorly played coda, but as Soren's health kept steady, and then as it improved even more, the feeling had been forgotten. Soren had seemed unmistakably alive again. But it was different now.

This time the sickness broke on a Friday, in the hourless half-light of the dawn. During the previous night the violence of Soren's sickness had subsided, and he'd slipped deep into a semicomatose calm. His breathing was so shallow it was nearly soundless, and several times Sambul startled awake at the quiet, making himself closely inspect the covers folded over Soren's chest for movement, fearing that Soren had drifted away while unconscious, half-dreaming. Before first light Sambul, growing more and more worried, decided to wake him and was unable to. The best Soren could do was to half-way open his lids, barely tracking Sambul as he moved around him.

Sambul gathered Soren up from the bed in his arms and carried him back into the bathroom, where he gently undressed him. Sambul filled the bathtub and lowered Soren, his skin cool and clammy against Sambul's forearms, into the warm water. It was clear, after Soren's face slipped immediately below the water level, that this wouldn't work. Without really thinking and without taking off his clothes, Sambul climbed into the tub, sliding himself behind and under Soren's body so that he was propped up against Sambul's chest, so that he rested in Sambul's arms.

There was no excitement, no electricity storming Sambul's skin at this full body press. It came to him as he lay there—Soren's body warm against his chest, his hair wet and stringy as his head lolled back on Sambul's shoulder—that this was more physical contact than they'd ever had, or at least, not since they were kids. The two men lay there like that for a long time, Soren dipping back into sleep, Sambul wide awake, thinking of the vague sense of disappointment he found in what this actually felt like, the lack of intimacy in the way Soren's limbs splayed against his. What had he thought it would feel like? What had he thought all those others had felt, mistaking this invalid husk for a body? Soren was a light and wispy weight against Sambul's chest and legs and lap. As he waited in the tepid water for dawn to fully break, Sambul closed his eyes and could barely feel him, simultaneously there and not there.

It was Soren himself who awakened Sambul, telling him from the doorway that he better get out or his skin might fall off. Sambul made Soren rest for that day, but his patient could eat again, and the cough was occasional, a kind of punctuation. He was resurrected, a minor miracle, again.

The whole estate was uneasy. It had been a week since the drowned man was discovered, and as time progressed from his entombment in the basement freezer, the idea had seemed to grow more and more perverse to the servants, the guides, and Sambul. The easiest and most obvious thing would have been for Soren, as soon as the next day's sun had risen, to order a few of the workers to load the body into the back of one of the trucks and make the long drive into the city, depositing the anonymous corpse at the municipal morgue. But this had not been ordered during Soren's incapacitation, and wasn't now, though Soren was now able to make the car ride to the village himself.

They stood in a dusty square that could have been any square

they'd been in so far that day, any place they'd stopped in Amdin or any of the other slums within driving distance of the estate. Colorful wash was strung across the roofs of the dun-colored buildings and flapped gently in the breeze. A group of old men sat in dirty plastic furniture and played dice games while drinking Coca-Cola from glass bottles. Sambul leaned against a building in the shade, keeping an eye on the car.

It had been agreed that this would be their last stop. Soren had made it known to all the servants and guides, some of whom were getting panicked and angry, that if he and Sambul couldn't find a relative or someone who could speak for the man this afternoon then he would take care of the body the next day and it would no longer be kept so unnaturally. As the locals who spoke to them had, slum after slum, proven unable to place the man, Soren had grown more and more moody and upset. A curl of pink had come into his cheeks, which in a different life might have meant good health but did not in this one, Sambul knew.

Soren, the woman he'd come to see, and a short, round man came spilling out of the shack.

"My sister demands to be compensated for her information!" the fat man was shouting melodramatically.

Soren ignored him. He held up the picture of the dead man's face and put it right in front of the woman's eyes. Sambul pushed himself off the wall.

"How do you not ask him where he's from? How do you not take his name?" Soren shouted at the woman over the fat man's protests.

The woman ran one of the illegal liquor bars that were rife in the slums. She'd apparently once rented the backroom to the dead man, or someone who looked just like him, for one night. This was all she'd managed to say, however, before her brother had gotten the idea of a reward.

"You didn't hear his accent, you didn't know where it was from?" Soren shouted at her.

"No!" the woman shouted back, half-nervous, struggling to be defiant about something, at least.

Soren was still holding the picture right in front of her face. The woman was ducking and moving, trying to look at him around it, but he only moved it with her.

"But you recognize the face, yes?" Soren said.

The woman stopped her bobbing.

"I don't know," she said, subdued.

"Now you don't know," Soren said.

The woman was quiet. There was a pause. Soren's heavy breathing was loud in the square.

"You're a liar," Soren said, and spit at the woman's feet.

At this the little fat man rushed forward and shoved Soren, who went flying, tripping backward comically before collapsing in the dry dirt. The fat man immediately began backing away, reaching for his sister and looking around wildly. Sambul started toward where Soren lay, crumpled. As he passed the group of old men, they laughed hoarsely at Soren, who was trying to get up and failing. Sambul hissed through his teeth at them, raising the back of his hand and juking his upper body sharply in their direction, and they shut up, looking up at him with drawn faces as they scooted their plastic chairs inside.

Sambul squatted to help Soren up but Soren pushed him away, so Sambul stood back and watched as Soren—now on all fours, coughing hard, saliva dripping in long strands from his mouth—crawled toward him. When Soren got close enough he used Sambul's body to drag himself up, finally getting himself to a standing position, where he wavered unsteadily. He listed forward and Sambul

caught him, helping him regain his tenuous balance. Sambul left his palms against Soren's chest, as if keeping him from trying to move. They stood there like that for a minute, Soren looking over Sambul's shoulder not at the building the man and the woman had disappeared into but instead at the center of the square, at the nothing of the dirt and the dust and the light. Sambul thought of Soren's face on the day they'd found Peter Oprong, of how much, perversely, he'd loved Soren in that moment, in the sickly hopefulness of his gaze, in the truth already dawning on him, his body already giving up the struggle to get past Sambul, to see what Sambul would not let him see. Now here Soren was, staring at nothing, seeing something else. The double vision commanded by memory. Sambul waited now, watching Soren for a sign that he was done, that he was ready to accept Sambul's assistance and go, and he thought of the pointlessness of struggling so hard to gain purchase on a world so thoroughly mortgaged by the dead.

In the car on the highway, they were quiet, Soren slouched low in the wide backseat, breathing quickly, shallowly, exasperated, stilled.

"It's not like," he said, "it's not like he doesn't have a name. It's not like there's no one who knows it."

They'd mistimed their final visit, Sambul could see now, as the sun swung low over the tree line that undulated beside the highway and dusk gathered itself up from the shadows. When the rusted three-wheeled matatu raised on a jack appeared out of the darkness in the middle of the road, Sambul slowed. He was thinking of what would happen to the dead man, the delivery to the dirty municipal morgue, the final slot in the big, ancient crematory oven the government had started using when the land allotted for a paupers' field had filled up. Sambul could back up quickly, retracing their path, and find a more rural way around to the estate, but the thought of

the body having to wait even a few more hours now that its destination had been finally decided seemed somehow perverse to Sambul.

The stretch of highway they'd stopped on was deserted and dark, the asphalt wending its way between the face of a rising bluff on one side and a drop-off on the other, below which the matte-faced waters of a large lake sat low and still in the dark beyond a pale, thin beach of mineral flats. The bulky matatu was angled directly across the narrow road, missing a rear wheel, a single dark figure sitting against its front bumper and smoking.

Sambul began to walk toward him and could feel Soren a few feet behind him. Neither heard what must've been the sound of the other men hefting themselves up over the ridge of the shoulder on the lakeside until their footsteps were right behind them. Sambul turned, looking from their blank faces and weapons to the man who'd been sitting on the matatu, the man who now stood and smiled widely, his eyes flashing in the weak light of the Land Rover.

They marched Sambul and Soren down to the mineral flats, which were stiff and crumbly underfoot. As they walked the tiny crystals of the useless chemicals caught the last light of the moon and seemed to lead their way in a shining path. The small band of men stopped them a hundred yards from the water and pushed the prisoners to their knees. Sambul and Soren were about thirty feet apart and Sambul heard Soren overbalance and fall forward, trying and failing to catch himself with his hands.

The leader of the band came and stood in front of Sambul. He had a thick, old machete in his hand and the steel was greasy and ill kept, the metal revealing itself only at the sharpened edge. They all had guns, but these would not do for what they wanted. The man paced a little, mumbling to himself. Sambul closed his eyes and breathed in through his nose. As if by peristalsis, the furrows of

the night and the water and the far tree line delivered a small, gentle breeze, and on it Sambul could smell the sweet rot of decaying fish. He opened his eyes.

The scrabbling sound of Soren's would-be scramble, of his lunging motion, so weak and slow it seemed not like a lunge at all, was strange in the quiet. Everyone watched him try to grab at the machete-wielding arm of the man who stood in front of Sambul, Soren's grasp so tenuous that it just kept slipping off as he again and again lost balance. The other men were laughing, one of them very loudly, but the man with the machete just seemed confused and annoyed. Every time he raised his arm to do anything, now stepping sideways away from Sambul, Soren grabbed at it with his skeletal fingers. The man shrugged him off easily a few times. Once, Soren got a good enough grasp to pull himself upright and, bizarrely, just for a few seconds, it seemed that the two were dancing. The man threw him down again violently. No one was talking now. As he rasped and rasped at the man's arm, the air filled with the sound of Soren's desperate, labored breathing.

Neither man would ever speak of this incident; not to the passing motorist who, at daybreak, let them use a cell phone, and not to Benny when he picked them up. The Land Rover was gone and they had been spared, without knowing why, and they were silent. Neither did either man speak when they arrived back at the estate, when Soren retired to his room and Sambul filled a jeep with split wood and gasoline, and set to work preparing a funeral pyre for the body, making sure to set it up within sight of the great house. Benny helped Sambul bring the body out and tilt more wood over it.

As it burned, Sambul retreated to the house and watched from the windows with Soren, who was laid up on a daybed. They watched it flare in the distance. Soren was just beginning a new course of

infection and sat gingerly, leaning forward awkwardly to breathe, lifting his eyes to the window. After a few hours it was clear Sambul
had made some kind of mistake and he had to go with Benny to put
more wood and gasoline on the pyre. As they approached, Sambul
could see the dark shape enveloped in light, the body unmade into
a skeleton, bits of liquefied fat that had dripped down now viscid
among the coals, almost nacreous in the light. It took a long time after
that. Eventually, Soren turned away from the window and went to lie
still on his bed. In late afternoon, a billow of dark, distended clouds
swept over the land, and Sambul waited until he could barely see the
outline of the pyre in the rain before going out to stir the ashes, and
see what was left.

In the Mosque of Imam Alwani

1.

This was when they lived in the eternal city. It seemed possible that the trio's little corner of the Kurdish spring—the square chimneys of the brick kilns unfurling their columns of black smoke high into the clear light; the sloped red sides of the river, seething with insects in the lambent dawn before the air filled with the clattering gossip of the washerwomen and the collisions of the silver-voiced children worrying its shallows—had, since the beginning of time, continued in just this way, relying on no allegiance other than the residents' curious sense of their own perpetuity. This was when Bajh and Asti and Araz all lived there together, when they were young and the fields and herds still seemed born entirely anew each spring. This was when it was still their city to have.

Bajh, Asti, and Araz were all born at almost exactly the same time, though this was a fact only Araz cared enough to note. Bajh Barzani had been born on his family's long, retreating descent back down from the mountains after the Baathists' Anfal campaign. When the family Barzani turned back, they removed themselves from the hundred thousand others who neither reached Turkey nor made it

back over the Iraqi border, the hundred thousand Kurds who disappeared into the Toros mountain winter or the big pit graves or the pocking of the mortar craters. The Barzanis paused long enough in their defeated return for Bajh to be delivered, and one night a few weeks after he was born and they were on the move again, Bajh's mother went down to the river for water and never came back. When he was a child, Bajh often said the wrong parent had been taken, that a widowed father was unnatural. He also claimed, at least when the three friends were still small, that he dreamed of his mother on the coldest nights of the winter, but neither Araz nor Asti believed him. After their mother's death, Bajh's two older brothers also disappeared, presumably to the ranks of the PPK. Bajh's father took his only remaining son back across the Iraqi border and down through Kurdish territory, skirting the slums outside Dahuk and Erbil before turning west and following a calm, flat little river into farming country and to the hem of the town, where he could see the green fields, riven only by the coruscating face of the river, offered like two upturned palms to the spring light.

Bajh eventually grew into a set of bold, clear features, a face that Araz, only many years later, on a rainy, nostalgic day of university classes, would think to call Romanesque. When he was younger, Araz only had the distinct feeling that Bajh was the twin of a nameless movie star from a bygone era, his well-defined brow and high cheekbones seeming to have come to life straight off one of the ancient cinema posters that had once been pinned to the walls of Uncle Nuri's shop when they were toddlers. Bajh was taller than Araz and Asti, and his providential history was the best known of the three. Araz felt electric in his presence, as if in meeting up on the walk to school or going down to bother Nuri for Cokes or sneaking past the baying herds at night, Araz was merely joining Bajh's ongoing story. But there were other times, walking back from where Bajh and Asti led

their midnight amblings, when Araz felt it was almost celestial the way Bajh, always and ever there with them, was also so often somehow elsewhere, as if romanced by his own occluded future.

It was a surprise, then, when Bajh proved to be particularly inept at school. By the time the three should have together reached the upper levels of the city's grammar school, Bajh had been held back twice and seemed destined to be stuck forever with the "babies" in the first level. Even more distressing, Bajh's academic failure (which seemed also to extend to the hours of after-school religious instruction) was not for lack of effort—if anything, Bajh was the most eager student in class. Araz often watched him from across the large, open room—Bajh's robust brow comically serious, crumpled with concentration, his hand waving high above those of the kids several years his junior—until the ache in Araz's chest got to be too much (Bajh's clear voice, so avid in its incorrect answer, an inexplicable heartbreak) and he had to look away. For Araz, whose great love was knowledge of all kinds, the world seemed to untwine itself everywhere before him, equations or words or poetry or ideas stepping down out of thin air, and he wanted more than anything to be able to give this vision to Bajh, for whom the world in their fourteenth year had only proven itself to be a more opaque mystery than he'd ever imagined. But Araz couldn't give it to him; there was nothing he could do, and they were out of time anyway.

"I gave two sons and a wife for God, and so I said I will give one for school," Bajh's father ended up saying, melodramatically and without elaboration, sucking his teeth at the table where Araz was making a final attempt to tutor his friend. So Bajh would not be a famed scholar after all; he would not be a leader of men. Instead, he would be a farmer for his father and would supplement his primary job of herding their sheep with the odd shift at the brick kilns. Both duties had increased that spring, and Araz and Asti usually

went after school to find Bajh high in the rising plateau of the fields upriver, where his silhouette slanted unmistakably against the sky as it pearled with rain.

This is what they were doing on an overcast day that spring, their last one all together in the town. The sky was furrowed with restless clouds that moved along on a steady, vernal breeze. The air was cool on Araz's face, and the wind made Asti's dress billow and gesture over her jeans in front of him. The irrigation levee they walked along was surrounded by the crops' waxy green leaves, which fluttered or showed their undersides in the occasional gusts. Together they worked their way up toward where the tiny figure of Bajh was grazing his little dots of gray on a grassy hill.

Araz enjoyed watching Bajh from a distance. There was something about the remove that allowed him to take in Bajh entirely, in one thrilling breath. Sometimes Araz even skipped school, coming out to the grazing grounds and sitting with his workbook in his lap, looking up after each problem to see Bajh whipping at one of the animals with a thin switch or calling to a ewe about the punishments that would surely befall her if she disappeared over the ridge she was presently considering.

Asti was a different matter, though. She seemed only able to believe Bajh was real by evidence of physical proximity. This made some sense to Araz, for whom Asti herself never seemed so real as when she was up close, her vague figure only resolving into calm green-brown eyes and black, lustrous, half-tangling hair at the last minute, when one was close enough to embrace her. To Araz this also felt true of her history in general, from her birth to an unwed mother of unknown origin to the subsequent death of that mother, supposedly in Sulaymaniyah, and through to the improbable adoption by the aunt who'd followed her husband to this town (Asti herself rendered in higher and higher definition out of the soft focus of

her baby fat with each passing year). All of which seemed almost purposefully engineered to deliver Asti, with her thin limbs and angular
body and high cheekbones, to this spring afternoon, to the space of
light and color that was Bajh's grazing hill, where Araz now watched
him receive her. The effect—that of a bodily vision coming suddenly
into focus—was the same now, as both Bajh and Araz looked at her
and as Bajh laughed and grasped first the back of Asti's neck and
then the back of Araz's, their old greeting. Araz thought of his own
face in his house's dusky mirror, the puffy flesh of it, as if there were
no bones in it at all.

These trips were a sort of retrieval, signaling the end of Bajh's
workday (at least on those days when he did not have a shift at the
kilns), and he was almost always in a good mood as they walked with
him back toward his father's compound on the edge of town. Even
the sheep seemed to acquiesce, traveling with relief after a day's
heavy business of grazing. Bajh allowed some of them to wade the
river at a narrow point, after which they streamed thinly along either
bank, occasionally pausing and looking across, calling to each other
before trundling ahead, only to stop again and look.

On these trips back, Bajh and Araz often took up a game they
sometimes used to play at night, when Asti could not be sprung from
the watchful, nervous sleep of her aunt. They did not call it anything,
not even "the game," only ever referring to it via the question "Do
you want to play?" as if the final word could mean anything, though
Araz knew it only meant one thing, and sometimes, the question was
wordless.

That spring they'd begun to play the game, or to attempt to
play it, almost every day, testing the still-frigid water with their shins
and feet. So far the season had not reached its hidden tipping point,
but today Bajh had grown tired of waiting and, as Araz watched, he
plunged into the cold water with a shout. He'd left his clothes in

a small pile on the bank as they always did, and Araz turned from where Bajh's pale buttocks had disappeared into the river, already unbuttoning his own shirt and stepping out of his shoes. Asti had begun picking up the clothes and stuffing them into her knapsack and she crouched, facing away, until Araz plunged in after Bajh, letting out an involuntary cry at the shock of the cold.

The game was this: one boy would float on his back as motionless as possible, simulating lifelessness, as the river's swift current whisked him along. The other would bridge the distance between them with heavy, strong strokes and attempt to support the first boy's body from beneath, making a sort of double-deckered raft. There was no goal, or sometimes Araz guessed the goal was to keep the other's body as high out of the water as possible; the test was to avoid all that might impede them: deadfalls, snags, small bars of sand or mud and whatever fleeting, rough fish sometimes glanced briefly against their feet. When they got to a calm stretch of the river or when the obstacles became insufficiently challenging, they switched. They traveled this way when they were playing, covering most of the distance to the town on the river's current.

Araz thought the game seemed for Bajh a natural extension of the playful feats of athleticism that his friend often displayed in the trio's boredom: vaulting over crippled fences or scrambling up the exterior of a small building and grinning down at Araz and Asti below. But for Araz, the game was different: a burst of sensation, a quickening of his pulse and breath—the basic state of being exhilaratingly present, alive.

Today, as Araz floated in the freezing water, his body numb, he watched the roiling clouds above the river, heavy and knuckling lower with the promise of rain. Their speed and course matched his own in the current and so gave the illusion of stillness. There was the suddenness then of Bajh's splashing, the surprise of his lithe body

drawing up against Araz's own from below, and then the delicate weight of Bajh's long forearm over Araz's chest, the tense knot of his penis (made small and dense by the cold) against the back of Araz's thigh, the warmth of Bajh's breath just past his ear. They moved like that, with the river, chest to back, chest to air. Bajh occasionally lifted his head to see an obstacle or, in an attempt to steer, waggled his free arm and feet, his breathing in the calm air something like laughter.

From his position, Araz could not see Bajh, only feel him, curiously stilled below, and so he watched the sky or the series of black faces of the sheep as they looked across the water, or he turned his head away, toward the bank, where Asti was walking as she always did: placid, arms folded with whatever neatly creased articles of clothing could not fit in her bag, keeping pace easily. She was quiet, wind flipping at her hair, and she looked either down at her path or ahead at the river or over to where Araz floated, meeting his eyes impassively.

•

That night the three were to make one of the long clothing runs up to Dahuk. There was a man there, a night watchman at an airplane hangar that had been converted by the Americans into a storage warehouse for the pallets of aid materials that now came over the Turkish border. As a toddler Araz had been adopted, taken from a religious orphanage by the widower Bertrand Baradost, a lawyer years ago returned from Beirut; the night watchman had once been a client of his, and it was understood that the clothing arrangement was in service of his fee. Bajh drove his father's rickety old flatbed pickup while Araz and Asti sat between the squares of stale hay in the back. By this time they knew what would be waiting for them after the two-hour chugging ride along the throughway into Dahuk: the gray canyons of

buildings; Bajh's craning neck as he carefully backed the truck up to
the side of the hangar; the watchman, rousing himself from sleep to
sip at a thermos of tea, watching them roll up the loading-bay door
with a series of metal clangs. And inside, the dark labyrinth of shrink-
wrapped pallets, stacked higher than their heads.

This warehouse was where the NGOs for the northern half of
the country stored secondhand clothing donated from America. The
tightly wrapped plastic glistened in the dark, catching the dim light
from the opened bay as Araz walked down the rows. The best pallets had many T-shirts of bright colors or thick clothes good for the
winter or anything that had a prominent logo, and the three had been
instructed to try to discern the contents of the pallets and pick one
that looked to have the most of these. Though Araz knew the pallets were basically all the same anyway; he had watched the children
employed by his father in the market hawking the T-shirts with large
seals of American sports teams, the endless Christian youth group
fund-raising slogans, the button-up shirts with armpits yellowed by
years of sweat. The warehouse was endlessly refilled, and the watchman insisted that the NGO in charge of distribution didn't even keep
records of what it received.

This night, the trip had been quiet so far. Twice before, on previous runs, they'd been stopped by local security of the towns they
guided the truck through (Bajh had been instructed to stay off the
main roads on the way back), but each time they'd gotten by with
only the loss of a few shirts and a blazer. They'd only had to go
through an American checkpoint once, very late at night, with Araz
whispering translations of the soldiers' orders through the back window of the truck's cab, where Bajh, fingers white around the wheel,
carefully obeyed them.

Now Araz and Asti lay as they always did on the return trip,
squeezed on either side of the mound of clothing (once the pallet was

loaded, the plastic had to be cut away and discarded so as to avoid suspicion), pressed against the low containing rails of the truck's flat-bed. On the more bumpy roads, they were to keep the clothes from flying off.

Araz sighed and put his hands behind his head, looking up into the litter of stars that shifted slightly with each jounce of the truck. In the cab, Bajh turned off the radio he'd been listening to and a silence surrounded the exertions of the engine. After a while there were the sounds of other cars, and distant voices, and the truck eased to a stop.

Araz sat up and looked around. The small side road they'd taken, which ran parallel to the highway, was full of headlights and the sounds of motors stopping and starting. There was a traffic jam, stretching as far down as Araz could see. Maybe a breakdown, or a convoy moving through.

"What's going on?" Araz said through the back window.

Bajh pointed to the slim, false horizon of the actual highway dimly glowing in the distance to their right. "It's stopped there too," he said. He opened the door and leaned out to look behind the truck. There was no one there. They were the last car.

"No problem," he said. "I guess."

Bajh got back in and reversed, using the shoulder to turn around. They traced back to the nearest turnoff and followed it, the tires mak-ing a dull thump as they went from the paved road to the dirt one. They traveled like this for a while, the roughness of the road causing Araz and Asti to sit up. The commotion of the late-night traffic jam eventually receded until its luminescence only barely troubled the dark of the sky behind them.

Araz watched Asti, who was sitting with her legs pulled up beside and under her. He thought again of her body, the form that her sim-ple long-sleeved shirts and jeans under dresses both embraced and

obscured, of the quality of her skin, the way it held light, its grace over her naked hollows and rises as he had seen her the afternoon two weeks before, laid along Bajh's body on the cot in the abandoned guard hut outside town. The afternoon light had been warm and came tripping down through the gentle movement of a tree's lower limbs outside, finally falling through the glassless window, making of their pose a shifting chiaroscuro, revealing then hiding Bajh's huddled nakedness behind her. They were asleep, pressed together in the slight chill of the hut's shadows, even though it was a balmy day. Bajh's face was turned down, nestled between the stiff material of the cot and Asti's shoulder blades. Asti's hair was folded under and hung over the metal brace of the cot, where the long sun of the afternoon alighted on it in bits and pieces, leaving the rest to sit darkly in the shadow of her body. Araz had stood for a second, stilled at the doorway, and carefully taken in the fact of her nakedness, letting his eyes run down to the dip of her stomach and the rise of her hip, Bajh's own hip behind hers, the slim line of his body, mostly hidden behind hers, grayed and blued by the foregrounding distance, even in that small room. There was the pocket of dark hair, surprisingly silky and flat, where her legs met, and the easy curve of her calf, her delicate ankles. They did not wake as he turned away and left.

•

The truck gave a wrenching creak and came to an abrupt stop. Bajh jumped out, cursing. A thin tree of smoke assembled itself out of the air above the cab. Araz got down and watched Bajh kick the front wheel, cough a little from the smoke and pace away, mashing down a button on the cell phone they carried for emergencies and waiting for its small square of light to come on. Asti stayed up in the truck.

The truck's interior lights then quit and Araz found himself in a deep darkness, able to see almost nothing at all. He strained to look around. They were on a farming road, and he thought he could make out the dull metal of an irrigation well-marker glinting flatly a little way off, though he couldn't be sure.

Araz turned to look back toward Bajh and the night came alive, breaking itself around Araz's head.

A skirling came out of the sky, a mechanical screaming, directionless, as if out of the molecules of air itself, its howling barely even a discrete sound. By the time Araz was able to process it at all, the sound was alive in his chest, his hands, his skull, his mouth—percussive, felt more than heard, as was his own voice; if his scream even existed, he couldn't tell. Araz only heard the blast once; the night was blown to a lucid muteness afterward, though he could not yet feel the wetness of the blood trickling from his ears and coating the sides of his jaw and neck.

Later, Araz would find himself unable to divorce his actual memory of what happened from the strange, otherworldly vision of the Internet video he would be shown by a roommate at his boarding school in London. Araz's memory of that night was thus perpetually recast in the shaky, falsely illuminated field of a helicopter's night-vision recording, the only omniscience able to sort the physical chaos. Though the particular video he saw was certainly not of his own night (and though no such video record of his own experience even existed, as far as he knew), Araz would forever afterward bear the acute feeling that he'd witnessed what happened to himself only through the real-time eye of the gun-sighted screen.

In Araz's mind: the glowing white shape of his own prone body beside the truck; of Bajh, statant, in the field's furrows; of Asti, limbs held close, a jumbled blob of the white that signaled body heat to the helicopter's lens. The trio had not been aimed at, so none of them

were hit. Instead, the rounds meant to disable the already-disabled truck (a hundred? a thousand?) found something (a half-full oil can forgotten under the truck's seat? a spare gasoline container wedged without thought under the hay in the back?) to alight on, and the viewfinder was quickly awash with a riot of heat-shapes, an amorphous monster mounting the vehicle—fire.

From the sky came more screaming of metal, though Araz did not hear it. Here, the false implantation in Araz's memory of the concussion of air made by the helicopter's blades. The truth, of course, was that he heard nothing.

Finally, the brief sensations that would not end up savaged by the violence of time passing: the load of clothes, half ablaze, lifting up and up into flight and falling, slowly, slowly, onto Araz's back, lighting his own clothes. Araz struggling up, wildly glimpsing what must have been the shape of Asti's body in the bed of the truck, where she was somehow embracing the clothes, the fire, to her; then Araz knocked flat by the collision of Bajh's panicked, tilting run. At some point, Asti was pulled down off the truck and landed near where Araz lay. A scurry of dirt as Bajh smothered her flames, Araz somehow still burning, the heat spreading up his side and reaching around to his chest like a grasping hand, then the feeling of Bajh returning to smother him again, the heaviness of Bajh's body landing on his own, seeming—because Araz never quite got his breath back—to last for hours and hours.

The afterward Araz would remember better, the coming of morning. He lay situated in a position where he could see only the flat expanse of the field and the horizon beyond. He assumed the truck, Bajh, and Asti to be somewhere behind him, but in the strange otherworld of his condition he did not really think of them, and the emptiness of his mind was even vaguely pleasant. He felt no pain (or he felt pain so completely that all other sensation was wholly

undone, and so did not suffer). There came a distant, rainless storm, and the brief office of lightning gave way to an ataraxic lightlessness just before dawn. The subsequent creep of color into the sky had a curious physical presence to it, limning the ridges of the field and the dirt nearest Araz's face. Just before daylight was full, a drizzle stung Araz's eyes, and he woke for a moment simultaneously into the effluvium of the morning and the insanity of his reverie, just enough to process the arrival of other cars and other people, after which there was only the long surrender of unconsciousness.

2.

Araz's return was inaugurated by a wet, lifeless spring, the air damp and torpid. Even the subdued light, which each day snuck obliquely into the town under the guard of the heavy, unsettled clouds, failed to obscure the glaucous film that covered the buildings and streets. In the middle of the town the river's surface was matte-faced, and its wavering pulse quickened, as if hurrying through.

Araz had arrived on one of the new, dreamily christened "Amman-Qum" expresses, its name suggesting the bus might continue on, long after all the returning Iraqis disembarked, all the way to Iran instead of turning back as everyone knew it did at Baqubah, not even within sight of the border, and refilling itself with dozens of Baghdadi businessmen eager to see the midlevel luxury hotels of Riyadh. After the express, Araz had to connect with a smaller bus to go north for the final leg into town, and as the aged vehicle growled and whinnied its way up the highway, dutifully collecting the tunnels of blast barriers at abandoned checkpoints and police outposts, Araz had the distinct impression that some kind of magic had been broken—specifically, that the spell which had kept the country of

his memory outside the passage of time had been lifted, and that all the built-up brutality of urban aging had, in the six years of Araz's absence, suddenly happened at once: the reclamation of concrete security dividers by sand and dirt, the winnowing to bone of buildings once thrown up for immediate use, the incidental artifacts of the American, then Provisional, then New Iraqi, then New Parliamentary authorities (the burned-out skeletons of Humvees, imported black SUVs, white Toyota pickup trucks, and cheap, Chinese-made taxis, respectively) all suffering what looked to Araz to be the deconstruction that time practices on civilizations over hundreds of years, but in the span of just six. It was as if Araz had looked away and turned back only to find himself adrift in a vision of the country's distant future.

The eternal city had changed too, though in less pronounced ways. During the six years Araz had been gone, news of the town's transformation had drifted to him—little asides and clippings from his father washing ashore in his Darlington Abbey Boys' College mailbox and then, after Araz had turned eighteen and departed for King's College London, via those abbreviated emails of rumors that had wended their way into the law office in Beirut, where his father had gone back to. Araz read every bit of information about the town carefully and each time felt a sort of wonder at the familiar foreignness, especially as he got older. This was the driftwood of his years in the town coming back to him, even in England, to reconsider; time and the distance these anecdotes traveled seemed to have softened away any real detail or utility. At any rate, he'd heard some things, learned them from his father's half-mentions or his own bored, late-night Internet searching. Though what he'd learned had not prepared him for the place itself.

The town had grown. It was now fully a city, apparently, the city center (now referred to as "downtown") built up with multi-level buildings and shops, all of which perhaps wouldn't look quite

so pointedly modern if they did not surround the original dun-colored buildings of crumbling local bricks, which looked posi-tively Neolithic by comparison. The farming compounds previously on the edges of town had been quietly taken in, assimilated by the city's amebic expansion, and were now just groups of low buildings unnaturally close together. What Araz felt on his first exploratory drives around with Asti, her ruined cheek turning this way and that to watch the simulacrum of their town pass by the window, was not so much that the home of their adolescence had changed (it was not a betrayal of time, exactly) but more that the town in some eerie way had approximated the change Araz knew he had experienced in him-self while thousands of miles distant.

This feeling was especially borne out in the strange balance of lay-out the city had settled into in his absence. In the north, the Kurdish farmers who had lived in the town of Araz and Asti's childhood had bunched into a loose agricultural suburb that got thinner and thinner the farther it projected from the city's center until it eventually just petered out, reaching wistfully back in geo-ethnic time toward Iran. In the south, there was a similarly nebulous comet-tail stretch back toward Baghdad, origin of the Shi'a money that was now developing the city, except that this trail was made up of shanties, as if many of the Shiite pilgrims streaming in from Baghdad's religious environs had simply run out of money before they could reach the city proper. And finally, in the west, gesturing toward Samarra and the Al-Askari, was the real cause for the town's increase: a previously little-noticed mosque, in whose tranquil courtyard the Shi'a Imam Al-Alwani had decided, during an American siege, to relocate the holy relic that now made the city such a destination.

All of which bore a curiously accurate spatial resemblance to the grounds of the Darlington Abbey Boys' College (an unassum-ing but respected catch-all for the children of foreign diplomats) and

the general world Araz had spent his first four English years in. He'd woken each morning in his cramped, separatist, scholarship boarder's room on the north end of campus and made his way to the dining hall in the middle, where he met with the devout children from the religious quarters on the south end (both groups eyeing enviously the spacious central dorm suites of the rich students) before trudging off to prayers at the small mosque, partially obscured in the west part of the campus by the larger, largely unused chapel building beside it. The whole time during this morning walk, Araz felt as if he belonged exactly no place, or rather to some undisclosed place nearby that he always seemed to be waiting in vain to stumble upon. He got this very same feeling driving around with Asti in his first weeks back in the city: full of hope that he might at any moment turn a corner into an unknown neighborhood that felt perfectly and finally familiar.

The popular mosque of Imam Alwani was situated at the tip of a fingerlike projection of new buildings rising from the city's chorion, and it presided calmly over a muddy stretch of rich soil, a panorama of the verdant, soggy fields stretching out behind it. Its entrance and the minarets topping the four corners of its courtyard looked back toward the city, and the curving, prehensile jetty of development that it crowned enclosed a small slum that had grown up around a wide nearby square long before anyone could remember. The slum had hung on, despite the best efforts of the mosque's wealthier pilgrims; the area seemed to have the power to revert any new venture or building to its natural, semidecrepit state. This was certainly what it had done to the Hotel du Chevalier, where Araz took a flat.

The Hotel du Chevalier had been built and then quickly abandoned and sold by a foreigner a few years before the invasion and had already, in the span of a little more than a decade, undergone several discrete phases of decay. By the time Araz rented a fourth-floor flat on an indefinite lease, it had passed from hotel to run-down board-

ing house to something resembling a Caliphate-era inn, and had become, finally, a sort of crumbling, late-empire Roman cathouse.

The building did tower over the uneven harlequin blanket of the surrounding slum's roofs, though, and if it had portions of ceiling or intermediate floors missing—the bits of concrete rebar exposed like nerves, hung with the residents' colorful wet wash—it also had rooms, mostly on the southeast corner, that were more or less intact and that, as Araz's did, even improbably retained bits and pieces of the hotel's old official errata, regurgitating them whimsically. Once, braced on all fours on the gritty floor beside the bed as a low-level officer of the "Imam's Army" thrust into him, Araz knocked into the leg of the room's desk and a piece of stationery floated down and landed in front of him. As the man's timid grunts (really he was just a boy, or maybe a late teenager) accelerated, Araz stared at the miniature, ridiculous hotel seal at the top of the sheet—not a knight, as it should have been, but a falcon—and recited to himself (simultaneously in this room full of late-afternoon sunlight and back in Father Vere's poetry class at Darlington) the Hopkins poem Vere had passive-aggressively demanded all the Muslim boys memorize. As the man-boy climaxed, Araz recalled the words: "Buckle! AND the fire that breaks from thee then, a billion / Times told lovelier, more dangerous, O my chevalier!" The man was silent for a long time before Araz realized he had spoken the last line aloud. The man's breathing was uneven and querulous, and Araz had laughed sharply into the quiet.

•

Araz saw Bajh again for the first time at the mosque, after prayers had let out and the courtyard was filled with people. There was a small stage set up just in front of the bright green structure that housed the

relic, from which every Friday a local imam delivered the khutbah. This Friday, however, Bajh was to speak, and Araz, pushing unnoticed through the crowd to stand just inside the wide courtyard's walls, could see him sitting on a chair at the edge of the stage.

Asti, preparing a hookah the night before, had told Araz about the change in Bajh. Even though Araz had taken in her information greedily, now, standing there, watching Bajh rise from the chair and approach the bundled microphones, watching the way the brisk wind revealed the shape and shadow of his body inside the brilliantly white (how did he keep it so, in all this mud?) dishdasha, Araz was conscious of all he knew falling away, leaving only the mercurial breath in his chest and the midmorning light that vaulted beneath the ceiling of clouds, gathering around Bajh's figure as he spoke.

The experience of Bajh's later sermons and speeches—they would become weekly—was so similar to this first one that, in Araz's memory, watching Bajh this first time was like watching the Unity of Bajh, or at least of New Bajh, as he was now, in his new world. Bajh was reading his speech haltingly from a piece of paper, talking about the religious theme of the day. Araz wasn't really listening; he stared at Bajh's hands and face, at his perfect skin. Araz had always assumed Bajh had escaped the night of fire unharmed, but Araz had also, if he was honest, occasionally hosted other hypotheses, which had only been encouraged by the news of Bajh's rise in the esteem of the great imam in Baghdad. Half of Araz thought Bajh must have some visible marking, a lesser version of Asti's, that let everyone who looked at him see the entire span of his lifetime in this country: the supple skin of a boy, the awful violence of his adulthood. This was the easiest way for Araz to explain to himself the news of Bajh's growing popularity in the city, among the Shiite pilgrims. But he could see now that Bajh was visibly unscarred. If Asti was to be believed, he had no trace at all of what had happened about his body. Araz watched Bajh pause and

look up, watched him smile a little sheepishly at the crowd's cheers, which grew wilder and wilder with the growing abstraction of his exhortations.

"The genius is that he never says anything about what happened," Asti had said, blowing on the hot coals of the pipe, and Araz saw now that she was right.

In the following weeks, moving among the crowd, Araz would hear countless versions of the story—the trio's story—most of the speakers curiously downplaying Bajh's actual role, Bajh always more one of the victims than the hero. "It's the same way with his family," Asti had also said. "He's Feyli, so he's OK in the mosque, but they never talk about him being their little Kurd."

On the stage, though, Bajh was as handsome as ever, almost defiantly so, though he now cut his hair short, and his skin was an even deeper tan, and his classic features seemed less striking on his adult frame. When Araz left, he could already hear the words of Bajh's speech being rebroadcast breathlessly by the muezzin's loud-speakers, as they would continue to be all afternoon until even when they'd stopped his voice seemed to echo in the streets, an inescapable diminuendo.

•

As the moist spring went on, Araz began to understand better the way the city had managed to preserve its unnerving sense of perpetuity. Araz had been invited to a dinner party by an old Kurdish politician, a friend of the man Araz had met in Kensington on a similar afternoon, the air relieved of its rain, the city quiet around him. Now, as Araz walked through the market district, he thought of how, while the town had been goaded into its chronological future as a

city, a bewildering sense of timelessness remained. People back in Baghdad used its traditional name now as a sly denigration for its residents. Yes, the *eternal town*, they said, meaning, *This will never be your city*. And yet Araz could not find a single person who could tell him the day or even the month that all the meat in the market had become halal or that Uncle Nuri's shop (now a corner super-market) had ceased selling the popular pirated DVDs from Syria, or that anyone, let alone fully half the women among the stalls, had started wearing her loose hijab pulled across the mouth and not just the hair. Maybe, he thought, it was more that the city was just over-full with illusion, as in the Shi'a-backed real estate companies that quietly bought up the big apartment blocks and upped the rent on anyone who refused to be observant. If religious families were all you saw on that block, and if you couldn't remember the change occur-ring, hadn't it always been that way?

The dinner party was in the north end of the city and the host, Araz realized upon arriving, had invited someone from every import-ant Kurdish interest or family left in the area. The men stood closely, their rounded bellies almost touching as they slurped in the tradi-tional way at their tea saucers, as if no one could see that the dark substance was actually American whiskey. Araz understood then that he was there representing the Kensington man's money. These men, these old local politicians and businessmen, knew Araz's story, knew he'd had an expensive English education paid for first by a settle-ment with the Americans and then, vaguely, by other interests. It was possible they wanted Araz as a spokesman or at least as a representa-tive to a large potential donor to the cause. They did not know Araz had been in love with the Kensington man, did not know that Araz had left him on a cold, lightless winter afternoon in the shared gar-den behind his flat a few weeks before Araz's reappearance in the city. They knew nothing about the kind of silence that had come

into Araz while the man, some twenty years older, had gasped and sobbed like a child.

Bajh had also been invited. Araz caught sight of him across the wide living room, his white taqiyah standing out, his hands clasped behind his back, not drinking, his face half-serious, half-amused as he met Araz's eyes. Araz had to wait to speak with him, a whole hour wasted between the host's little speech about loyalty as a new government coalition was formed (delivered pointedly in Bajh's direction) and the nattering of Asti's husband, who was an uneasy, very poor man whom the other men allowed because he supplied the alcohol. Asti helped his little shifting operation in the market sometimes, selling the residents of the Chevalier's slum aged cans of Turkish beer and crumbles of the hash bricks that Asti wheedled out of their supplier and split between Araz and herself.

When Bajh finally did come over, he turned to Araz as if continuing a conversation that had been interrupted only minutes ago.

"So I go on these walks," he said, and smiled playfully. "I find they clear my mind."

And so they walked, not just that night but each night they could escape early from the biweekly meetings in the Kurdish politician's house, which were becoming tenser and tenser, and eventually on days when there were no meetings at all. They rounded the city, Bajh showing up in the square in front of the Chevalier or Araz waiting patiently for Bajh to get out of one of the Sura study sessions he led a few days a week at the mosque. They walked in the cool spring nights and the humid, breezy afternoons. In the north of the city there was a small laundromat (everyone used washers now, due to the city's new, larger electricity ration), and sometimes they followed its scent of jasmine and linen as it wafted out into the fields, mostly abandoned now, until it mixed with the smell of the real flowers that grew in the fallow tangles. They didn't talk all the time, but

sometimes Bajh asked about what it had been like in England, and Araz told him about the sallow-faced, Yemenite Muslim chaplain at Darlington because he thought Bajh would like to hear about that. Other times Araz asked about what it had been like in the town while he'd been gone, but Bajh had difficulty answering this, and the conversation usually devolved into Bajh simply listing the fates of people they'd known as children. If they'd started out in the afternoon they came back to the slum just before last prayers, Bajh returning to the golden bulbs of the minarets' spires, Araz to the fuzzy, colored lights strung over the market in the square at dark.

The days began to slip away from Araz. His money, which had been mostly exhausted just getting back to the town, dwindled to nothing; the lease on his flat was the only thing remaining, a final parting gift from the man in Kensington. Araz reclaimed consciousness each morning to the distant calls and chittering insults of the other residents of the Chevalier as they stirred. The hotel had become a sort of refuge in the slum. Aging Syrian prostitutes with thick black eye makeup mixed with the fey boys who put on dance shows in the square on weekends. There was Araz, the half-foreigner, on the fourth floor, and Asti and her husband, the alcohol seller, on the first. The days became hourless. Araz was not even able to say when his and Asti's hash sessions got earlier and more frequent, eventually lasting more or less all day. Neither could he say when the visitors started appearing in his living room. Of this especially, scenes became inseparable from their own recurrent memory, causing them to surface, reexperienced, with the whim of Araz's boredom or moods.

The visitors were almost always from the mosque, members of the "security force" that people were already calling the "Imam's Army," referring, of course, to no real or local imam but the lost imam, the yet-to-come imam: the army, then, of no man. Araz saw

them sometimes as he and Bajh inspected the city near the mosque: teenagers mostly, lying on the ground behind ancient, bulky-looking machine guns, aiming them into the empty twilight. Then Araz would see them again the next day, in late afternoon or night, before or after final prayers, hedging back and forth in his doorway. They were timid as they had sex with him, or, if the only way they could bring themselves to do it was in a fell swoop of violence, sometimes they were rough. Araz didn't care, didn't ask questions. He made them do it in front of the long, dusty mirror he'd propped against the wall, so they had to look down at the awful geography of his back.

The Kensington man had refused to look at the sea of mottled skin while they had sex, but Araz knew from his experiments at Darlington what it looked like. Whoever was behind him would try and fail to ignore the scarred field, the landscape of it, blotchy with faded yellows and vermilion, the swells and vales of it, uncanny membrane that both resembled and did not resemble skin. A failure to look away was sharpened by the final discovery of the flesh near Araz's hip that had taken on the grid imprint of a medical wrapping left on too long in the early weeks. One visitor, older than most, lay on his side on the floor and cried afterward, until Araz threw him a towel and told him to stop embarrassing himself.

Though he asked for and required nothing, the visitors brought Araz little gifts: food, clothes, or sometimes just money, placing whatever they'd brought on the small table in the entryway where Araz left it all untouched, taking only the money to use with Asti to get new and purer supplies from her husband's connection. Araz ate little and slept less and lost weight. Each time after a visitor left, Araz lay with his back against the cool, dirty tile of the floor and felt the swelling in his chest, the one he'd had since he'd first seen Bajh again: the feeling that the world was accelerating around him, not in time but in pitch, in intensity, a terrible inertia, as if together he and

Bajh were approaching some small apocalypse. Araz felt a terrible drive in himself to be owned by his desire, to continue until nothing of it was left, until he had no money, until there was no one left to sleep with, until the not-skin of his ruined back stretched taut over his ribs. He imagined, lost in his drugged reveries, that the entire town was wasting away just as his own body was, until all that would be left in the slum's square on the last day would be himself, barely there, and Bajh, in perfect condition, the leveled buildings and fields presenting him like a statue.

•

The city seemed to be holding its breath. On their walks, the people in the streets no longer joked or called to Bajh and Araz as they passed. Bajh also grew quiet in the Kurdish meetings and during their perambulations.

One afternoon at the end of their walk, Bajh offered to come up to Araz's flat with him to wash the mud from their feet—this instead of obeying their unspoken rule of doing it separately: Bajh at the mosque's ablution fountain, Araz in the communal bathroom at the end of his hall. Araz watched Bajh as he made his way through the halls and stairwells of the Chevalier. Those who saw him were silent at first, standing tensely in their doorways or stilled with laundry baskets in their hands, their eyes guarded. But Bajh was kind, oblivious, respectfully greeting everyone he saw and making conversation with anyone he could until, by the time they reached the second floor, the hallways were alight with his presence.

In the flat, after they'd washed the dirt from their feet, Bajh stood and watched while Araz changed his splattered clothes. Araz turned away from him as he pulled off his long shirt and watched Bajh watch

him in the mirror. Araz stood still. Bajh's gaze had dropped to the middle of Araz's bare back and was hovering there sadly. He stepped forward and stood close behind Araz. Araz closed his eyes and imagined what Bajh's breath would feel like on his shoulders then, if he still had any sensation there. Bajh reached out gently in the space between them and traced very lightly the longest blooming ridge of scar tissue. He leaned forward and down in an awkward sort of bow, and Araz could feel the cool weight of Bajh's forehead pressing against the back of his neck.

"Oh, Araz," Bajh said quietly. "What on earth are you doing here?"

•

Araz was drinking tea in a café at the edge of the slum's market square on the afternoon of the dog's head, and so he saw it happen. It unfolded so easily that it was almost unsurprising, like watching something many times imagined suddenly happen in real life. Though no one could have imagined it, really. A group of chanting, jumping children dressed in the uniforms of the religious school came singing and dancing into the square. At first among the vendors there was the air of pleasant excitement, as if this was some new version of the occasional Saturday-night parades in which the teenaged boys from the Chevalier formed a dancing line, dressed as famous women from history. But then, as the commotion progressed into the center of the market, Araz could see people pulling away. When the group of children arrived at the unmarked alcohol table, which Asti was manning while her husband made a trip out of town, the severed head sailed into the air out of the blob of little bodies, appearing to do so of its own accord. It hit Asti on the shoulder, the dog's blood

streaking across her dress, and fell loudly to the table in front of her, its glassy eyes gazeless, muzzle hanging slackly open. She looked down at it, and as she did they threw cups of dirty, red-dyed water on her—apparently they'd been unable to gather whatever was left of the animal's blood.

"Praise be for the death of the dogs!" they were singing. "Praise be to Allah who saves us from the nastiness of the dogs who corrupt us with their filth!"

That night, Araz helped Asti undress and clean herself. Her voice was even and quiet as she told Araz the plan she and her husband had decided upon on the phone.

In the dim light of the room, Araz could see the queer geometry of her burn scars, almost symmetrical, worst up and down the middle of her torso and getting less and less pronounced farther away from her heart, until her hands were almost normal. On her stomach were chunks of uneven, missing flesh where infection had been excised, and her bra hid the irregular shapes of her mangled breasts. Helping her like this was not for Araz to do, but her husband had begged him on the phone, and Araz did not blush.

There was a quiet after she'd changed and had explained the plan, as she leaned into her small mirror and tried to fix her hair. Araz looked at her face, the snarl of taut, shining pink skin.

That night the whole Chevalier was quiet, possibly out of respect, which only had the unintended consequence of making Asti's cries of pain and the strange pattern of her husband's crashing blows and apologetic sobs even louder, until they seemed to fill every open space in the hotel, drifting up through the decaying floors and ceilings to where Araz lay, flinching. Their plan had been simple: they would contend to anyone who would listen that the husband had no idea that Asti was doing something so terrible as selling alcohol in the market, and that he'd punished her severely with a brutal

beating, hoping this would be enough for the powers that were in the mosque, those who had sent the children.

The next morning the men came for him anyway, dragging Asti's husband out by his shirt and hair just before first light, not even looking at the proposed penance of Asti's swollen face and beaten body but kicking him right past where she lay on the couch and beating him into the back of a white pickup truck. It would be half a day before someone thought it was safe enough to go into the flat, where they found that Asti's husband had, in his fear, done his part too well, leaving Asti still drifting in and out of consciousness. A few of the older women were left to care for her, and it would be another ten days before someone found her husband's body, partially submerged in an irrigation ditch, half his face missing from the exit wound, shot through the back of the head.

●

In the weeks that followed, the city became populated by shadows. Only small caravans of speeding vehicles chanced the street. Bajh was missing; people were saying that word had come from the imam in Baghdad that, of all the lieutenants, Bajh had been chosen as the new security commander of the district. Word had also come from the north that the Kurdish parliament would be joining the new government after all, ceding, as part of the agreement, its claim to all towns bordering the Shi'a territories to do with as the religious liked. The mosque gathered its boys from the city. Araz's visitors dwindled to almost none, until finally there was only one boy left: a skinny, affectionate, nervous teenager with a ghost of a mustache who called himself a soldier and came only in the dead of night. Sometimes the boy fell asleep afterward in Araz's bed, and Araz, lost in the waves of the hash, would get up very

close to the side of the boy's face, trying to focus hard enough on some tiny part of it, his canthus, say, to transform it into Bajh's so that he might be there with him, even falsely, just for a few minutes.

When the men came for Araz, he did not resist. The two men, their faces obscured by the black wraps of masks, had to carry him down the stairs. They bound his hands and laid him with a surprising gentleness in the bed of the pickup, and Araz wondered briefly if they knew him.

At the bank of the river, Araz fell on the wet ground. He could feel its cold firmness beneath him, yielding slightly to the shape of his body. Above the men's faces, the sky wheeled with sharp stars. One masked man went back to the truck; the other watched him go. Araz heard the door slam, the engine start. In a sudden motion, the man above Araz lifted his gun and fired a single shot. Araz felt the sting of dirt against his cheek, and his head filled with a pure ringing. The man put his gun down and hefted Araz up, Araz realizing only with the slosh of blood rushing to his head that he was uninjured, that the man had fired just to the right of Araz's ear, deafening him. Then there was the sensation of falling backward and the splash of cold wetness as Araz was dropped into the river.

He did not know how long he floated. He felt the motion of the river's current, the clinging of his clothes in the water. He felt like nothing in the water—weightless, directionless, as if with the next gurgle of the river pushing around a snag he would find himself without a body. Above him the sky shifted. Eventually he felt himself bump gently to a stop, beached on a sandbar. He rolled awkwardly and sat up, working his hands loose.

From his path along the irrigation levee, Araz could see the dim, colored glow of the fire leaping and hovering in front of the city's constellation of lights as he made his way back. The leaves of the old crops left in the fields rustled in the cool dark. The wind stung the

deep cuts around Araz's wrists where he'd worked the plastic zip-tie handcuffs free. The ringing was still there, though it had quieted and moved outside his head so that it was like he was rediscovering it in each stretch of field or huddle of abandoned farm buildings.

The square, when he found it, was lit by the flames, bright as if at midday. There were people everywhere, small knots of religious men cheering, others racing to and from various places carrying water, bandages. Araz looked around. There were people clustered around bodies where they lay on the ground. Araz recognized one of the dancing boys, a huge portion of his thigh missing, the skin and flesh flensed to the bone, a jagged edge of fat glistening yellow-ish into the wound.

As Araz stepped away from the boy, he felt a light grip on his neck. He turned a little to see Bajh standing beside him. Bajh let go. His face was calm and flat, completely without affect. He did not seem surprised to see Araz, and Araz knew then that Bajh had saved him. Together they turned, watching the figure of the Hotel du Chevalier unmade into its skeleton frame, now only a darkness at the base of the riot of color, the smoke an oily blackness listing in the night, the air above them turned to a sucking, gasping maw. The two stood and watched the towering face of the building, roaring with its burning: huge, almost regal, raging, unconsumed. Suddenly a bolt of brilliant fire bloomed high above the hotel's roof, and Bajh and Araz hushed with everyone else in awe. And that age was gone for-ever between them.

The Territory of Grief

As the ship carrying his new wife crests the wavering horizon of the gaseous sea, Gershon again checks the foyer mirror, and rubs his hands vigorously over his face. He is standing in the consular unit, the "penthouse quarters" as Ofer, his supervisor at the diplomatic corps back in Jerusalem, once called the apartment. And while it is true that these rooms do preside at great height over the stone buildings and roadways in the settlement below (as might befit the Government Administrator of the Northern Territories), the effect is not really one of luxury. Instead, the wide glass windows with their panning views and the smooth modern surfaces of the rooms' décor only emphasize, to Gershon anyway, the solitude of the post—a kind of experiment in bright monasticism. He does not think about it much, usually, but the prospect of the new woman's arrival has forced him to cast his gaze anew.

Gershon stands at the edge of the foyer, stands in front of the bay doors, which will at any moment slide open to reveal his new wife, the one they've sent. He wonders briefly if this woman will look like Yoheved, and, if so, if this will seem more cruel, amusing, or sad. "Well, you know," Ofer said on the video-link when they told him

about the new woman, "they're starting to use the word *rehabilita-tion* a lot in these meetings about the new territory." Then, after a pause, "It was that or reassignment down here. Which, you know…" And Gershon had nodded, understanding. In the window beside the bay doors, the Earth burns with its color high above the territory, a steady blue moon.

•

"Did you sleep?" Gershon says, the next morning.

He's found her standing in front of the widest window, the one in the sparsely furnished living room, looking down, or out. She turns to him slowly.

"You should sleep, if you haven't," he says. "I know it can be hard. People have trouble, because of the sky."

The sky: clear, cloudless, a piercing black at night while at day only ripening to a lightless cobalt, insinuated with vaguely amethyst underhues at dawn and dusk. The impression, especially upon new arrivals, is of limitless depth, or height, and sometimes the new set-tlers experience a kind of vertigo. But he's talking too much.

She turns to him, is facing him now, silently, her eyes wide, though not with fear. Instead, it is a sharp look, one of alert appraisal, and somehow this in conjunction with her delicate attractiveness feeds Gershon's anger.

"I'm ready, if we need to do something in the city," she says softly. "They told me we'd probably need to do something in the city."

Gershon nods, his jaw tight and aching, and tries to keep from speaking again.

•

Gershon has always been surprised when he's come across a very attractive Orthodox girl, though they are not so entirely rare. Stepping off a creaking Egged bus back in the real Jerusalem, he'd catch a glimpse of an upturned face in the line waiting to get on: smooth skin, perfectly symmetrical features—a kind of sloe-eyed beauty that passed briefly through his day like a ghost. These fractions of visions became even more disconcerting after he and Yoheved had Shmuli, and moved to the apartment above the hostel just inside Jaffa Gate. Gershon, out walking in the Jewish Quarter with Shmuli in his arms, would see one of these *belles filles* hurrying along the narrow, cramped Old City market streets, three or four small children wheeling through the crowd before her. It always seemed impossible to Gershon, for a moment anyway, that such an attractive woman—a girl really—could have so many children, though the kids themselves also usually seemed beautiful in that crystalline, epicene way of small children.

"That's the whole point, though, isn't it, with those women," Yoheved once said when Gershon tried to describe it. "All that obscuring: the wrist-length blouses, the wigs and scarves, the denim dresses they're always tripping over. Men are so predictable. Let them see only your face and they'll see a fucking Vermeer. Men. It's because you're an immigrant, really. It's because you didn't grow up here that you can even see it." And Gershon wonders now, glancing every few minutes at his new wife in the seat beside him as he navigates the terrain vehicle away from the Government Tower, what Yoheved would make of this girl, this woman, this Hava. What did Yoheved see before her when the two women met to sign the rabbinical agreement allowing the new marriage? Though that must have been four years ago, Gershon supposes, just before the beginning of the girl's long trip. What would he have done if they'd told him in real time, if he would've had four years to prepare himself for

her, instead of just the six months? Still, the meeting, the document between the two silent women, feels to Gershon tenderly recent, as it must not to Hava herself.

Gershon glances at her in the passenger seat again and forces himself to see her; he can resist it no longer. Her jaw and high, delicate cheekbones make her face angular, Hava benefitting from Ashkenazically emphasized eyes and balance of features while escaping somehow the elongated face. Against such clarity, the head covering she wears seems particularly ugly. The few tendrils of her hair he can make out (real, it looks like) are a deep and rich brown.

Yoheved was never as attractive as this Hava, Gershon can admit that, not even when she was that age, which was some time ago. Gershon met Yoheved a couple years after immigrating, when he'd wandered accidentally into a near riot between protesters on the campus of their university, so he knew well what face it was that ended up gently ruined by time and motherhood: the strong jaw, the shrewd eyes, the defiant, almost martial cheekbones, the dirty-blond hair. Yoheved was plenty attractive in her unconventional way back then, but never in this mode of fully realized features, never with that small, tight body, apparent even beneath the modest layers of Hava's clothing. Yoheved must have hated her, Gershon thinks, hated the insult of her youth. But her internal flinch of disgust would've been balanced by the knowledge of the fate she was signing this girl off to, and besides nobody stayed beautiful out here; not with the dry air, the silence, the empty city sucking one's mien—especially with women—of its marrow. Let her see what comes of beauty, Yoheved would've thought, and Gershon's anger dilates now to take in Yoheved herself, along with Ofer, and even the family of this Hava, for whatever monetary or social disgrace resigned her to him.

They are traveling to the first mourner's tea of the day, which is in an apartment on New Ben Yehuda Square, and Gershon is driv-

ing their exterior terrain vehicle with unnecessary, aggressive speed. Despite this, Hava looks around carefully, her respirator, which she'd tried to put on inside the vehicle before Gershon explained she only needed it outside, forgotten in her lap.

"It's really eerie, isn't it," she says, as if to some absent third person. "I mean, of course they prepare you, but it's . . . it's completely imaginable, I guess, which is what makes it so odd to actually see, if that makes sense. It's just so accurate. I mean, it's real. The same thing. Stone by stone, almost."

She is talking about the settlers' city, which Gershon forces himself to see again now, slowing down. Here, in the outskirts which they have been traveling through, the doubling is less noticeable, just as in the real Jerusalem the modern buildings are less distinct, fading in one's mind to a gaunt blend of cityscape. But they are approaching now the environs of the Old City, or the New Old City, which is what has moved her to speak. Because wasn't it something to see for the first time this simulacrum of familiar buildings, streets, the pale Jerusalem stone—in the distance the Old City walls so real—and to realize it is not actually a simulacrum but a doubling, an impossible physical recurrence, just unpeopled. It is the first appearance of any inhabitant at all that emphasizes the larger emptiness of the city. As Gershon slows to park on a deserted side street, a little band of four small, dark Palestinian kids rushes around the corner. They begin dancing around the vehicle, goofing off. The youngest one presses his face, shielded by the stolen respirator's plastic, against the driver's side window.

They've been having this problem lately. The distant Free Territories Settlement was launched two years ago when a vessel financed by Saudi, Arab League, and Red Crescent monies more or less crash-landed in the unoccupied plain out in the unassigned, unclaimed quadrant over the horizon. According to the briefs

Gershon received in his office, their supplies, which had been inferior in the first place, were now running out, and this was inspiring many of them to attempt the long trek over to the Israeli settlement. Though it seemed for some reason only the children were making it across.

Gershon looks at the boy's face, the small hands cupped around the respirator's shield, trying to see in, and can feel Hava looking too. Everything but the dancing boys is still. Then the boy draws his head away and takes half a step back, turning his face to say something to his friends, and Gershon seizes the opportunity to open the door quickly, thunking the boy's head hard against its metal. As Gershon gets out and adjusts the rubber rim of his own respirator, the boy staggers into the street, shaking his head like a dazed animal, then disappears around the corner where his friends have already fled. Gershon turns to where Hava is sitting in the vehicle, and waits.

●

In the widow's apartment, Hava is speaking to the group of women in the living room, suffering their oblique interrogation. Gershon isn't listening. He's standing at the window, looking down at New Ben Yehuda Square: deserted, the replica store windows dark, the signs unlit. The most prominent storefront, stretching on two sides of a corner, is Giorgio's, the famous chain pizza place, its big plate-glass windows smoky at this angle. The tall, old-fashioned stools along its counter, where people back in the real Jerusalem are even now sitting and eating, are made into solemn, shadowy figures.

Gershon was there, maybe a block away, when the Giorgio's bombing happened, on a dull assignment babysitting a group of American diplomats' wives and children, showing them the real city. They'd all wanted to eat at the Hard Rock Café: Jerusalem,

and Gershon had only just shepherded them out of the restaurant after the meal—they were headed to the market on Ben Yehuda, actually—when there was the concussion of air, the tremendous sundering skirl that seemed to emanate from the very buildings themselves, then the unearthly moments of silence. The first thing Gershon heard: the querulous wail of one of the American kids, a little blond girl, crying, or gearing up to cry. Her mouth was upturned cartoonishly, without thought or understanding, in a way that made Gershon's sternum ache. Within ten minutes the American security detail for the diplomats' families had whisked them all away to the safety of the embassy, and Gershon was left there, on the curb, alone. He did not run toward the carnage, as most of the other men on the street did. Instead, he turned and walked all the way home, to his and Yoheved's apartment at the Jaffa Gate, where Yoheved had locked Shmuli in the bathroom, of all places, for safety.

And Gershon thinks now, as he does consistently when his business in the New Jerusalem brings him to the square, that if he *had* rushed toward the real Ben Yehuda Square, if he had rushed into the abstracted concrete and savaged urban errata of the bombing, there is a good chance he would've seen or ran into the very widow whose apartment he is now standing in. Her, or any of the other mourners who live now above or beside the New Ben Yehuda Square—the recreated, reconstructed site where, all that distance away, their husband, or wife, or child, or whole family bled to death on the concrete, in the road. He doesn't want to explain this truth about the New Jerusalem settlement to Hava, though she must've been briefed. Let someone else tell her about the passenger ships full of those mourners, the way they made their lives as near to the simulacrum locations of their respective violences as possible. Gershon doesn't want to try to explain to Hava their strange, dissonant belief. This planet, this settlement, this doubled city, where entropy is stalled, reversed.

The women are quieting now, and Hava has started in on some kind of speech, something that sounds prepared. She will announce herself as Gershon's new wife, and the mourners will make of that what they will. They will understand what it means as well as Gershon does, he suspects, once they discover her lack of a tragic history.

He was initially chosen as the Government Administrator of the Northern Territories for a reason, everyone knows: he was emblematic of the population; he would understand them, would be suited to the diplomatic post; he was already alone. So what it means that they now want him here with a wife—a young wife, and (it is implied, eventually) children—is that the Israeli government is not satisfied with having only a mourners' colony any longer. The religious settlers (the Israeli Space Administration's first idea) had been unwilling to come, unwilling to turn away from their divinely mandated, illegal constructions in Gaza and the West Bank. The military could not justify the budget to establish even a minimal presence here. And the original, notional idea that this outpost was built up to be a final resort, a sort of final galactic keep of Jews in case of largest-scale catastrophe, while still popularly held in Israel, is ultimately not enough. What will come—what will soon already be arriving, Gershon knows from the shipment manifest schedules he receives—is business, commerce (and so jobs, money, and people: Israelis sick of Israel, or Olim for whom the land of Israel's promise has been dwarfed by the greater promise of a new frontier, a bigger adventure). The Giorgio's below the window where Gershon stands will within two years or so be open, be alive with customers, workers. But so what, he thinks. They reopened the real Giorgio's in real Ben Yehuda Square a month after the bombing, and there was a line around the block.

"And I'm just so glad and honored to be a part of this special community," Hava is saying. She doesn't understand what the women really want to hear: which tragedy it is she will be the mon-

ument of here. Why it is she's so suited for Gershon, ultimately. Gershon turns momentarily toward Hava where she stands now in the center of the room, the women sitting here and there around her, listening. She takes a breath. She has been coached.

"I myself have never experienced a loss such as any of yours, but I want to say that you all—that the people here—that you were never forgotten by me. I think the settlement is a wonderful opportunity for a new life, a new kind of life, and your interests, I can assure you, will always be at my and my husband's hearts."

Gershon turns away. Below, in the square, he sees the band of dirty kids again. Two of them are sitting on the curb. The others are walking back and forth in front of the replicated shop windows, peering inside. They won't break the windows: the stores are not locked, and hold nothing of any use inside, and the kids must've explored all of them already anyway. The Administration's stance, as Gershon has been euphemistically instructed via memo, is basically to let them run out of supplies, at which point they will either die or turn themselves in for deportation back to their settlement, which amounts to the same thing. But Gershon thinks the Administration underestimates how apolitical, how apathetic to politics the Israeli population settled here is. The refugee kids' respirators, Gershon has noticed, are Israeli-issued, the backup sets that would be nearly impossible to steal. And they have to be getting food from somewhere. Mostly the people here, Gershon wants to say to Hava, to Ofer, to nobody, just want to be left alone.

•

Back in the car, Gershon loops around on the streets without really knowing why.

"We have to pick up something for the next visit," he says, though Hava has not asked.

The silence in the vehicle is suddenly oppressive. Gershon flips on the streaming stereo console. It begins where he left off listening in his study, how long ago—days? weeks?—picking up in the middle of "Mars, Bringer of War."

Hava gives an abrupt laugh.

"Holst!" she says, surprising him. He feels himself color.

"Yeah, well," he says.

She laughs again.

"Very apropos, I mean, you listening to *The Planets*. It's just funny," she says, losing heart at his empty face, trailing off, "I guess."

It wasn't the first thing he'd listened to. After his first year in the post, he'd decided to sacrifice each subsequent term to a different composer. By the time it came to this year, there were only two composers left in the giant box set of vintage vinyl he'd brought with him, stubbornly refusing to download anything. He didn't think he could bear Mahler. He is saving Mahler for the end of something. And so it is Holst this year.

He feels self-conscious now, as they listen to the music in the vehicle's cocoon of quiet, about just how much there is to dislike about Holst, and particularly this movement—the insistent chees-iness, the way it telegraphs its effect, etcetera, etcetera—and for a moment Gershon wants to explain to Hava why it is he loves it. Which is, mostly, its time. The recalcitrant 5/4 time signature that one is *meant* to be unsettled by, that one is meant to recognize on some plane of consciousness as otherworldly: violent, but an odd, stumbling sort of violence. Gershon loves the shifting character of it too—giving the section that is now filling the silence between him and Hava its limping, reeling motion. It builds to a climax that never comes, that is instead interrupted by the piece's own blunt, mar-

tial, off-kilter theme. He especially likes the contrapositive effect that occurs when listening to it while driving through the city, its insistent tones set against the nothing-scape, the empty buildings. How long, if ever, will it take Hava to understand?

The movement ends, the piece's final crisp blasts giving way to the quiet thrum of the vehicle's electric engine, which declension of silence rushes back in around them. They round a corner and pass along one of the small bus depots, four stops in a row. Hava turns almost sideways in her seat. Gershon slows the vehicle, then stops, though he's not been planning to.

This is the scene of the first of the new bombings, of which there have so far been three. The sites of the bus bombings are always more pointed, Gershon thinks, because they are on exactly the right scale: the mangled industrial metal and shattered plastic of the small shelters and stubs of benches clearly imply the size of the absent human figures; the bus (which is not there, which will never, in fact, arrive) easily present in the imagination. And afterward, back in the real Jerusalem, when things are quickly cleaned up, when the bus shelters are immediately and officiously rebuilt, there is no sight that so clearly demonstrates the aggression of the quotidian, the way the world just goes on with its commute, urban regeneration swallowing memory whole. What is left—what has always been left for Gershon, even before everything happened with Yoheved and Shmuli—is a residual sense of the city's sadness: nonspecific, drifting at the margins of a beautiful, light-filled mid-afternoon in the square in front of the Jerusalem Ballet, for instance. This is a quality that is absent from the New Jerusalem, where even an actual event such as this new bombing is only re-creation, re-created history, as if anyone needs further proof of terror's lack of imagination. The real city's sadness is comforting, in a way, is also what he means to say. But he can see Hava doesn't recognize the location.

"Didn't you ever see the bus station during the third intifada?" Gerhson says now, sharply.

"No," Hava says, not looking at him. "My parents lived in the suburbs. We didn't go into the city for maybe two whole years, during the worst of it. Or I didn't, anyway."

The reference to the suburbs throws Gerhson off for some reason. Unbidden, a memory: only a few months after immigrating, Gershon walking for hours and hours through the suburbs to get to the Israel Museum in order to see the Dead Sea Scrolls; mid-morning, the city absolutely deserted, Gershon strolling through the stillness, not having any idea why there was no one around until the woman at the ticket office reminded him it was Tisha B'Av. Gershon leans forward a little to see around Hava, to see exactly what she's looking at, and is distracted instead by the crumbled concrete curb at the epicenter of the explosion.

Who was doing it, bombing the New Old City? When it began, Gershon simply assumed it was one or several of the packs of Palestinian kids, rigging oxygen tanks to explode, which had seemed poetic in that they needed the oxygen tanks as much as the Israeli settlers did. But after the second, and the third—the bombings always in the old places, the corresponding places where, back in the real city, there'd been real bombings—Gershon is not so sure. It seems unlikely that those Palestinian kids (unorganized, wild, mostly diffident) would even be able to come by the oxygen tanks and whatever else was needed to manufacture and set off a single such bomb, let alone three. Who then? Briefly, Gershon has entertained paranoiac visions of secret (subterranean?) bands of adult Palestinians, having made it across the gaping gulf between the settlements, surfacing to plant the explosives. But no, the unblinking eyes of the government satellites, with their heat-imaging and Gershon can't imagine what all else, would never miss them. And there is the fact that there was never—

or hasn't been so far—a single casualty, a single person even injured. Who then? Who did that leave?

But to be honest, Gershon doesn't really care. He visits the bombing sites, writes his reports back to the diplomatic corps, and follows the slight change in the cityscape with a detached kind of interest. Sometimes, as now, he thinks about what the New Jerusalem will look like in ten years, in twenty, with the bombings continuing; if, at some point, the New Jerusalem will resemble exactly what the actual, amnesiac Jerusalem really should look like.

Gershon sighs and realizes with a start that Hava is watching him. He has been staring off into space for he doesn't know how long. He gives a little cough and puts the vehicle in gear.

"Some tour guide," Hava says flatly, and Gershon can hear her steely anger.

•

Hava follows Gershon up the steps in the empty building just inside New Jaffa Gate. Catty-corner across the street, the Tower of David's brutal features emphasize the heavy quiet, never stranger than when one is actually standing inside the abandoned, the never-occupied New Old City.

To get to the new old apartment, they have to follow the wide staircase of decrepit marble up two flights, passing through the lobby of a dank, empty hostel with vaulted ceilings. One floor above, Yoheved and Gershon eventually got used to foreign backpackers and American college kids trudging up the stairs which passed through the real apartment's wide dining room on their way to the cheapest sleeping mats on the roof. Shmuli used to look up from his food during dinner and wave to them, beaming.

Now, as Hava and Gershon climb up through the hostel lobby, Gershon says, "Mark Twain once stayed here. Well, not *here*, but, you know. There's a picture of him in some book standing right there by the desk."

Hava nods.

"Who's Mark Twain?" she says.

In the apartment, Gershon goes quickly to the kitchen, dragging out the heavy crate of sweetbread and grabbing a bottle of liquor. He is suddenly embarrassed, flustered to be here. He doesn't know why he's brought Hava here. It was a stupid idea.

He comes out into the living room and sees her standing at one of the tables along the wall, picking up the framed pictures and looking at them. Gershon has forgotten all about the living room, forgotten his own recreation of it—a weak moment during those desperate, lonely first months that he's never gotten around to undoing. He doesn't spend much time here anymore.

She sets down the picture of Shmuli, his face pushed close to the camera, filling the whole field of vision. His expression is almost one of wonder, though he knew what a camera was, of course. Silly.

"I'm not so totally stupid, you know," Hava says now, turning to him. "I've seen the documentary."

Gershon is stunned, and feels his face pounding with blood.

Back in the vehicle, Gershon thinks, Of course she's seen the documentary. Of course. Of course. Most of the country has seen the documentary by now, Gershon would bet.

They gave him a tiny grave on the Mount of Olives, of all places, among the war heroes and ancients—a big, quiet show. The government. Gershon and Yoheved never would've been able to afford it. And so they'd buried him and gone to Italy. That was Yoheved's idea and Gershon, standing in St. Mark's Square, wondering at the uneasy huddle of so many pigeons, had thought it a good one. They

were there, together. Yoheved had wanted to be there, together. He had no problem fleeing grief. He knew it would catch up with them, but why make it easier? Why not let its full force find them there, amidst all those delicate, unaging marble children?

And though Yoheved did not begin filming the famous interviews for the documentary until much later, well after they'd returned to their apartment in Jerusalem, Gershon knows it really began then, with that trip, knows he should've been able to see what was coming. And now the insult of her "healing process"—of the interviews and the documentary, and really of Yoheved herself, of what she's become—has finally reached Gershon here. His suffering and his wife's—ex-wife's—simulacrum of their suffering have been brought into this world only so that the fragile, indignant mouth of a twenty-two-year-old girl may open in this pathetic recreation of his own living room, and her eyes may narrow, and she may summon her pith to say, *I've seen the documentary.*

Back in the car, continuing, changing the subject, she says, "I like the bits that talk about the nomenclature of this place." She says the big word carefully, seems pleased with herself not to have tripped on it.

Gershon is driving swiftly out of the city. The buildings become more and more widely spaced, the verisimilitude falling apart as the construction project outpaced its budget and, back on earth, the opposition government gained power.

"It's stupid, the nomenclature," Gershon spits out, because it is. Officially, the city is called "Jerusalem North" ("New Jerusalem" finally too political for the offices that made these decisions), situated in the "Northern Territories." The technical ridiculousness of this term, this wholly inaccurate nondimensional appendage—*northern*—is a perfect synecdoche of the basic failure of imagination of those back on earth. Where did their mourners live, if it could not be

found on a compass? "Just idiotic," Gershon says. "You get used to it, unfortunately. You call it what you want."

He's trying, and though they are now passing the final retaining wall of the city and the vehicle is shifting its suspension to suit the pale dirt of the unpaved road as it descends into the canyon that leads away from the settlement proper, he still can't get past Hava having seen the documentary. Him standing there, back in the living room, his mouth hanging open like a fish. Blushing in—yes, he must say it—shame. Shame! To be caught unawares by this nothing of a girl!

Gershon guides the vehicle up a series of rough switchbacks and they begin to slowly rise up out of the canyon. When they crest the edge, and Gershon speeds the vehicle onto the flat, empty road, Hava turns in her seat to look back at the low gray line of the distant city, its ambient glow seeping into the darkening sky.

•

"We're unprotected out here, officially," Mendelbaum says, indulging Hava, once they've all settled into the den. "According to the Administration, it's basically the city or nothing. But it's not been so bad with old Gersh here in charge." Mendelbaum smiles sadly. "He comes to see me every now and then—says it's to share his sweetbread and whiskey, because he's just too polite to admit he's checking to see if I'm dead yet."

"We?" Hava says. "*We're* unprotected? Who is we?"

Mendelbaum shrugs, gestures with his glass.

"There's a few of us with homesteads out here. Every couple months we get a memo from the Administration, telling us about the terrorists from the Free Territories coming to cut our heads off."

"Not me," Gershon says from where he's making the drinks, though he knows Mendelbaum knows. "I don't write those things."

"Who does?" Mendelbaum says, sighing and smiling kindly at Hava as Gershon steps around the kitchen island and reenters the room. "Some computer, probably. They always sound like a Mad Lib done by a very boring little boy." He crosses his legs, shakes his head at Gershon's offer of a refill. "But then, you probably didn't have those, did you?" he says to Hava.

Though he's made her one, Hava surprises Gershon by taking a drink off the proffered tray.

"We had those," she says. "Or I did."

"Mad Libs," she says to herself.

Mendelbaum lets his eyebrows rise and fall, once.

"Nostalgic amusement," he sighs. "What an industry."

Gershon likes Mendelbaum, a gentle, intelligent man. He was an old professor at the University of Haifa, back in the world. Gershon actually met him once, there. His office had been on the very top floor of the university tower, on top of Mount Carmel. A spectacular view, suspended there over the city, the twirling skirts of roads and buildings decorating the mountain's slope, and, of course, the sea, always the sea. During his first few years in the post here, Gershon often stood at his quarters' window in the Government Tower and looked down and out past the city at the hazy, unclaimed desertscape extending to the horizon, where he knew somewhere was this low, flat house, Professor Mendelbaum in his den. It was like they'd switched places.

"You gave it all up?" Gershon had asked him back then, on one of his first visits in the territory.

"I gave it all up," Mendelbaum said distantly, and gave a wan smile.

"Are you really in danger, though?" Hava asks him now, concerned.

Mendelbaum takes a drink, lets out a breath.

"My daughter would say so, I think," he says. "She's a professor as well, at the Technion."

Gershon watches him. Hava senses something, but only looks down into her glass. She's drinking from it using the ridiculous little straw which Gershon doesn't have the heart to explain is really for stirring. She looks like a child. She actually looks a lot like Mendelbaum's daughter, in the low light.

"Is a professor, was a professor," Mendelbaum says into the quiet. "She's dead, anyway," he says flatly, not changing his posture. "So I guess that makes her emerita. They didn't take the title away from her, at any rate."

Gershon used to be chilled by Mendelbaum's odd, blunt way, by his hauntingly affectless statements, but now it is vaguely comforting somehow. Gershon stands up, begins walking around the den. Hava continues to drink her drink incorrectly. Gershon wonders if she's ever even had alcohol before.

Mendelbaum settles for a while into his old professorial voice and answers Hava's questions, tells her a little about the brief period of "New Wave" settlers who refused the city. She keeps circling back to the issue of whether or not he's in danger, living out here.

"So, I mean, are you, though?" she says now. "Would you agree with your daughter?"

Mendelbaum glances up at Gershon, who is sitting on the edge of the wide bay window, eyes unfocused, face trained on the carpet between Mendelbaum's couch and Hava's.

"I take it our friend didn't bring you here the scenic way," Mendelbaum says dryly.

"No?" Hava says, and Gershon can feel her looking to him.

"Well, there's some tumble-down shacks along the route—some of the first people to make it across from the Free Territories

site threw them up. They used to live there. There was a time when the other settlers out here were very afraid, probably justly."

Hava is looking at him, her eyes wide. Gershon can see her face is flushed, and he realizes, with a paroxysm of anger, that she is drunk. He finishes his own drink in one swallow and crosses the room to make another.

"But they don't live there now," Hava says. "The Free Territory people."

"No," Mendelbaum says.

"What happened to them?"

Mendelbaum finishes his own drink. He motions to Gershon for another.

"Well, you know, I tried to help," he says. "Every year, when the backup respirators came, I signed for them, took them right out down the road and gave them to the first few kids I saw. It was the only way I could figure to do it fairly—no system, just random, just give it to them. Sometimes I'd give them food. I'd leave it out there and in the morning it'd be gone."

Gershon, as he works the gimlet into the synthetic lime from Mendelbaum's greenhouse, thinks of Mendelbaum back in Haifa beginning his nightly stroll down from his office to his apartment, seeing halfway there the rush of ambulances and military vehicles, then having to walk the rest of the way home, a good half hour, in silence. His daughter the professor was killed by a suicide bomber (also female, also a professor, at Palestine Polytechnic, also the daughter of a professor) who'd convinced her to meet up at an intercultural music festival being held that night at a local park. Eighteen others had been killed as well. It was a famous incident in Israel, for its symmetry.

"Well, that was kind of you," Hava says.

"You think so?" Mendelbaum says. "It didn't help much, in the end."

"You mean, what?" Hava says.

"They all died. From that wave of crossers, anyway. Except a few of the kids, who, sensibly, moved on. Maybe you've seen them in the city. Maybe they're not the same ones. Who knows."

Gershon finishes making the new drinks, comes back in, and sits down on the other end of Mendelbaum's couch.

"Let's have some of this sweetbread," Mendelbaum says, leaning forward to the coffee table. "Did Gershon tell you he designed it? It's like a multivitamin, it's so good for you. You can live off it for weeks, no kidding. Never goes bad, either."

Hava smiles in surprise, looking at Gershon, who wishes she wouldn't. He takes half of his new drink in one swallow. Hava and Mendelbaum natter on good-naturedly about the wonder of food engineering.

I've seen the documentary. Her voice defiant, defensive. The shame of his surprise.

In the footage that makes up the documentary, Yoheved looks like herself, but her voice is different—no thin wire of grief in it, no vulnerable undercurrent of querulous tone. His choice when he saw the footage was to either interpret this, her interview voice, as a performance—the performance of bravery, of poise—or to interpret the voice he knew, the Yoheved voice, the voice of his wife, as a performance—the performance of grief.

They're talking about documentaries now, Mendelbaum and Hava are, about Jerusalem North's portrayal in the media, which is changing, Hava says. Gershon can feel himself bloat with anger, his face puffy with liquor.

First, Yoheved began with the Israeli military commander of the settler area in the West Bank, the man who had held his soldiers back, mistakenly believing that the disturbance was a village matter, though why he would think a village matter would be occurring in

the middle of the road running only between the protected knots of religious settlements is unknown. Yoheved did not ask him this. In the video, Yoheved does not ask what he could've done, or what he did not do. She asks him what happened that night, from his perspective, and she listens patiently, leaning forward, her hands steepled beneath her chin, her eyes clear and calm. Then, as will become the pattern, she forgives him, three times repeated, and there is a long shot of them sitting together in that complicated silence after her voice has stopped. Then it cuts to the next interview.

How did she go along with such a thing? What is Gershon talking about, *go along with*—she came up with it in the first place. It was her own literally incredible idea. Like it would be hard to find some young, unknown documentary filmmaker ready to eat the story up, to do exactly what she said. For a while, Gershon was convinced it was the idea of her therapist, whom he'd always mistrusted, but watching the actual documentary, watching interview after interview, his wife moving closer and closer to the epicenter of the trauma, unflinching, her manner in the interviews so assured it was almost self-satisfied, he knew, finally, that it was all her doing. First the military commander, then the soldier who'd called the disturbance in, then the Palestinian mother who'd excitedly sent her son to join the fray. On and on and on, the interviews. No, only Yoheved herself could realize such horrible will.

"So where's your monument here," Hava says to Mendelbaum, meaning to ask, Gershon guesses, where it is his daughter died, back in the world.

For the first time, Mendelbaum looks away.

"Well, you know, a park in Haifa. It could've been anywhere, really."

Hava nods thoughtfully, leaning forward. She cups her hands around her empty glass. She looks up and regards Gershon, her face empty.

"And where's yours, then?" she says.

What does she want him to say? There is no analog really, no simulacrum. That, or they drove through it to get here. But she knows that. *I've seen the documentary.* Mendelbaum is looking at Gershon quizzically.

Her face is even, patient. The quiet aggression of the question takes him aback. What does she want him to say?

My wife was visiting her brother in Ma'ale Adumim, in the West Bank, she wants him to say. Yoheved wanted him to say this for the documentary, for the camera. *My wife's brother was driving with her to a nearby settlement for a wedding. Our son Shmuli was in the back seat. He was two years old.*

Hava must think this is some exercise; maybe they've briefed her for this, for the recovery into new marriage of a man in grief. But she doesn't understand. He could say what she wants, but she wouldn't understand the flatness in his voice. He has no trouble saying it.

Midway between the two settlements, in the darkness, they heard something hit the car, or the car hit something, and though they'd been warned not to, they stopped. Apparently my wife Yoheved made her brother stop the car. She believed, in error, that they'd somehow hit a child walking in the dark.

But the affectless voice is what she wants, isn't it? His pretension of having confronted the trauma, the loss—just another kind of repression, Hava's handlers would have told her. "It's just another kind of repression," Yoheved said to him in her steely voice, during one of their many fights about the documentary, "but it's worse because it's willful."

As they searched the shoulders of the road for the injured child, a small crowd from the nearby village gathered. My wife's brother, who spoke good Arabic, made the mistake of trying to explain. Men in the crowd began to shout and cry out about a child struck and killed, and the crowd grew.

She couldn't think he would say this, not on camera, not even now, in Mendelbaum's living room. By that point, Yoheved had turned their apartment into a jungle of her beloved houseplants, though. "Doing these interviews," Gershon had screamed back, staring into the leaves and tendrils of green, though he had seen none of the footage yet and did not know what she was saying in it, "that's what's willful repression! Repression by force!"

Later, the official investigation, aided by informants, would discover that a good deal of the agitation was accomplished by a small core of men, which group had thrown the large rock at the passing car, creating the illusion of impact in the first place.

"My monument?" Gershon says now, out loud.

Hava's face is changing, she looks confused. Mendelbaum is looking at her now.

Gershon could say it, if he wanted to.

People in the crowd, which was by now a mob, grabbed my wife's brother. Then they grabbed my wife. Someone was shouting about them being Israeli spies, my wife's brother managed to tell her, but then they were beating him. Spies? my wife shouted uselessly, in Hebrew. Spies? Spies? An unknown member of the band of men stepped forward as my wife's brother was dragged out of sight.

"You haven't told her, then?" Mendelbaum says to Gershon.

Gershon feels very tired. He sets down his drink. When Yoheved gave him the rough cut of the documentary to watch, she'd left the apartment to give him privacy. "I want to talk about it when I get back," she said. "I'll be home in two hours." He'd watched the first few interviews, then digitally skipped ahead to the last one, the only one that really mattered. When she came back, he was gone.

"They beat my wife's brother with their fists and feet, and then beat him to death with stones until his head caved in," he says, looking at Hava. "Somebody stepped forward out of the crowd and threw

a Molotov cocktail into the car. I don't know whether they knew Shmuli was in there, strapped in his car seat. I don't know if they saw him. He was burned alive in the car. While this was happening, they dragged my wife Yoheved away into a building where she was beaten and violently raped, repeatedly. Thirty-two hours later, when the IDF moved in, they found her there, barely alive. So I don't have a monument here, I guess."

Hava is sitting very still, her eyes unblinking. She looks ill.

"But then you knew all that," Gershon says. "You've seen the documentary."

There's a pause.

"The foundation documentary," she says quietly. "*Ad Astra Per Aspera*. About the first settlers here."

Mendelbaum rubs his eyes.

•

Outside the low-slung house, Gershon hurriedly resecures the crate of sweetbread to the cargo rack on the back of the vehicle. He has been spun into a stunned silence at his own mistake. He hops down and waves once more goodbye to Mendelbaum.

His friend is standing at the window of the house, watching Gershon get into the vehicle and prepare to leave. Gershon was undecided for weeks as to whether or not to come and speak to Mendelbaum about the tiny line item, the request for one more kind of seed in the customs and horticulture delivery invoice, which Gershon came across purely by accident.

But on this visit, before coming out to the car to leave, Gershon went through into the greenhouse, Mendelbaum explaining to teary Hava back in the living room that he and Gershon were going to pick

out some of his synthetic produce to take back with them, it'd just be a few minutes.

Mendelbaum had found Gershon standing in front of the plant, its droopy flowers a brilliant, unbelievable purple.

"That color," Gershon said, not looking at him. "That color is just . . ."

Mendelbaum stepped around him and lightly touched a few of the petals.

"I didn't think it would actually look like a monk's hood," Gershon said, his voice skating as he looked at his friend.

"This," Mendelbaum said, holding one of the bulbs delicately between two fingers, "is only one tiny mutation away from being a tomatillo. Can you believe that?"

Neither man said anything, both looking at the plant. Gershon could stop this, they both knew, could stop Mendelbaum from harvesting the rare plant, from poisoning himself with it. But Gershon knew he wasn't going to impede Mendelbaum, had always known the appalling mercy he was capable of, and now Mendelbaum knew it too.

"What a place we've come from," Mendelbaum had said, quietly.

And now Mendelbaum's figure in the darkened bay window recedes in the rear camera of the vehicle as Gershon drives into the desolate landscape, the town burning electrically in the distance. When they trace their way back to the canyon, on an impulse Gershon turns away from the road, and steers the vehicle up a steep crest.

"Where are we going now?" Hava says, the first time she's spoken since the living room. She sounds exhausted. Gershon doesn't answer, but speeds up.

Soon they're on the old road, which curves before one last ridge. Nestled along the elbow of the path are a few dark, angled shapes huddling against one another, vacant sockets of shadow against the hill.

"Oh," Hava says quietly. "There they are. The shacks."

Gershon catches some movement out of the corner of his eye and is trying to process it when they both hear the bump and crunch, something changing, momentarily, about the vehicle. Gershon slows but doesn't stop, though both he and Hava look around. Two very dirty children are sprinting out from the hollow behind one of the piles of wood that used to be a shack, oversized respirators slipping on their faces. The vehicle's slowed progress has brought it to the top of the ridge above the ruins of the encampment. Gershon stops sharply.

They both look down at the stretch they've just come from, following the path of the two children—boys?—to their objective: the mangled crate of sweetbread that has come untethered from the vehicle's cargo rack and crashed down into the dust of the road. The two kids struggle to drag the pallet back into their hidey-hole. It's slow going but they're getting it there, throwing wild glances at the stilled vehicle above them. Gershon exhales and looks forward again.

"There's also this," he says, nodding to the view out the windshield.

Hava gives a little gasp.

It is night now, and the sky is laid out before them in its penetrating blackness. Beneath it, revealed by the ridge's elevation, is the great liquid sea, its darkened silver face waveless, vast and inconsolable before them.

And Gershon wants to tell her, wants to tell Hava about that final interview in the documentary it turns out she has not seen, wants to describe what it was like watching his wife sit there with the man—the boy, really; fidgety, nervous, scared to have been pulled out of his cell for these cameras, for this woman whose face he doesn't remember—who lit the rag and flung the bottle of alcohol into the vehicle where Shmuli sat, strapped into his car seat, screaming in terror. What it was like watching her sit there with him and hear him out,

hear him admit what he did. And then Gershon wants to tell Hava what it was to watch his wife lean forward and forgive him.

Hava is already distracted, though, turning around to look through the back of the vehicle at where the two kids are still dragging the box, a little quicker now. Gershon looks out at the sea, the blue moon of the Earth hanging still above it. Where is Yoheved at this moment, he thinks; what is she doing? It's four years in the future where she is, four years since she's sent this girl, this Hava, to him on the ship. Hava, the last insult, Gershon suddenly understands. Pretty, unmourning Hava is Yoheved's last forgiveness, sent out to him across the unbridgeable distance. Hava is her way of forgiving him, and he will have to suffer it.

Gershon turns the vehicle around and then stops. Below, the kids have almost got the crate to their cave. They'll live on that bread for months, Gershon idly thinks.

And how could Hava ever understand that it was, all of it— New Jerusalem, yes, but also Earth, also the real Jerusalem; Yoheved combing her hair slowly by light of his dorm room's open window the morning after their first night together; Shmuli trundling around the small apartment, his laughter rising, rising; also Hava's own life, the slightly sweaty scent of the first boy from school that made her smile, her father's rough hand in the garden as the late afternoon sun slid past the brim of his wide hat; and also the future, the years and years to come, Hava's skin cool against Gershon's in bed; and still somewhere, continuing, Shmuli's squeals of delight at being chased around the kitchen—all of it was the territory of grief. You are always living in it, he wants to say. You have never lived anywhere else.

One child has disappeared into the cave. The end of the box is still visible. Gershon can see they are already celebrating.

Elegy on Kinderklavier

A child is sick. A child is sick. You open the door to the room, or you look up, or you wake up and there is your son, sick, changed, and even with the scaled-down hospital bed they use in the pediatric oncology unit, even though he's been there for months, there is still a micromoment of near panic, of your reptilian brain sending up the signal, running the sentence through every level of your mental processes. A child is sick. A child is sick. You want to tell someone. Though, of course, they all already know.

Sunday breaks on the pediatric oncology ward; I can see the sun, with its tired golden aspect, creeping down the wide corridor from the huge windows at the end of the floor, where the playroom is. Some of the children have been encouraged to paint the smaller windowpanes over with pictures that are supposed to "best represent themselves" in the words of the "play specialist," a woman with short, auburn curls whose whole body seems to have been wrinkled, like a balled-up napkin. My son Haim painted his square of glass completely black; he did this with an undefined level of self-satisfied humor, depending on how much irony you believe an eight-year-old to be capable of. It seemed at least clear that he meant to piss off the

play specialist. "It's too bright in here," he said flatly, when she asked him to explain his work.

In his quiet, angry humor he is most like me, though this seems to be merely an unfortunate genetic accident to everyone (my mother-in-law, my own mother, a plurality of the nurses) except my wife, Charlie, to whom it is a continuous insult. "Is this real life?" Haim sometimes deadpans as they wheel him back from the radiation therapy, parroting a popular Internet clip. "Will this be forever?"

The first time Charlie heard him do this she looked right at me, made her eyes go hard and flat, glaring. There is too much awareness in his tone when he says this kind of thing, his face held too purposefully empty, affect disarmed, hollowed out by what seems to be his unnervingly firm grasp of his situation. This disturbs the nurses, either because this prescience in an eight-year-old is spooky, or because it undermines the game we're all playing, pretending he might get better.

I think they're also unsettled by how it's never clear how much he really means by what he says, how much he seems to be accusing whoever is listening of some responsibility for his sickness—a sense that is both discomfiting and mysterious even to me. This is another way that Haim is like me, at least to Charlie: the way he guards his thoughts jealously, until often when he speaks it's like a judgment is being pronounced, though you can never be quite sure what the ruling is, exactly. I go back and forth about whether or not it's terrible that I find his caustic, indicting little one-liners funny.

This morning I've not noticed Haim waking up, the gurgle of him trying to remaster his throat and breathing.

"Where is Charlie?" he asks, groggy. He's called his mother by her first name ever since she stopped coming to the hospital consistently. It's clear he means this as an insult to her, though when she does show up he offers the formality dully, like instead of meaning it

to really hurt her he just wants the situation between the two of them to be clear.

His question, though, is really meant to be a jab at me. A taunt, maybe. It's useless to try to tell which one, how much malice this stormily intelligent young son of mine can muster. He asks where she is every morning, mostly because he knows that I don't know. It's his version of a benediction for the day, a dry thesis for the kind of uselessness his hours will inevitably prove to be. I don't know where Charlie is. I don't know if she's on one of her jags, in which case she is probably wrapped up in the covers of our bed or cocooned on our couch in front of the TV, paralyzed by depression; I don't know if she's not left the flat for days, if she's eaten this week. Or she could be gone, vanished during one of her different periods, wandering any of the tourist sites of our little island country, as she calls it.

When I answer I try to say something different every time.

"She's on a sailing adventure," I say today. It's unclear how much I'm taunting him back, how much I'm just tired. "There's a squall kicking up. She's somewhere cold, somewhere where the tips of the waves are being sliced off by the wind and stinging her face."

Most days I don't say anything.

We're waiting for the people from radiology to come get Haim for his targeted therapy. He has to be under sedation for it, which he likes; a few hours' escape from full-blown consciousness. But this means he can't eat anything beforehand, so we don't talk much until it's time, because not being able to eat makes Haim miserable. When he wakes up afterward, after sleeping off the sedatives for a few hours, the imagination in his food order will be something to behold. Breakfast burritos! French fries! Sardines! Each time when the food comes he marshals the cart in with fussy waves of the laminated menu, an annoyed maître d'. There is a moment, once I've got the dishes arrayed out in front of him on the tray of his hospital

bed, when he regards it all greedily, not touching anything yet, and he seems, for a few seconds anyway, to have been completely transported, to have come into some other kind of life entirely.

•

These things don't have a beginning, not really. I've reached now the age of narrative, and it's important to remember that this structure is false, an imposed will, quirk of myself as a thirty-four-year-old man, of an age (reached perhaps a decade or so prematurely) when I have begun to be concerned with the story of what's happened to me. I once heard an old writer say that the problem with the young is that, for them, the past is still only what's happened. That is, that they have yet to be drawn into the necessary sadness of thinking about the future with the anima of nostalgia. And if this is so, then I've certainly reached that age, which is never made more clear than when I think of Charlie—Charlie who one doesn't meet but finds oneself in the middle of, like an unannounced storm; everywhere, suddenly, the light is just different.

It's a clear, freezing night in the minutes after a long snow has ceased, deep in the bowels of an upstate New York winter. I have wandered into the darkened shadows of the old abandoned buildings on the far side of the river that halves my campus. I am twenty years old; I will graduate on my twenty-first birthday. I have come from a party where I spent an hour watching a young female poet attempt to snort the dust of a pulverized pharmaceutical from the rug where it spilled off a hand mirror. I've spent the last twenty minutes standing on the riverbank, thinking about the conversation I had with my mother on the dorm phone that afternoon, looking out the lounge's window down at the nearly iced-over river and telling her

I was lonely, admitting it to her, even though her blunt concern felt worse than the loneliness.

These buildings are the old, abandoned incarnation of the university whose lights now twinkle with modern life on the rival bank of the river. The university and the university. The past little city ghosting itself uselessly onto the future one.

Usually there are a few small groups of shadows smoking pot behind the crumbling brick in the openings here and there. Tonight, though, there seems to be no one; the old campus is silent, dark, the half-glow of the snow and the washed-out sky reflecting each other.

What draws me to the old auditorium is the muted light rippling out from its high, thin windows—a kind of colorless aurora over the snow. One of the side doors is unlocked and I slip inside to see what where it comes from but as I do the light, whatever it was, abruptly flips off. There is the spooling sound of a movie reel flapping at its end, then resetting itself. I notice, breathing in the dark, that the old whooshing furnace is blasting the room with an extreme heat.

When the light flashes on again I can see that it's the ambient glow of a black-and-white movie being projected onto a ratty, hanging sheet of muslin at the back of the stage. From the throw of the projector's beam, someone must have situated it on one of the seats in the tiny balcony behind and above me. Its illumination is so striking in the dark that at first I don't even notice the girl at the center of the stage.

She is standing, head down, arms stiff and flat at her sides, feet together, as if waiting for a dance to begin. She is almost naked, wearing only her underwear: a matching, simple white bra and briefs. Just as I'm about to say something, the first tripping, swooning notes of George Gershwin's *Rhapsody in Blue* fill the room, emanating from two dark shapes in the balcony that look to be speakers. Against the muslin, I can make out the skyline of a black-and-white New York

City, which soon switches to shots of blinking neon parking garage signs and markets. It's *Manhattan*, or at least the first reel of it, which, as I will find out later, has gone missing from the campus student theater's collection.

As Woody Allen's voiceover sounds, the girl's head snaps up; her entire body changes, comes alive. On screen the shots of the city are still playing out, but here is the girl, opening and closing her mouth, miming the film's narration so perfectly it is like the voice is coming from somewhere inside her, a funny, entrancing ventriloquism no less real for its perfect memorization than for the deft bodily mimesis, the ticks and expressions and gestures all spot on. I'm sitting down, about halfway to the stage, without even realizing it. It is almost a dream.

"He adored New York City," Woody Allen and the girl say with one voice. "He idolized it all out of proportion. Uh, no. Make that 'He, he romanticized it all out of proportion.' To him, no matter what the season was, this was still a town that existed in black and white, and pulsated to the great tunes of George Gershwin. Uh . . . no. Let me start this over. Chapter One. He was too romantic about Manhattan, as he was about everything else."

As the light from the scenes, shifting faster and faster now, plays over her body and there is only the bombastic surfacing of the Gershwin, she turns her face out into the audience that isn't, the torn rows of seats missing covers, and looks right at me, holding my gaze perfectly steady, though I know in the darkness I must only be a shadow, a shape. She does this until the movie proper starts and she begins parroting Woody Allen's character's movements and lines without a single mistake, with impossible ease, until it seems that the figures flickering on the rotting muslin are being led by her body.

Later, I will find out many things about her: that she stole that reel, fixed the auditorium's ancient furnace herself, and learned *Rhapsody*

in Blue by heart at ten years old and loved it so much she played it nonstop every minute she was home until her mother threatened to sell the piano, which didn't matter because by then the music had, in her words, passed into her entirely, until she could reenter the composition at any moment, on any note, and play it through in that mental theater all the way to the end, for instance. I will learn that she loves Woody Allen, both Gershwins, and Buster Keaton movies, and that somehow, in her solitary, culturally sentimental self-education she picked up several outdated idioms (like saying "I'm all wet as a science major") that still slipped out occasionally, helplessly, or that she'd once slept with one of her professors and that this professor had one night described her as "a girl lost in space and time" with a glazed look in his eyes that she had not liked at all. I will learn that she was once, in the sciences, mathematics, and musicianship, somewhat of a child prodigy, and that by the time I met her she'd had enough of describing the world in impossible equations, Schumann overtures, or predictive theoretical physics models, and was now beset on all sides by a terrifying aimlessness, a suspicion of the lack of primary meaning and genuine experience in this world. And I will learn her name, Charlemagne Rosen, the girl I can never keep out of the present tense.

But for now there is the movie proper, with its better lighting, and, offered up by this, the revelation of her body.

There is a thin luster of sweat on her skin, and her near-nakedness is explained. The old boiler heater's gusts have forced me myself, even with my coat shrugged off, to sweat through an undershirt and sweatshirt, and for a moment, watching the suite of human motion that is laid bare by the sheer fact of her skin, of her flesh, pale and taut, it seems we are sweating together, connected in our agitation.

She is short, with chin-length blond hair pulled austerely back away from her face. Her shoulders are sturdy and square, but her

torso tapers down away from them shyly, into an impossibly delicate waist. There are the legs all out of proportion; the long, slick thighs; the abbreviated curves of the calves. Her silhouette seems to belong in a ballet. I am transfixed by a large freckle hovering catty-corner to her bellybutton, which itself sits strangely high on her stomach, as if to accentuate the faintest glance of tiny, downy blond hairs on the stretch of skin held taut between her hips.

There is also, of course, her underwear, the way the briefs seem to almost float on her up there on the stage, as she turns this way and that. They are not loose enough to be unsexual and not form-fitting enough to be a thrill, exactly. She is not quite vulnerable in this state of undress, but yet there she is, mid-performance, reenacting perfectly, without ever turning to look, the screen behind her, and there will be nothing more intimate in our life together than her body in this stretch of minutes, than the discovery of the way she unconsciously stands with one foot turned outward like she might plié at any moment, just for me.

And who could ask for more chance, for life to prove itself more the curiosity that one in one's youth always secretly hoped it will be?

Arbitrary a point of experience it might be, in the scheme of things, but here persists that night, reaching out for me again. It's nostalgia that holds me at such a delicate remove from that feeling, that night in the ruined theater. It is this age of nostalgia—maybe the only true age—which casts the sense that the episode is not yet completed, that I may, in my present or future, be somehow reclaimed.

How does one tell oneself such a story, if not to pretend a beginning? It is inescapable: her body, organizing principle.

It is at least true that what jetsam of memory left unruined by what came after is ensouled by her body, particularly this pale bough of a body in her youth.

"Well, don't you just hate people who come into movies late?" she said, when the reel was done. "You're not off to a very good start."

•

That night she took me to her apartment. It was in a nice complex, built up just on the edge of campus in that bright, blocky way that often makes student apartment buildings indistinguishable from prisons.

As we took the first few steps into her apartment, I looked around. The entire apartment was empty—not a stick of furniture, nor decoration. When I turned my face to Charlie's I remember the look on her face. It seemed such a vulnerable, honest expression— an ingenuous shame.

It turned out she spent all her money on rent, knowing she'd be able to afford nothing else, just to claim a space in this upscale complex. It turned out, as we sat on the carpeted floor Indian-style, like little kids, that she spent half the night in the old auditorium to minimize her own heating bill, which she could barely make. In the fridge there was nothing but a magnum of vodka and a bag of thawing corn, the former of which she retrieved.

Later, when we finally stood next to her surprisingly ornate bed ("moving day dumpster dive") I moved to kiss her. With a graceful motion, she locked my face into a tight hug, pressed side by side to hers, her grasp strong. I blushed.

"I'm nervous, OK?" she said.

"*You're* nervous?" I said, her soft, anxious breath in my ear.

To what end these sentimentalisms? To what fire go these uncorrupted bits of memory? I suppose Haim was there, even then, mixed up in all of it, our little homunculus observer, energies still coiled in a quiet, patient ovum inside of her, years away from his birth. He will

not even live long enough, it occurs to me now, to posses it as his own story, privately recalled.

But that night I looked down at Charlie under me, her leg bent slightly to the side, us both moving, her eyes glued downwards to where we intersected, mouth and brow formed into (mysterious to me, even now) surprise, and I remember the way the air seemed to crackle with a kind of ambient electric static as I looked down at her, as I watched her body as it moved and writhed and squirmed, unbearably sensate, alive.

•

Let me be clear about what kind of world we now find ourselves in: Haim's stretch marks have opened. Haim's stretch marks have opened, meaning that the long-term use of the steroid meant to control the swelling around the glioma in his brain has caused his skin to thin out from the inside, forming open wounds all over his stomach, back, and thighs.

The steroid is also what causes him to always be hungry, and to have gained tremendous amounts of weight (thus the stretch marks, thus the open wounds which, because of his chemotherapy, refuse even the basic bodily dignity of closing).

I can't say what this small detail of his medical treatment has done to him. I can't tell you what it is the first time you don't recognize your own son.

Before his diagnosis Haim was a small child, skinny but also short for a seven-year-old. We have a picture of him getting ready to go to Hebrew school one Sunday where he's wearing only a new polo shirt and underwear, and it almost looks like an optical illusion, the way the shoulders of the shirt fit him perfectly but the collar,

even buttoned to the top, hangs off his neck and the rest of the material billows down over his thighs. For boys that age, their size balances out their novel, baffling personalities (their features starting to resolve and solidify into what you think, for the first time, they might look like when they're men). This reins in the slightly terrifying suspicion that they're really adults-in-miniature, that you've failed at protecting them, at preserving that unknowing age when their love for you is still focused, can still be seen, you are convinced, in everything they say or do.

And so at first the sickness is an insult because of his size, because it seems impossible, no matter what the pediatric oncologists say, that a brain so small and malleable could harbor anything of real magnitude or strength, anything that could survive the vast powers that twenty-first-century medicine might bring to bear on it, but also simply because it seems unclear, exactly, what a human being so physically minute might possibly do to defend himself. It's only later, in this second year of treatment, when the steroids begin to unmake Haim's body, that I begin to understand the real insult, the way in which he would be taken from me even as he lived.

It is an indignity to require of yourself a certain kind of double vision in order to see your son when he is lying there in front of you. To see him with the grace required of an aging lover; to see the once-body inside the thing you are presented with now—to see past and present at once, and have the latter not ruin the former.

First, Haim's face billowed out, his two cheeks like twin sails catching a sagging wind. The rest of his body soon followed, inflating almost cartoonishly. There were the steroids, but also the fact of his decreasing mobility (not even, at first, due to the left-side weakness caused by the glioma, but the pain of several secondary infections—UTIs from all the catheters, kidney stones from some of the medicines, and so on) until he could not (and still cannot) move

without a wheelchair. Strangely, even the size of his head seemed to change until it appeared, as it does now, vaguely monstrous, disproportionate and swollen.

The changes to his face are the most insulting fact to Haim himself. There used to be a mirror on the wall to the left of his bed and when he had visitors he'd stare past them as they spoke, focusing on a spot slightly above their own heads, where the specter of his ruined features stared back, but after a while he made the nurses take it down. He's right that it is his face, or, more accurately, his eyes, that make the dissociation so striking, so final. His bulbous cheeks and neck-fat change, helplessly, his gaze, give it the slightly addled strabismus of the morbidly obese, and for whatever reason this is a look so antithetical to the six-year-old waif whom I last knew without a glioma on his brain stem that the two seem, most of the time, irreconcilable.

I think it is his face that Charlie could never quite recoup either. I remember watching her take him in, after the change had occurred, when she returned from the holiday. (We called it "the holiday" because at one point during those long, desperate months of her absence, Haim and I watched *Roman Holiday* together on the digital projector he and I had rigged up in his room. The room is of a size and orientation where it only really worked if Haim held the digital machine on his stomach as he reclined and the thrown picture was allowed to take up most of the wall he faced, including the door. He picked the movie out himself, out of the midst of another of his unknowable seas of contemplation. Unlike all of the other kids on the ward, Haim never wants to watch movies. We've only ever used the projector for two things, that screening being one of them. I don't know if someone told him about the movie, or if he clued in just from the title. It seemed clear at first why he wanted to watch it, the parallels to his mother too apparent, but then halfway through he asked

me to turn the sound off and we just sat with the flickering picture, Audrey Hepburn and Gregory Peck's cavorting turning vaguely sad, in silence.)

When Charlie entered the room that time after her return, I watched her stop short a step inside the door. She didn't look at me, and didn't say anything. Instead, she gathered herself and went to Haim slowly. In his fitful sleep he had kicked off his blanket, and she started with his leg, the fat beneath bulging out in rolls. She put her hand out as if to gently touch his body, allowing her fingers instead to hover carefully a few millimeters above. It was like she was, piece by piece, retaking his body from the distortion of his sickness, reaffixing the original in the system of vision she seemed to understand would now be required of her. First was the leg, then the sides with the violent stretch marks, then the arm.

It reminded me of the way she used to do more or less the same thing when he was a newborn, the way she spent hours gently feeling and moving his tiny legs and arms, which had seemed to be almost all fat and no bone then, the way he let her, looking in confusion at her hands. Now, when she got to his face, she stopped.

If I am to be brutally honest, I admit to taking some pleasure in her difficulty, her struggle in that moment. I wanted him to be foreign to her in the wake of her desertion, unrecognizable. For Charlie, for lack of better words, to understand that he was now more mine than hers.

I also wanted her to see what was the cruelest bodily insult of all, which was that instead of the wan, ravaged, rail-thin body of the child with cancer nearing death, we had been given the opposite: a robust, bloated, outsized child, an embarrassment of flesh. I wanted her to get that we would not even have the small mercy of watching our own kid live and fade; that, instead, we would only have the queer neutrality of watching this Other, this boy whom some persons else had

allowed to grow so fat, to become so lost in his own body. Of not even being able to recognize him, really.

Because, of course it's true that you can't see him within that body. I had to admit that, even then, watching Charlie staring down into his changed face. You can't see him as he once was, you can't see and love the passage of the years, not really, if you're being plainly honest. You see only what's before you. The foreign body, the sickness. It's impossible to see what you've already lost.

She stood beside his hospital bed, stooped over him for a long time. Eventually she closed her eyes and put her hand lightly over his face, touching it like a blind person. I understood then that things would not go back to their erratic-but-more-manageable normal with her. That her holiday was not the single act of brinksmanship she needed to enact with herself in order to bring herself back to us. Haim had entered the hospital as one boy, with one body, and she had left that child, not this one. To her, he was simply not there to return to.

Haim had to have been awake by then, had to have felt her hand there on his face, but he refused to open his eyes until a long time after she was gone.

Nighttime here, especially on Sundays, has its own kind of timelessness. It's winter now, so the light goes quickly, and by seven o'clock it is so dark through the windows you can't even see the outlines of the mast tips at Cadogan Pier needling the sky. Eventually it is so dark that the windows reverse themselves and only show the long corridors they face, giving the shapeless dark beyond them the false depth of the hallway's lights. It's late now. Sundays are the hardest nights to get through.

The day has been quiet—they try to schedule all the kids' therapies so that they feel like they have a real weekend, can recover a little bit—and the only thing Haim has had to do today is suffer a

dressing change for the stretch marks. These re-dressings used to be so traumatic that they couldn't do them without sedation, but Haim eventually chose to refuse the anesthetic. This amount of pain seems to be interesting to him, even if he is sick from it afterward. Today he watched as he usually does, looking down at where the "wound team" worked: curious, wincing, not really breathing. They've had to switch the dressings to non-adhesive foam pads because of "skin breakdown," meaning they had to stop pulling off the gauzes that were taped to the skin because the skin would come off with them. Nobody says anything, but there is a finality to all this. The nurses with their hyper-focus on Haim's wound care. Three failed "avenues of therapy" for the pontine glioma and we're left slathering onto his body something called MediHoney. Two different Phase II clinical cancer trials (one that was supposed to recognize and block the chemical signals that lead to the generation of new blood vessels in the tumor, and one that was supposed to damage DNA at certain guanine locations so as to trigger death of the tumor cells) and months of targeted radiation/chemotherapy later, we are using honey—actual honey—that bees make from a certain tree in New Zealand to hopefully give us a few more weeks.

I come back to the room from a coffee run in the deserted cafeteria and Haim is gone. I find him a floor down, in the pediatric intensive care unit. The lone nurse at the duty station gives me a sad little smile as I pass, as if to say she's sorry.

Haim has been back and forth between here and the pediatric oncology ward so often that everyone knows us. The only real regulars in the PICU are from our ward upstairs; most everyone else on the PICU floor is already close to the end of their story, happy or sad, and, one way or the other, doesn't return.

Haim met Ava on his first return from the PICU, when they'd both gotten C. diff after starting chemo. They were each in contact

isolation rooms which were situated next to each other at the end of the ward. The bathrooms, which they both occupied a lot, had extremely thin walls, and at some point they realized they could hear each other. Dozing beside Haim's bed I would hear their tiny voices talking for hours as they each waited out the diarrhea, the tinny laughter echoing strangely, always sounding so surprised. Each time the IV team came to access their ports, the nurses moving back and forth in the lock between the two rooms, Haim and Ava craned their necks, trying to catch a glimpse of one another when the doors opened, and sometimes waved. Ava got cleared to leave contact isolation first and Haim moved into her room. She'd spent a lot of time writing random phrases and words in dry-board marker on the large windows that looked outside. Her handwriting was rounded and girlish and after she was gone, Haim changed her letters into numbers, solving the complicated equations idly against the furrowed clouds.

Ava, who has acute lymphoblastic leukemia, is not doing very well. Haim asks for updates about her every week and I usually tell him whatever the nurses tell me when I pause at their station. He has his own information-gathering services, I guess, because lately I've just told him I'm not sure. He's not really allowed down in the PICU, but he knows this and usually goes at night, when the nurses are too tired or defeated to stop him from wheeling his chair along to Ava's room. I nod to Ava's mother as I pass her in the lounge, but she is sitting forward, perfectly still, elbows on her knees and face completely covered with her hands.

I don't disturb Haim. I lean against the wall in the hallway and watch through the doorframe. The only light on is a long, tubular fluorescent one above Ava's bed. She is lying flat on her back, beset by the Lilliputian tubes, wires, and monitors. Her mouth is taken up by the breathing tube, but she is looking up into Haim's face with her sharp, clear blue eyes, her small brow rising, steepled in what seems

like fear. I don't know if she recognizes him. It probably won't be long now.

A man has places in his heart which do not yet exist, and into them enters suffering in order that they may have existence—I can never remember who wrote that.

Haim strokes the girl's white-blond hair, so light a color that when it miraculously remained through round after round of chemo-therapy it seemed providential, a gift. Now, though, I can see it coming off in Haim's hand like spent animal fur, as he does his best to pretend that it's not, and continues his smooth stroking in the imperfect quiet.

•

There is a time in the beginning of a marriage when your wife's body is still a discovery, when—at least if you were married young—the changes you notice on certain nights as her flesh begins its shift to the denser, solid tone of mid-range adulthood are to you still a delight, something new to learn and take pleasure in. This is almost evolutionary, you might understand later, after the birth of your first child, a graceful biological swing to the kind of ruddy corporeality that can best protect and deliver a pregnancy, but there is a period when her body is not yet on this spectrum, is still only made up of the surprise of a cupped buttock or thigh, a new fullness in your hands in the dark.

We'd been married for two years when Charlie's body began to change. Up until that point, she had looked more or less like she had the night we first met; if anything, she'd lost weight, seemed to have become younger somehow. In the eighteen months between our first date and our wedding, she had grown more and more animated, her neural circuits blinking faster and faster, her hair becoming relaxed

and silken, her skin smooth and clear, full of color. Most days during our time together in college, I dropped her off in her study room, an abandoned office in the graduate mathematics department (the office where, lost in her depression the year before, she'd spent months of long afternoons lying flat on top of her big desk, asleep), only to return after class to find the big chalkboard that dominated one wall filled with complex systems of numbers, symbols, and signs. By the time we were both graduating, Charlie had won a prestigious mathematics prize from an international science organization for her thesis work, which turned out to be the hypothetical solution to a problem that had stood unsolved for seventy-five years. This award came with a large cash award, but in order for it to be granted the judges' committee wanted a fuller work, a long paper to be peer-reviewed, a more elaborate proof.

We moved that fall after graduation to Attica, Missouri, home of Attica State University, which had offered Charlie a fellowship with a large stipend in order for her to complete her work on the proof under their auspices. It was a good university—one of those tiny schools with a handful of highly specialized faculties, largely supported by very specific government or corporate grants for research or innovation. The only catch was that we had to move to Attica, Missouri.

It was a very small town in the southeast corner of the state, with four restaurants, a mall, and one movie theater whose reels always seemed to be slightly damaged. I was still a little in shock that for all my worrying about what we would do after graduation (what job I could get with my literature major, how we would ever be able to start paying off our student loans in six months, when they began to become due) it was Charlie—Charlie who preferred not to talk about a "careerist future," Charlie who seemed to just drift forward in her academic life with the fickleness and detachment of a child—who ended up with the good job, the good paycheck.

Because of the low rent in town, we managed to find a small house with new fixtures and a room in the half-finished basement that Charlie, in a gesture of support, agreed could be my "office." We took walks to the nearby city park, which had a duck pond. I spent the days staring at my computer during the hours I was supposed to be working on a novel. Charlie called it our "starter town." If we can learn to be married here, she often said, we can be married anywhere. When I complained about things like the lack of culture in the area or the fact that the nearest bookstore was forty minutes away, she tsked and smiled, shaking her head, not looking at me. "The writer in exile," she said.

What does one remember of the collection of selves one must inevitably prove to be to sustain a marriage over the years? The story of our time in Attica, Missouri (and even that of the years afterward, in Iowa) is so tired to me, so oft-repeated and reduced down into the kind of cocktail party summary that proves to be so startlingly effective that you eventually forget that the things which made the experience meaningful are exactly what you now excise, all the details that would most likely matter to no one else but you.

I remember spending those two years marooned in small-town Missouri learning and relearning Charlie's body, falling in love over and over with the angularity of her jawline as it drew close to me in the morning just before she left for work, with the pulsing, contracting spasms around my fingers as she orgasmed when I went down on her. There always seemed to be something to learn. I remember leaping, shoeless, from our wooden stoop onto the hood of Charlie's moving car to keep her from driving away after a particularly bad fight. Our fights were not even saved by being interesting, or original, and Charlie was always leaving. She'd come back a few hours later, never saying anything about where she'd gone, and be silent until she'd slept, after which it would be like it never happened. We

thought we were learning how to be married. "Think of us living here," Charlie said, "as performance art."

Then, of course, came the things not so easily protected from the logic of narrative memory, from the construction of theories and psychology. I remember these things helplessly, and with no small amount of reluctance. An awkward visit in the middle of the day from a university administrator. A call from a colleague, urging me to come to Charlie's office, where she had locked herself inside, and the whispered conversation that followed through the wood of the door, where I could feel her just on the other side, crying softly.

Then the day before she was to present the first half of her paper at a regional mathematics conference in Kansas City, she didn't come home from work. At first I assumed that Charlie was punishing me for some perceived slight, perhaps going out for a celebratory dinner with some of her research assistants without telling or inviting me, and then, as it got later into the night, I thought that maybe she'd left early for the conference, gotten the dates messed up. It wasn't until I pulled into the highway rest stop and saw her sitting there on a bench with a state trooper on either side of her, one of whom must've been the voice on the phone a few hours earlier telling me my wife had been found wandering the shoulder "confused," that I even believed it wasn't a joke. And I'll admit that what I thought of on the ride back was the shame, the humiliation of walking toward them, of claiming Charlie, who looked so happy and surprised to see me (looking at me with, unmistakably, the wonder of a child) that it utterly broke my fucking heart.

The thought of Charlie talking to a therapist—Charlie, who, when I pressed her, often gave a survey-course-in-miniature over Nietzsche, Kierkegaard, and nihilism as well as depression psychology, and applicable ontology, not to mention the medical science and epistemological implications of antidepressant, antipsychotic, or

mood-stabilizing medication—was so ridiculous that I couldn't even bring myself to demand it. The next day we got halfway to a local therapy office before I pulled the car over to the side of the road and looked out over all that blank snow and punched the steering wheel over and over again, the ancient horn bleating ridiculously. This was Charlie, whose soft, pale flesh of thigh and gluteus and back pressed into my nuzzling body in bed each night and fell asleep that way, in that hold; Charlie, who stood on Saturday mornings with her back to me in the kitchen, in T-shirt and underwear, with one hip cocked, foot turned out to the side, her legs seeming oddly short and thick in the blue light. This was my wife. I knew her.

She did not go back to work. When I went to collect her things from the office, I found the room almost completely bare.

Charlie ended up going to a psychiatrist by herself, of her own accord. In the months we spent holed up in the house, waiting for our savings from the fellowship to run out, we made rules to get through the days.

Mathematics was the great enemy, it seemed, and one rule was that Charlie was no longer to work with numbers, to do any kind of math at all. Somewhere along the line, Charlie told me during those months, she'd become lost in the world of digits and signs, symbols and systems. She tried, as we took walks down to the duck pond, to explain, to point to a small group of children and talk about the systems of equations that could describe each of their forms and chances, about the algorithms that they—their human selves—made up, the least of which could be found out, could describe simultaneously their fetal development as well as their choices in the game they played as they ran past us, and how this was essentially the same math that can be used to describe the shape of the universe.

Sometimes, when neither of us had spoken for a while as we lounged around the house or went for groceries, Charlie would

speak differently, trying to reach into my world. "Imagine a forest where all the trees are made up of numbers," she said. "Imagine you have to build a boat out of their boughs." There at the end of her work, she'd begun to think of the collections of numbers and symbols as little machines, and in the single box I filled with the contents of her desk's drawers from the office, there were hundreds of white sheets, each with a small ink drawing of withered, maimed numerals that tangled together to make sinister-looking spiders, tractors, airplanes, landscapes, and cars.

Charlie seemed embarrassed by the diagnosis of severe manic depression her therapist-psychiatrist team came up with and, as if to show its inaccuracy, she refused to display any of the classic side effects; she did not gain a pound, and if anything her sex drive became more consistent, on the whole more lively, spurred by our boredom. Every third weekend our mothers would visit and I'd talk to them while they sat with Charlie in the living room, both of them eyeing Charlie uneasily, as if something unexpected might happen at any moment.

Of course, the fellowship dried up and the promise of the cash prize receded, but after a while it seemed to us just a small part of all the money we would never have. I'd made a late application to several creative writing schools, and we agreed to move wherever I got in. That summer, after twenty months in Attica, Missouri, we celebrated our second anniversary, and two weeks later moved to Iowa, for me to go back to school, and us to have an honest restart.

It was easy to start over in Iowa, to pretend that the fever dream of our small town psychosis had simply never occurred. Charlie had a stable summer, and took a lot of interest in the new house. In essence, we switched roles: now I had the fellowship, now she was the one with the office in the finished basement, and the free time to pursue whatever she felt like. And she went out of her way

to assume the kind of normalcy we had never really had in Attica; now she found obscure apple orchards in the farmland around Iowa City, planned whole day trips as if they were apologies. And it was in Iowa City that I first began to notice the changes in her body.

Charlie's breasts and ass deflated slightly, descending from their nubile perches just a little bit, settling in comfortably to the hold of a mature body that no longer needed the taut energy of lingering adolescence. The skin beneath the complicated eye makeup that she no longer wore became puffy in the mornings, making her eyes reassuring in their calmness. And it was only then—as if to prove even further her stability and optimism, as if to finally regain our purchase on the kind of marital story we had once believed ourselves to be a part of—that Charlie began talking about wanting to have a baby.

•

I woke up this morning because an alarm on one of Haim's screens was going off. It was his oxygen levels, which I knew by the alarm's tone, and by the time I could get my eyes unblurred they were down in the 80s. A nurse appeared in the doorway, and together we turned and looked at Haim, who was trying to roll back and forth, his pupils wide, eyes glazed. When we went to him, he grunted and looked wildly up into our faces in confusion, recognizing neither of us.

Last night, after we came back from Ava's room and went to bed, Haim had to get up three times to vomit. In between he moaned quietly and complained about his head hurting. At two in the morning I called the doctor who is overseeing Haim's treatment at his home number, and he said some things I was already thinking about possible increased cranial pressure.

The nurse asked him where he was and who we were, and Haim still didn't seem able to answer. Two more nurses and our doctor showed up. By this time I was standing nearly in the hallway. You learn to stay out of the way. "He's unresponsive," I heard the doctor say to someone, and then a nurse turned around to tell me we were going to the PICU.

In the PICU I really did stand out in the hallway, watching through the room's big corridor-side window, as if keeping a couple feet outside of the room would make it impossible for anything too serious to happen inside. I could just barely see part of Haim's chest through all the nurses' bodies and medical detritus around him—its rise and fall was almost imperceptible, one of those foci that make you distrust your eyes and the world in front of you. I counted his breaths. In two minutes he'd breathed ten or eleven times, and I stood there thinking *which one was it, ten or eleven, ten or eleven,* until they went to intubate him and his entire pudgy body began to strain violently, and I stepped back inside.

At one point a screen high above Haim's bed began beeping and flashing and, as if in concert, the doctor and all of the nurses stopped and looked up at it, in silence, just for a moment. This was his blood pressure skyrocketing. Then they all began doing things with an even more frenetic fervor. I could see the doctor leaning down over Haim's face, pulling open his eyelids. Haim was having a seizure, I would be told later. The doctor would say later that he'd never seen a child's pupils so big, as if there were no irises, as if they were not eyes at all.

There are no small emergencies, of course. There are no close calls. For Haim, being alive at all is a close call, a chance escape. This is what this time is now, as I'm sitting here in his room in the PICU watching the sun set over the Thames and the little boats nodding against the pier—a gift of unknown providence, a chance only to escape one kind of waiting for another.

They've just a few minutes ago brought back the test results from earlier today; a resident explained them, occasionally glancing up at me and then at Haim's still, unconscious body, like he might be listening. Haim's sodium level is now at 123; since it was at 134 earlier in the day, a sudden drop seems to be the key medical clue. The numbers themselves (and all the infinite scales they assemble) are so arbitrary that, even now that I actually understand them, I often imagine, half sleepless, that they should bypass their medical literality (which means nothing to a parent anyway) and reach instead to a description that could approximate the level of emotion the numbers should be communicating. For instance, the resident could have said that the amount of sodium in Haim's body dropped from the amount of salt one might cup with two child-sized hands to the amount one might cradle in one child-sized palm, and, moreover, that it had not been lost slowly but all at once, as if the hands had been parted unexpectedly, and that Haim lying there now is desperately trying to keep his little damp palmful of salt from blowing away in the bodily winds that are threatening to carry him right out of this room, this night, this tired conversation. A test result like that might mean something to me.

So it is, as the resident explained, actually SIADH that caused the emergency today, that made my son fail to recognize me. SIADH, or Syndrome of Inappropriate Anti-Diuretic Hormone Hypersecretion. They don't use the real names of these things because they're ridiculous. *Inappropriate hormone secretion, or, as it's otherwise known, ninth grade,* I wanted to say to cheer Haim up, but he's unconscious, and it's a lame joke that he will never be old enough to really get anyway.

There's not much to do now but think about the words, as if breaking them down or playing a kind of sleep-deprived free association might change them into something more logical, something

one might understand. In the wake of his morning of medical activity, Haim is now hooked up to an EEG to monitor brain activity, a ventilator, and a catheter, and has an arterial line in his left wrist and a central line in the right side of his groin. He has been given one medicine to seep fluids from his tissues into his veins, and another to make his body rid itself of the excessive fluid through urination. The body, even when it is more plastic tube and chemical molecule than flesh, persists in being a body. Haim is under sedation now, but doing better, and is scheduled, if everything continues to improve, to be extubated tomorrow. I already have a Popsicle ready for him for after they do it, have already stashed it in a small fridge in an empty room two rooms down. It's purple.

Of course, no one tells you how to feel about this, how much this minor crisis signals our proximity to the larger one, the crisis that is not a crisis, the end. I try to call the number that, through several relaying connections, is supposed to connect me to Charlie, but it only rings again, as it has all day, to no answer.

Diffuse Intrinsic Pontine Glioma. Imagine a morning fog spreading through a dense forest, insinuating itself until its opacity is the very space between the trees, until its wispy presence exists even in the delicate distance between the needles of two overlapping fronds. It is a betrayal of one's own flesh, growing as it does out of the glial cells, which are the ones in the brain that are supposed to protect your neurons. It is inoperable.

The first time we almost lost Haim (to a bad sepsis that developed around the medical port that had been implanted in his chest) I was still stuck on those words, "pontine" in particular. You read up on everything, at least until the medical labyrinth loses you. You do what you can. The pons is tightly held in the brain's fist, encased neatly, maddeningly, by the meat of the cerebellum, midbrain, and medulla. It deals with sleep, breathing, swallowing, bladder con-

trol, hearing, taste, eye movement, and facial expression/sensation, among other things. The frontal lobe may be the seat of abstract consciousness, but it is the pons that is the seat of the bodily existence, the brain's brain. Pons means "bridge" in Latin, and its matter bridges many things, like the signals for voluntary action and the motor cortex that allows one to act in the world, or the act of (in the sad, unintentional poetry of the medical textbooks) inspiration and expiration. The pons is there right from the beginning, in the folding of the tube that will be the fetal brain, gathering at seven weeks, just about the time you find it safe enough to tell the world that you are pregnant.

At the time, I could only think of the Ponte Vecchio, which I once saw as a child. It's impossible to separate what I knew that first time, in the long hours sitting alone by Haim's bedside in the PICU—not used to the kind of low-grade panic that never quite recedes and compulsively dialing Charlie's cellphone number to no avail--from what I know now, from all the subsequent Googling, the madcap late-night efforts to draw the connections. *A tumor on the pons, full name pons Varolii after Costanzo Varolio, the 16th-century Italian who discovered it and who worked and died in the country of the Ponte Vecchio, where four hundred years later I stood as a boy on a dreary, wet fall night (my own pons at that moment safely coming to the last stages of its development and yet even then containing the very DNA that would recombine with Charlie's, adding the future groundwork for one tiny disastrous mutation) thinking only of how the bridge's many vibrantly golden lights leaping in the water made it look like the whole river was on fire.* This all in order to somehow, someway understand even a little bit of what it was that was being visited upon my little son.

That was the night the holiday started, that night of the sepsis scare. It was the first of September, Haim had only been sick for

about four months, and everything still seemed manageable. Charlie and I spent all day every day at the hospital with Haim, taking turns nights with one of us sleeping on the small foldable cot in his room and the other making the tired walk back to the flat in the cool dark.

A lot of the other families on the oncology ward could only have one parent there at a time, while the other was forced to spend the day working and visiting for a few hours before bedtime and on weekends. By this time, though, Charlie's art shows (the reason we moved to England in the first place) had made so much money that neither of us had to work.

First grade, and Haim being gone most of the day for the first time, had been hard on both of us. We took Haim for little adventures after school, catching a train and getting as far out from the city as we could without coming back too late. Once, we went to a Zen garden way out in the country and walked around for hours, Haim pointing things out and naming them quietly, insisting that his made-up name for each tree or stone was correct, and we tried not to disturb the few other tourists with our laughter. On the ride back in, Haim fell asleep on Charlie, who fell asleep on me, and I stayed up to watch the dark farmland give way to the concrete and brick of London. The train was empty except for us and I remember even its hum of speed sounded pleased, contented.

So in some way during that first era of Haim's sickness the days felt almost OK, like we'd gotten our little boy back somehow, like he might never get any older, might never outgrow us or this trusting age. We started out in the hospital the way that all the families on the terminal end of the oncology ward start out: the diagnosis is bad but your child is alive, is right now alive, and though in a vague, abstract way you understand the fear, here is your little boy, begging you to play futsal on the hospital's miniature enclosed court, and how bad could any world be when he is running toward the goal, his head (no

matter what grows inside it) tilted back to watch the ball arc through the air toward him, his tawny hair, half stuck to his forehead with sweat, catching the long golden sunlight of late afternoon. This is, of course, before his eyes begin to drift independently, before his left-side weakness becomes so great he cannot make a fist, before his speech so often dips into a slurring, coughing Hebraic stammer that when he does manage to get a clear sentence out it rings in the air as if someone else has said it. Before his body, bloated and ravaged and drained and filled with medicine, is so weak that he cannot stand to kick a ball, even if he ever showed enough interest in the world again to want to. This was before all that, when he was still recognizable, only a boy, a miniature bodily vessel brimming with the discovery of each day.

The sepsis emergency was the end of all that. It came on so quickly and completely that the doctor in the PICU said that he'd thought they'd sent Haim there to expire, and was confused when he found no Do Not Resuscitate order.

I wasn't there when the crisis started, because it was Charlie's night to stay in the room. She'd paced the room all night as Haim deteriorated, torn over whether or not to wake the doctor who was overseeing treatment, or to bother the nurse, who was overworked at the end of a double shift, and worrying about being a "problem parent," trying to decide if it was all in her head or if this was really happening. This is what I imagine. What I know is that Charlie was alone with him through the night and there when he coded, and there in the PICU when he coded again. What I know is that I got a phone call at four a.m. from Charlie saying that I needed to get to the hospital right away, that Haim was dying. I don't know if she waited somewhere to make sure I got there in time before leaving. I don't know where she was calling from. The last time any of the doctors or nurses saw her, a Patient Care Liaison was putting the DNR form in her hands. When the doctor came to talk it over, she was gone.

And so the holiday began, though we didn't call it that until a few months in, when Haim wanted us to watch that movie, and I didn't really understand until a few days after Haim recovered, until I sent for the mothers (both of whom had, since we first moved to England, been clamoring to be allowed to visit together) and went to the police station to report Charlie missing. The report took a long time and the officer seemed to grow increasingly confused. He left and came back nearly an hour later with his supervisor, an older, red-faced man who patiently explained to me that their passport records showed that Charlie had left the country. He seemed sorry to have to tell me this, to have to reveal to the clueless husband his loss, and we sat there for a minute in silence. "Is there anything else I can do for you?" the man said sadly, in a way that seemed full of his disappointment at what this life had turned out to be.

We got the first video a month later. To be honest, I was not all that surprised that Charlie had fled. Some part of me knew it when I came in that morning and saw Haim in the PICU, alone, unconscious. Seeing him like that, almost comically undersized amidst all the machines and screens and even the scaled-down hospital bed, was like getting punched in the stomach. Nothing could have pulled her away from him when he was like that—no abduction, no accident—except volition. I was told at one point a nurse was on top of Haim, straddling him; she did a compression too hard and one of his ribs broke, and I often wonder if it was this single muffled snap of sound that brought Charlie out of it, that propelled her out of the building in shock, against what should have been all her instincts, and down the streets (perhaps even passing me, without either of us knowing it?) and eventually to her suitcases and the airport. *I have seen the gaping maw of the world*, I remember her once reciting to me when we were still in college, *and am fit no longer for heaven or hell*. And so I wasn't terribly surprised when we got the video either.

The video was a short clip, about twenty seconds long. It arrived on my phone from Charlie's email address, and I stared at it for a long time before opening it. The body of the message was blank. The attached clip was taken from a handheld video camera and shook slightly. There was the glossy square of a picture, a postcard being held up to the lens. It showed a photograph of the palace at Versailles. The camera then panned up from the postcard to the actual building itself in the distance, roughly in the same scale as the picture. There was the distant sound of someone's laughter. When the camera panned back down, the postcard had been flipped over. On it there was writing in thick black marker. DO YOU KNOW, it said, THAT I LOVE YOU SO MUCH?

For the first few days she was gone, before I'd made the police report, I'd refused to look at our credit card charges. I believed that if I didn't, she would come back. That the act of not looking would make it impossible, in some Schrödinger's cat kind of way, for there to be charges from the airport, from foreign ATMs. When the police captain eventually told me the truth, that she was gone, not even in the same country, I felt that kind of magical thinking disappear from me forever. The same day the video arrived, I got a call from our bank inquiring about some suspicious charges and asking if I happened to be on a trip—I could have stopped it all right then, explained that I needed to freeze our accounts for legal reasons, settled something between us then, but I didn't. I didn't say anything, except to tell the man that my wife was traveling, and I wanted to be sure she had everything she needed.

Do you know, I thought, that I love you so much. What does that even mean.

Charlie would have been aware of the pithy irony of it, would have known the mixture of insult and hollow sentimentalism any

man in my position would be forced to take it as, would have known all this, and sent it anyway.

Of course, I spent the days as Haim came back into life searching my memory for clues. As more clips came in especially, one every two or so weeks. There was one from a Portuguese lighthouse, the camera finding DO YOU KNOW in rickety letters of scrawled graffiti on its interior stairwell, then THAT carved into the door with a pen, then I LOVE YOU, in girly script near the base of the re-created torch light, then SO MUCH at the end of a sentence in fat black marker by the stairs, the beginning of which, I could just make out, was DRU FUCKS BITCHES. How long did she have to look, I thought when I watched it, to find all of the words in English?

"Don't you know that I love you?" Charlie used to cry when we were younger, when we still had dramatic arguments that so exhausted us both that by the end we'd just be leaning into one another, and she'd be lightly beating my chest.

The holiday lasted all the way through the fall. As it went on I kept track of her with the credit card bill online, going back and forth between the electronic statement and Google's satellite search function. But you can't make a real path out of the random constellation of cashpoints, of obscure historical sites' gift shops and train stations. At any moment while I sat there in Haim's room late into the night, while he slept and I bent over the glow of my computer to save him from waking, Charlie could've been headed in any direction, could be on any train streaming through the Nordic or German or Russian or Spanish countryside, or in any room of a cut-rate left-bank flat, could be in the company of any man, any woman, any lover or friend or fan or critic of hers from the art world, but certainly not in the company of any child, certainly changing train compartments if one arrived, oblivious, in the company of a traveler. It didn't mean anything, really, to follow her.

At the end of October I had to get one of the nurses to help me paint Haim's face with orange, white, and black because he wanted to be a tiger. He insisted on waiting until the last second before the hospital Halloween party to put the paint on, in case "someone who really knows how to do it comes on the ward." As the play specialists took the kids from Pediatric Oncology around trick-or-treating to the various nursing stations, I watched Charlie's latest message. It was from the square in front of St. Mark's Basilica in Venice. It was longer than usual, almost four minutes. It began with an old, hawkish woman in a long, weathered fur coat singing with an open hatbox in front of her. Her voice was high, vibrato-rich, operatic. DO YOU KNOW, she warbled shrilly, stumbling on the syllables, not looking at the camera, THAT I LOVE YOU SO MUCH?

The camera panned out to the rest of the sprawling square, which was gray and empty in the faltering autumn sun. It seemed to be afternoon, and there were hardly any tourists. The many groups of pigeons shrugged in the cold. I sat there in Haim's empty room with the laptop on my lap and watched the clip again and again, eventually closing my eyes and listening to the long stretch after the woman stops singing, the digital roar of the wind gusting against the camera, thinking of the camera's closeness to Charlie's face and trying to hear, in the long space of ambient noise and quiet, the sound of her breathing. I had to stop when Haim wheeled himself back in, crying. His chewing ability had been gradually deteriorating and finally, in one of his first denials, it meant that he couldn't have any of the Tootsie Rolls he had been given.

By Thanksgiving, when Charlie did not show up, I decided to let Haim watch the videos. Because I didn't know how much longer we'd be allowed to leave the hospital, Haim and I went to his favorite restaurant, a tacky Italian chain imported from America. I told him about the videos, and asked if he wanted to see them. He thought

about it for a minute, poking at his chicken parmigiana, and then said that he'd like to watch them. When we got back, Haim was already very tired but we set up the projector anyway, and he held it on his stomach, watching the string of clips silently several times through, until he was asleep.

Every once in a while another of Charlie's paintings would sell and I would get an international money order from her with a strange remitter's address. Because of this, I knew she must be telling her dealer, the one who handled her paintings and finances here in London, where she was staying each time she moved. I knew that if I went down to his gallery in Chelsea, he would probably tell me where she was, and I could do almost anything; I could even go to wherever she happened to be at that moment and confront her, could bring her back, or, at the very least, get a real telephone number with which to speak to her.

But I understood, watching the clips with Haim, strung back to back on an eternal digital loop, that the entire point of this was to avoid speech. That had been her great indictment of me every time we argued, that I made every little thing that should be a four-minute conversation into a forty-minute argument (things which, I knew, in her mind should really even be a forty-second back and forth), that I talked too much, was rude, cut her off in midsentence. "It's an arrogance," she said. "You think you know what I'm going to say, but you don't. You have to think that, because otherwise you'd have no choice but to see that you're really just afraid that I'm going to say something both true and diminutive about the way you are." Of course all of this was true. I wanted to keep her bright, quick mind from leaping forward, beyond, with its terrifying ability to articulate with an almost autistic disregard the quintessence of someone as a person. There're some things, I often thought, that you can't ever unhear. Most of the time when she said things like this, I told her that

I thought it was petty, that I thought we should be talking about more important issues. "What's a petty problem?" she said. "What else is being married?" And so the video clips were also a rebuke, a punishment. The only way she could live without me talking. The only way she could get me to shut up.

The day after Thanksgiving Haim wanted to watch the videos again. He ended up watching them several times a week, the whole time taking a small stack of secretive notes, as if the clips contained an intricate system of subtle clues with a hidden message only for him. Who were these videos meant for, really? Had Charlie just assumed that I would show them to Haim as they came? I'd told him about where she was after I received each clip, but I hadn't really explained and he had, self-protectively I think, not asked many questions. I didn't want him to see that adults could be this way, that they could be so wrong about what love is.

It had been a mercy, anyway, for Charlie that when Haim got sick I didn't want to talk about it. "Some people talk," Charlie used to say when we argued, patiently, like she was explaining it to a child. "And some people live." But during those long months of the holiday, I thought about how it was dying that was really the anti-speech. The great authors in their twilight produce books that grow shorter and shorter, and nobody has much to say about a child with a terminal brain tumor watching the first snow of the year collect on his windowsill. The story refuses to assemble itself. Dying defeats all plot. What would I possibly have had to say to Charlie, even if we did talk?

On the first night of Chanukah I found out one of the nurses on the ward had been giving Charlie information. I had assumed somebody was. I thought about complaining, putting a stop to it. People should have to earn information about the terminally ill, I thought. People should have to come here and stare into the face of it. I didn't

want her to come swooping in if things got bad all of a sudden, as if she'd been here all along. I just wanted her to come home.

The mothers were here by then. I'd set them up in a small flat that they could share near the hospital when they visited. They were both quiet, nervous women, and for most of our marriage they had harbored a congenital dislike of each other, but they had been united in the cause of a sick grandchild and were mostly glad, now that we'd put an ocean between our little family and them, for the chance to see Haim. The nurses and the other families, who, of course, all knew my and Haim's story, knew about Charlie leaving, were glad to see the mothers around, and gave me big, knowing grins every time they saw me. I couldn't talk to any of them.

And Haim through all of this? It was hard to know what Haim thought during the holiday and when he thought it. He was quiet most of the time, kept his questions to himself. It helped that we'd started on a new therapy, one of the clinical trials, and it seemed to be working, keeping the size of the tumor stable, though it required a brutal course of infusions, and a host of medicines to counteract its side effects. Right at the beginning, as he was being prepped for one of the scans that would start the trial, he said, "So Mom's not going to be back for a while, huh?" As if she was late returning from getting takeout. It was so unexpected, I almost laughed.

It has crossed my mind that Charlie's holiday was not the same thing for Haim as it was for me. Haim understood the sadness of it, for sure, but what is betrayal to a (at the time) seven-year-old? And she did come back, eventually. Do you know that I love you so much that I will show you the world that you cannot see, it might've meant to him, and he might be too young to ever understand the sad miscal-culation of that, that the world he could not see was the one where he didn't have an unstable mother who would leave him to die because she could not bear to watch it happen. At the very least by the time

the holiday was over, Haim seemed to have aged years, though it was unclear, like everything else, how much of it was due to me, Charlie, the holiday, or his new body.

Charlie came back the day after Christmas, as if that timing meant anything. Haim had gone into respiratory distress, and been rushed down to the PICU. This was the episode where we figured out he would have to sleep with a bi-pap machine from now on. The mothers had been exiled out to the lounge a floor below the PICU, and I was with Haim. One of the nurses told me later that Charlie had just walked into the ward, leading two men who were helping her with a large crate, then dismissed them. The nurse had come in and told her where Haim was, offered to take her down to me in the PICU, but Charlie politely refused. The nurse said Charlie waited in the empty room until she heard Haim was going to be OK, then, before the mothers or I could return, she left. It was two days later, when Haim was back on Pediatric Oncology and doing better, that she came in while he feigned sleep, and I watched her try to reclaim his body from the distortion of flesh.

When Haim and I finally came back to the room after he'd been released from the PICU, we found a present. Standing to the side of the space where Haim's bed was to be rolled was a shiny, red piano-in-miniature. Both Haim and I stared at it. It had a small red bow on its top, the letters *kinderklavier* spelled out in fancy, golden cursive along the side. It was of a certain size, an in-between scale, not small enough to be a toy, not large enough to be a piano. Haim's body, bloated, voluminous, could not have even sat at it, let alone played it. There so close to Haim's pillowy hands, the miniature keys looked impossibly exact. It was too small for Haim to play, too much an imitation of an instrument for us to play for him. It had only three octaves, the tuning nothing if not approximate. What, I thought, could be suitably played on such a ridiculous thing?

It's now been six months since all of that happened. The story of time, when it is limited, when it is measured in the expansive quality of a child's experience, is impossible to tell. Time is the story, in a way. The relentless march of it. I never imagined this time I'm living through now during Charlie's holiday, never thought of it any more than when, in the moments of my worst anger, I tried to imagine what it would be like to divorce her, to greet her on her return, if it ever came, with the papers. But I never imagined what it would be like six months after she came back, never realized that yes you have to live each dramatic moment of your life, but then you have to live the day just after it, and the one after that.

Charlie comes to the hospital pretty consistently now. Twice Haim has had emergencies, been rushed to the PICU, and twice more Charlie has disappeared. But twice she has come back, each time staying away only a week or so, returning when Haim stabilizes. "At this point, I feel like I'm doing more harm than good if I stay," she says, and I don't point out to her how ludicrous this is because I know that she knows it, that she is saying this just to bridge the gap, just to speak, to tell me that these times won't be like the holiday, that she will no longer disappear into silence. She's also given me the international cellphone I hold in my hand now, and though she hasn't today, she usually answers it. The times she has answered, I haven't asked her to come back. I've tried to keep my voice even, tried to dryly just tell her the medical details, what's going on. I would still probably be too angry to talk to her on the phone when this happens, but honestly, I'm just too tired.

She came back to me that night after the holiday ended. I could hear the key turning, the door to the flat opening in the dark, as I lay in bed and pretended to be asleep. This was the last question I had, the only one seeing the kinderklavier had not answered.

Of course, later we'd argue, my feelings about things swinging wildly, the memories of bitter lines of thought that I'd strung together

in the long, lonely hours sitting in Haim's room surfacing, reanimating me with anger.

"You think I don't know what this makes me?" she said, on one of the nights the mothers were staying with Haim, in order to give us "some time to talk some things out." "You think I don't see how everyone in that hospital looks at me, you think I don't know what even my own mother thinks of me?"

"And Haim," I said. "Let's not forget him. How does he look at you?"

Charlie exhaled, frustrated. I don't know if she could even hear that I was trying to be cruel.

"He looks at me like I'm his mother, he looks at me like he loves me just as much as I love him; he's our little boy, I know he is, I know that, but what am I supposed to do? What am I supposed to say? That I'm a good mother? That I'm the kind of woman who can stand there and watch this thing, this little thing that is my whole heart, flesh of my flesh, that is years of our life, suffer and seize and bleed and die? I'm not that woman, I can't do it, and do you think I don't know that there's something wrong with me, that there's something wrong with me that I can't fix, something so wrong with me that I didn't even know it was there until the clearest possible situation, until he needed me the most and I couldn't even look at him? You think you're the only one that's suffering because you stayed, because there's nothing inside you that keeps you from watching that, but here I am: I have a little boy but I can't be a mother, can't even deny that there's something completely lacking in me."

Here she paused, bit a fingernail, looked out the window.

"And the thing is, the really tortuous thing is, Haim's the only one who doesn't look at me like that, he's the only one who looks at me like that deficiency isn't all I am. He's the only one who even looks at me like a human being—the irony being, of course, that I'm not,

that I'm the opposite, inhumane by anyone's standard. But maybe that's something about children, especially maybe terminal children. Maybe they are the only ones capable of true mercy. Maybe he can look at me and sense that I am fucked up, but still his mother—still *want* to be his mother. Maybe he can sense that the whole reason I had to leave was because I love him, because more than I couldn't stand the thought of having to see the worst things happen to him, I couldn't stand the thought of it happening and him looking up at me at maybe, I don't know, like his last second of consciousness and seeing my pure horror, this panicked horror instead of love, this thing that I can't hide."

And on and on and on. I spoke very little during these conversations, eventually not even curious to see if, like a tunnel through the center of the earth, her endless in-turning, her frantic affected deprecation, her spiraling mental contortions might surface somehow back into the daylight of reason. There is nothing sadder than egotism in a partner you have given your life to, because it speaks mostly to the even greater egotism true of yourself in loving your partner in spite of it. Once the heart is colonized, you can't ever get it back, not even by killing it.

"I mean, you think I don't know what I've done to you?" she said, on another of these nights. "You think I can live with myself knowing what is probably the truth about all of this? You know what I thought right at the start while I was traveling? I thought, this is what I have to do because of the day after, you know, Haim's suffering is, you know, over, and the day after that and the day after that. I thought this is what I have to do to still be with *you*, this is what loving *you* really is, because I knew you couldn't be with me if something bad happened, if the final, you know, emergency happened and we were standing there in the PICU and you looked at me and saw that I couldn't han-

dle it, that I'd checked out, that I was not moved by any of it but horrified—filled with horror at the sight of our own son—I knew that you'd never be able to be with me after that, that even if you loved me you wouldn't be able to be with me after that. And I didn't want to start over. And I didn't want you to have to start over. And I thought that maybe, just maybe, this is what really loving you required: sacrificing myself, my character, taking myself out of it and letting everyone think I'm horrible—in fact, *being* horrible—so that you and I may live after Haim doesn't. And this is what I had to think about the whole time I was gone, this is the truth I had to face then and that I have to live with now—that it's possible—I can barely even say it—that I love my husband more than my son, if only because my son is barely getting to live. There, it's horrible, unbelievable, but I've said it, because it's more important than anything to be honest."

That time I stood up and grabbed Charlie's face with one hand like you would a child who has something that should be spat out. I could feel her teeth through her cheeks.

"How about we try something new," I said. "How about this: no pity. No pity, not for you, not for me, and not for Haim. No pity. And no forgiveness."

That was all later, though. That is our recent history. That first night, when I heard her come in, as I listened to her undress in the dark of our room, I didn't say anything. She slipped into bed, and I could feel her heat—her body always so warm. And she settled in to the position in which she always slept and, as we'd done when we were younger, I felt her leg slide over, barely touching her skin against mine. I let her, felt the warmth enter my body, though later I would feel stupid about it. What can I say? There was only so much room on the mattress with which I could escape her, and I was already as far as I could go.

•

There was a time when we were not yet these people. This is how memory works, resisting your own meaningful organization. For instance, if you asked me to remember now a single day from the heady period when, simultaneously, Haim was a newborn and I was getting the bulk of the rejections for fellowships, teaching jobs, and my novel manuscript, I couldn't do it. But if you ask me about when Haim was a toddler, when we still lived in Iowa and I thought I might still be a writer, I am immediately back standing in the small canyon of buildings in downtown Iowa City on a brisk September late afternoon, watching the sun alight on Charlie's reddish-brown hair, which she'd dyed darker because it was cheaper to maintain, as we waited for the homecoming parade to start and Haim ran around, weaving between the families in lawn chairs in front of us and babbling loudly.

He'd just turned four years old, one of those birthdays where we along with him were suddenly older. Charlie had avoided gaining too much weight while she was pregnant (even though I told her that it didn't matter, that she should be eating double whatever she wanted because it was what Haim wanted too) but it'd been a long, difficult delivery, and she'd lost a lot of blood and was confined to bed for several weeks afterward and then extreme caution for months after that, during which time her curves became fuller, and small rises of fat began collecting at her lower abdomen, arms, and thighs. This had seemed a gentler body, one suited for the mothering of an infant. Now, though, in Haim's fourth year something had made her decide to regain, as much as she could, the body of her own youth. She found a gym that had a good daycare, and, at about this time, began talking to me about what we should do next, in terms of me teaching high school or doing any of the things I'd promised to try if writing didn't work out. By this, our fifth year in Iowa, I'd been

out of the masters program for as long as I'd ever been in it, and, in both Charlie's and my mind, the luminous encouragement and private assertions of confidence the faculty had once confided in me had faded, until it almost felt like I'd dreamt them. Charlie made a modest salary as an assistant in a law office, and I had a small stipend teaching Comp 101 at the university, but we were still depending on money from my mother, which shamed us both.

Charlie's body had, by the day of the parade, tightened and streamlined into an attractiveness that owed more to fitness than out-and-out sexuality. We were thirty years old, and I marveled at how her legs, bent in my periphery during sex, had completely changed, become slender, thin, graced with toned muscle instead of the full curves of her college years, as if this were an entirely different person than I'd first slept with. Her skin, which once seemed to lag behind her in the aging process, blushing smoothly with the cherubic health of a child, now seemed to have gotten ahead of her, and, standing there as the music of the marching bands approached, I could see again how in certain lights it seemed thin and almost grayish, the small fingers of red spreading over her cheeks sharp-edged with capillaries in the cool air.

As the floats and squads from the local baton-twirling studio passed along, I had been distracted by a small boy in front of us, sitting calmly on his father's shoulders, watching the parade with what seemed like an intelligent reticence. Every once in a while, he'd reach out and pat the top of his father's hair lightly, as if to say thank you. Haim was in and out of our sight, Charlie doing an awkward side-step thing along the back of the crowd to keep an eye on him as he moved. I could see some of the other parents eye the crowd in the direction he'd rocketed from, looking for someone to give the disapproving glance to, looking for me. Finally Haim came back to us and watched, leaning backward against Charlie's legs.

When the drunken middle-aged alumnus, leaning out from the top of a passing papier-mâché "hawk's nest" and wearing a black and gold jester's hat, threw the necklace of beads toward the crowd I saw it falling directly to me against the blank gray sky, and I reached up and caught it. The beads, I could see now, were actually tiny plastic black and gold football helmets. I can only guess that I must've forgotten that Haim was back with us, or maybe that I assumed that by then he'd run off again because, in a daze, I reached up to where the small boy perched, where he was turning to see who had caught the prize, and gave it to him.

I looked down at the sound of Haim's wail. For a moment he wasn't even crying yet, just looking up at me in shock and betrayal.

"For Christ's sake," Charlie said, picking him up and looking at me. "Really? Really?"

Sometime around the middle of Haim's second year, something had changed. He would only let Charlie help him with his food, only let Charlie put him to bed at night. He began to follow her around the house, and screamed and screamed when she left for work. As she cooked dinner, he would stand, leaning against the side of her leg, turning the thick pages of one of the picture books silently, occasionally glancing up at her, as if to make sure she had not disappeared when he was not looking.

This was also around the time we began to understand his mind, what gifts he had inherited straight from Charlie. The only thing he would do with me (and then only if I faux-pleaded) was to let me watch him turn the pages of one of his books. Charlie and I had also begun noticing right about this time that Haim seemed to have, without any real help from us, intuited the alphabet, and was beginning to read. It was small words at first, but then when he added larger ones they were all the words that were supposed to be the hardest, the ones not spelled phonetically. He loved books, and would

carry stacks of them around to wherever he was playing in the house. Charlie had worked with number cards when she was little and so she decided to try this with him, and by the time we were planning his third birthday party he could do simple addition operations with single-digit numbers. Our daycare reported that Haim cried from the moment I dropped him off until the moment Charlie picked him up, with only a few breaks for sips of water in between. His face became red, dry, and chafed. Charlie decided to cut back on her hours at the law firm in order to stay home with him more. She couldn't stand the thought of him toddling around ready to learn with no one there willing to teach him.

On the night after his fourth birthday party Haim had woken up crying, and wouldn't stop until Charlie came in, even though I'd gotten up to see to him, and wouldn't calm down enough to tell her what happened until I left the room. I stood in the hallway while Charlie talked him down. He'd had a nightmare.

"Daddy's gonna, daddy's gonna leave me all alone," he said, with barely enough breath. "He's gonna leave me and replace me with a different boy."

"Why would you say that? Don't say that honey," Charlie said, rubbing tiny circles on his back. "Daddy loves you very, very much. Daddy would never, ever leave you."

"I dreamed it," Haim insisted. "It's gonna be true."

"Well, I've known Daddy a really, really long time, and he's never left anybody," my wife said. "So I know he won't leave you. You're his favorite. What kind of boy could ever replace you?"

"It was, it was a robot boy," Haim sniffled. "Except it—except you can't tell, because they look, they look like—they look the same."

"No, baby," Charlie said. "Robot boys aren't real, and Daddy wouldn't trade anything for you."

Haim shook his head.

"You watch," he said. "You watch."

After that we'd made a deal with Haim, made a goal of one whole day with no crying. We would try to make sure we were doing things where he felt comfortable, things that didn't make him feel afraid or anxious, and he would try to be a little calmer. Charlie even took him to work one day at the office, and he wrote quietly on papers spread out on the floor behind her desk, filling page after page with the scrawled numbers he was just learning. The homecoming parade had been the closest we'd come to a cry-free day.

In the car on the way to the restaurant after the parade was over, I was thinking about the way the whole world seemed to be on the verge of great change—the fields into the winter anonymity of snow, Haim into a prodigy, premature school-goer with an acute self-awareness, a separate person from us, the qualities currently in concentrated miniature ready to swell, gain volume like one of his tiny plastic dinosaurs that, left for an hour in water, was suddenly too big for the bowl; its terrible, squishy body somehow all contained there in its condensed beginning. I was thinking about how strange it is that you can't really see even two or three years into the future. That you go through each of your days having no idea toward which sadness you are headed.

"Why should I have to guess at what you're upset about?" Charlie was saying in the passenger seat. We were continuing the argument that had begun in the parking garage after the parade, in which we'd cursed at each other in the few seconds when Haim was settled in his car seat in the back and we'd closed the doors before getting in the front. ("We should talk about this," I said. "Why, so you can go on telling me why it's OK that you're such an asshole?" Charlie had hissed over the top of the car. "You can go fuck yourself," I'd hissed back, and grabbed open the driver's side door.) Now she said, "Why can't you just tell me?"

"What I'm upset about," I said, "is that you have to ask. That's the whole thing you're failing at; that's what empathy is. You're supposed to imagine yourself in my emotional position in a real enough way to not only know what it is I'm upset about, but to anticipate it. And I shouldn't be having to explain this to you."

"Oh, is that what empathy is?" Charlie said, and sighed.

"Jeddey, jetty, jedi," Haim said. He was just getting into the *Star Wars* movies, and liked to try to say the harder words over and over again to himself. Despite his intelligence, it seemed his speech development had been skipped over in the hurry, and he often had trouble.

We were quiet for a minute.

We slowed to a stop in a long line of traffic, and Charlie put her hand over mine on the knob of the gearshift. "I don't want to be angry," she said.

And isn't this what we wanted? Hadn't this been the plan? We'd talked and talked about having a baby those first months in Iowa. It had seemed like a crazy idea at the time, but then at the end of one long argument about it, Charlie had sat down on the couch and cried, her shoulders heaving, trying to turn in on themselves. When she calmed down enough to speak she talked about her various failures: in being the concert pianist her early instructors had wanted her to be; in finding the mathematical proofs whose moving pieces she could no longer all hold in her head at the same time; in being a happy, well-adjusted wife. At the time, she'd just gotten the job at the law firm, which handled only family law, and spent most of her day filing, copying, and talking on the phone to confused, enraged women and men who had just been served divorce papers, or watched their children be taken from their own home.

"And maybe I'm just not one of those people who can find in a career the kind of meaning that can sustain a life," she said that night of the decision, her face drawn from crying. "I just think, I just really

think that maybe I'm supposed to find meaning in something else—that maybe what I'll be really good at will be loving our little kid. I can feel that. I just know it's true in my heart."

For weeks I said I didn't know; I talked about how we didn't have any money, how if we had a kid now we'd have to take money from my mother for a long time. I talked about how much we fought, how we weren't quite ready, and Charlie listened but then she said, "I think this is one of those things where you're never quite ready. Where the only way you learn how to have a kid is by having one. You figure it out as you go, I think. For instance, I think we'd fight less if I was pregnant. I think we wouldn't want to fight. I think we'd be better people because that is what our lives would require of us."

And she wasn't wrong, really. We had only the one bad fight while she was pregnant, and never argued at all while Haim was a baby. It was only in the middle of his second year, when he started to resemble a separate person, no longer our little ball of love and chubby rolls, that we began to fight again.

There was only one time that I doubted anything in those years. Charlie was five months pregnant, and going through a phase where she was so fatigued, she climbed into bed at about six p.m. and slept through the night. Usually, I lay with her for an hour or two because she said this was the only way she could fall asleep. It was a Saturday, though, and I had been invited to a party thrown by my fellow students in the masters program. It was at seven thirty, and after ten or so minutes of lying still with Charlie, I got up. I felt anxious. I wanted to take a shower and get ready.

"What are you doing?" she said, and I told her. She didn't say anything after that.

The party was in an old, warm house. A cool drizzle had begun to fall in the twilight as I pulled in. Inside the front room a couple amps and an electric organ were set up and a few of my colleagues

were playing together. In the kitchen a group of women were pouring bottles of alcohol into a pot on the stove, making something they called "blood."

After about an hour I texted Charlie. I was thinking that I wished she was there with me. There was something refreshing about the way these new people looked at her, about knowing they were looking at her and not seeing Attica and all that had happened there.

What are you up to? I sent her, hoping she was still awake.

After a few minutes she texted back. *I've packed*, it said. *By the time you get back, I'll be gone.*

I suppose I should have thought she was joking, should have paused at the unbelievable, melodramatic way she was doing this. But a few weeks earlier, Charlie had come home and not been able to recognize my face.

"It's different somehow," she'd said, looking at me almost with wonder. "It's like, you don't look like you. Or you do, but just not you you."

"It's like," she said later, "imagine if you had an identical twin. You look like your own twin, if that makes any sense. I know it's you, but for some reason it doesn't feel like you. Like you're an impostor of yourself."

This kind of dissociation had happened once before, in Attica, right before everything fell apart. Back then I was obsessed with the medical implications, an official cause, maybe Capgras Syndrome. Then, when everything happened there, I spent days wondering if my wife was schizophrenic, if she had some kind of early-onset dementia, if maybe even she'd had some kind of traumatic brain injury years ago without knowing it. But by the time it happened again, by the time Charlie was saying this pregnant, I understood that she was not sick, that there was nothing actually wrong with her. This was not dissociation, I thought, standing in the bathroom door,

watching her watch me. This is the imitation, subconscious or not, of dissociation, of delusion. Just as back then her wandering down the shoulder of the highway had been, this was Charlie getting scared, and attempting to leave me.

That was three weeks before the party. Then I got the text. *I've packed*, it said. *By the time you get back, I'll be gone.* I wasn't even surprised, just ill. I stepped outside of the crowded kitchen, into what was now a steady rain.

"Where are you?" I said into the phone. "Tell me where you are, and we'll talk about this."

"No more talking," Charlie said. "I have nothing more to say."

"Come on," I said. "Just come back home, I'm going to my car now, I'll come back and we'll talk about it."

"I don't want you to try and bully me out of it," Charlie said. "I've decided."

The wife of the poet who was hosting the party stuck her head out of the back door.

"Come in, come in!" she called. "You're getting all wet!"

I waved to her that I was OK.

"I won't try to talk you out of anything," I said. "I just want to see you."

Charlie didn't say anything. There was the sound of children laughing. Until that moment I'd thought she was bluffing, was sitting in our bedroom, the suitcase open dramatically beside her.

"Come on, Charlie," I said. "If we sit down and see each other just for a few minutes before you go it's one thing. If you leave like this, via, via text message and a phone call, it's something else."

Through a side window I could see one of my classmates playing guitar, his eyes closed, face gesturing with the emotion of the riff.

"I was very angry when you left," Charlie said after a while. "When you get back home go inside and see if you still want to talk."

Back at the house, her closet was emptied out, her suitcases and car gone. I thought she might've broken my laptop, but it was safe on my desk. In the living room, though, our TV stand and the shelf underneath it were bare; only a few jagged, smashed pieces of plastic were left in the places where our television and my expensive game system usually were. The hammer was sitting in the middle of the coffee table. Everything was strangely orderly. This missing television and game system was what I'd been using to kill the long hours between when Charlie fell asleep and when I went to bed.

"I can sense you're gone," she often said. "Even in my sleep."

I called Charlie again.

"I still want to talk," I said.

"I'm on my way," she said.

And it was in these few minutes before she got back to the house from wherever she was that I thought all the things I had not allowed myself to dwell on. I remembered her face in the queasy lights of the rest stop, the two policemen bracketing her. I thought of how desperate I'd felt when we'd moved here to Iowa, how much I thought that if something drastic didn't change, I would lose her. I remembered thinking that a baby would be the thing, maybe the only gesture crazy or grand or selfless enough to jar us both out of our failing, competing ideas of ourselves and our marriage and make our life a life spent together, about something more than our problems. And it was only when I heard her car pull up, and tried to imagine how it would work for the rest of the pregnancy, if someone would have to call me to tell me my wife had gone into labor, if she would even still be my wife by then—it was only when the door opened, and I saw her empty, even face that I thought, just for a moment, to my great shame, that she was carrying my mistake.

"I'm so manipulative," she said later that night, almost laughing. "The TV and your system are in the basement. The plastic bits were

from an old shower radio. I bet you didn't even really look in the closet, did you? All my clothes are still there, I just pushed them way to the ends of the bar, behind the doors. You know where I was when you called? I was at the movie theater. I thought I might see a movie, to keep myself from answering when you rang. But I couldn't choose one. I couldn't go in. I'm sorry," she said. "I'm so sorry. I walked in and I saw you and you looked so . . . and I thought, I thought that I'd really done it this time, that you were going to leave me and that would be it. I was so angry, and I didn't realize until I saw you how stupid, how totally stupid it was of me."

There may have been a time when we were not yet the people we are now, but we certainly always contained them.

Now, in the car, the post-parade traffic was letting up. Charlie's hand was still on mine. There is a time just after your child is born when you fall wildly in love with your wife all over again. There is something new in this world only because you have loved her, and that fact is its own kind of rapture, with the squealing, squirming proof right there, always, in your arms. For the first three months, when Charlie's breasts swelled with milk and all you could see of Haim's limbs were the rolls of fat, I couldn't take my eyes off of either of them. I don't know what happens to this feeling, if it simply fades or if it just breaks apart, letting its embers fall and be buried in the middle of other, different feelings that trouble you years later.

We were almost to the restaurant's parking lot when I said it, as if I'd been frustrated the whole time.

"You're emotionally illiterate," I spat, continuing the conversation that we'd both agreed to leave off.

"I *know*," Charlie said, frustrated. "That's why I need you to tell me why you're upset."

This was only a year before Charlie began painting, before a dealer from New York discovered her at a local show, before her first

painting sold for more money than both of us together had made in our whole lives, and Charlie had the idea of moving to England so that we might be "closer to the world." This was not even a year before I would fail to realize that we were at the exact middle of Haim's entire life. And this was four years before he started babbling again, the tumor muddling his speech gradually, taking back the exotic words first.

"I'm just so tired," Charlie said, and out of nowhere I thought of the first few weeks after we'd brought Haim home from the hospital, the way he could never cool down. It seemed to be keeping him awake, so I'd sit up with him all night, holding him in only his diaper, his body impossibly small in my hands. The only thing that ever made him feel any better was when I lifted him up and put my open, wet mouth on his stomach, then withdrew and blew on it. His skin was so hot, even though he didn't have a fever, that I could feel it radiating into the air inside my mouth. He'd be quiet until I did it again, and I'd do it all night, all over his body until he fell asleep. And for days afterward, even when he no longer needed me to do it, I would still feel that kid's warm skin against my lips.

"I'm tired too," I said lamely, into the quiet.

"Ewok ewok ewok," went Haim.

•

The medical team has come and gone, and Haim didn't struggle at all against the extubation. He's awake now, though something seems to have been lost in his long period of unconsciousness, some part of his health that will not be recovered. All day he's been listless, slow-eyed, and quiet. They say that Haim's status is "declining" and even though what they really mean is "descending" or "deteriorating," it

does seem to be the act of declining, of not wanting, of withholding, that tells you that you're finally in the woods you will not find your way out of. Charlie has still not answered her phone, as if she can sense how serious things still are.

There is one last hope, which they told me about at Haim's "Care Conference" this morning. Haim's name has finally come up for a late-stage clinical trial that I signed us up for a week after his diagnosis. It is at the National Institute of Health in Bethesda, Maryland, and would require us moving back to the States and living there for a few months. The doctors and nurse and technician representatives and hospital social worker were all sitting there at the conference table looking at me after they explained how long the trial would take, sitting there look-ing at me like I should not want to do it, should just want to take Haim home to die. They'd already given me the "goal checklist" of medi-cal things that needed to happen before I could take him home, if I wanted to take him home. But how can you want to do that? Maybe I've missed some important step or process in being the parent of a ter-minal child, maybe that's what everyone else would have been going through during the holiday, but how can you want to do that? How can you ever hear someone tell you that there is something you might be able to do to have even one more week with this kid, this little boy whom you have fed, whose shit and vomit and tears and sounds of delight and mysterious, incommunicable discomfort you have known, whose impossibly rapid growth you have measured against your leg, whose tiny hands have grabbed desperately at your face and then your knee and then the bottom of your shirt wanting always to tell you some-thing, to show you something, to call you to the things of this world— how can you have woken to the sound of his laughter, his crying, even sometimes just his labored breathing and not want to do it, to pump whatever vile thing into his changed body in the selfish hope of having even one more day, one more hour full of that unrelenting life?

Though, of course, you know you are selling him out, that this is a selfishness. You are thrust into the parsing of guilt, afraid of echoing to yourself the thought that you "just want it to be over" because you do want your son's suffering to be over but you also want him back, specifically you want him back the way he was, and both things are impossible, and both ways is the only way you want it.

"At some point," the doctor said, sighing and leaning forward. "You may feel treatment is going to do more pain and discomfort than good."

Like I don't know that. Like that isn't the great suspicion about all the treatment he's had since diagnosis.

We decided to let Haim decide. The care team followed me back to his room and explained everything as best they could, looking uncomfortable. I told him to think about it, and to talk to me when he felt like he was ready to.

In the meantime I signed the DNR form and also instructed them to rush the scans that are required to start the NIH trial. These are the little games you play with yourself, every bet hedged. Because Charlie wasn't there, the nurse had to sign as my witness.

Haim is sleeping now, worn out from all the scans. When the nurses laid him out on the white tablet that would convey him into the MRI machine, the technician cut in over the speaker to say that he should try to keep as still as possible and Haim laughed, once, mirthlessly, almost a bark. The technician looked confused.

The last procedure he had to go through was a physical evaluation by a neurological specialist. We hadn't met this particular doctor before because she mostly evaluated children for brain surgery. Uncharacteristically, Haim was talkative with her as she went through the little reflex and movement tests with him, his little voice sounding strange and fragile in the overly lit examination room.

"So you just work with children with brain problems every day?" Haim said, struggling with the "j" of "just" until it came out with a *sh*-ing sound.

The doctor, who was a tired woman with dry, wiry brown hair, gave a wan smile.

"Yes," she said. "More or less. I usually try to see what all's going on between the brain and the body so that the children I treat can have the best surgery possible."

"But not me," Haim said.

"Well," the doctor said, glancing up at me. "I'm trying to help the doctors you might go to see at another hospital understand what exactly is happening with your brain."

"With my brain and the tumor," Haim said.

The doctor glanced at me again.

"Yes," she said. "With your brain and the tumor."

"Doesn't doing this all day make you sad?" he said.

The doctor sighed and smiled a little again.

"Of course, a little bit," she said. "But I've been doing this for a long time, and you just can't let it get to you. You have to focus on the boy," she said, squeezing his knee, "and not the sickness."

"But it still makes you sad," he said.

"As much as it would anyone, I guess," the doctor said.

Haim was quiet for a while, not looking at anyone.

"How do you live with your sadness?" he said after a long time.

The doctor paused where she was standing and looked at Haim as if she were suddenly afraid of him, as if she'd just realized he was sitting there.

Now the nurse comes in and tells me that it's time, and I stand up and go to Haim to wake him up. Outside his windows, it is the middle of winter, gray snow against a washed-out night sky hung with thick clouds—a terrible season in which to be dying. Haim has

made me turn his bed sideways so he can look out the windows without craning his neck. I gently cup his face in my palms and straighten it out from where it has fallen to the side in sleep, because I don't want the first thing he sees on waking to be that failure of a dusk, the light not even gathering itself enough to be blue with the cold.

"Haim," I say gently, over and over again. "Haim buddy, wake up. It's time."

The PICU is quiet, as it sometimes gets when this happens, as if the broken vessels and infection and blood clots and confused platelets in the other critical patients can sense the sundering that is about to occur and grant their hosts these few minutes, if no more, of calm. Though this doesn't always happen, and may never happen, really.

My wife is not here, so she cannot see our little boy instruct his motorized wheelchair to take its place next to Ava's bed, cannot, along with me, fail to hear whatever it is that he says to her, though she is beyond response and understanding. My wife cannot then see Haim roll out of the room and take up his position against the corridor wall, across from the big window that looks into her room and that the doctors sometimes use to do rounds with their students without waking her.

He does not sleep or ask for anything, even though we are there for two hours. He only watches as Ava's mother kneels beside the bed and cries, one hand grasping hard the bottom of the lowered rail, the other holding Ava's, which sits limply on the cover. Finally the doctor comes in with two nurses and says something to Ava's mother and then she stands up and it is over, the monitors are turned off and the nurses begin disconnecting the many apparatus that have, until these few minutes, succeeded in keeping her alive.

Haim stays until long after, until Ava's mother and the doctors and nurses and even the covered body have passed by him.

He watches each one go and then continues to look in at the room, which looks strangely empty without the hospital bed, the several black screens still angled down to where it should be, blank faces turned to the absence, to air. Finally, he looks up at me and asks to help him get back to his room.

I think he's asleep, think he's been asleep for some time, his face turned slightly away, to the window with its vista of nothing, when he speaks, quietly, trying to stave off sleep.

"I just want to go home," he says slowly, barely getting it out. "Don't you?"

•

These things don't have a beginning, not really. One day you're at your son's soccer game in the park, you're sitting in the stands and the aluminum is cool beneath your thighs and the sun is high and beautiful, your wife is beside you, and the park's green, which has been divvied up by a long procession of pitches where other boys move and shout and leap, is laid out before you, and there is the white of the ball distantly arcing through everything, the flash of jerseys vibrant with color, and then you notice that your son is lagging behind, is wandering in the empty area near his own goal-keeper; you notice he's detached himself from the small knot of other boys around the ball, and you are about to call something out, afraid that he has become distracted, has lost interest in the game, and you are about to shout, to put your voice in there before the other boys notice, before your son can become embarrassed by his mistake, you are about to save him when you see that he is faltering, that his steps are uneasy, and then he is falling down even as you are rising, and he is rising slowly, pushing himself up from the ground as you step

down off the bleachers, and then he falls again, and cannot get up, and there is something obviously wrong and you are on the pitch, you are in the grass next to him, you are cupping your hands around the back of his little neck, and his eyes are rolling, unfocused, and he turns his head and vomits all over your hands.

This was in April. The September before, our family doctor had mentioned that there was a tracking problem developing, and encouraged us to schedule an appointment with an ophthalmologist, which we forgot to do. Around February, I'd seen Haim's eyes shake back and forth while he was watching TV, and Charlie and I agreed that it was odd and that if we saw it happen again, we'd take him to a doctor. These were the only things that could have told us.

We went from the soccer game to the ER. They did some scans.

"The brain stem shows a large area of swelling," a short, olive-skinned doctor said. "We suspect a mass."

"What?" I said.

"We suspect a mass," he said.

I could only think of a Mass in church. I could see all of the petitioners, dressed in dark clothes, their pale, drawn faces.

"What?" I said.

•

The end, as it turns out, is lost in details. It's only a few blocks from the hospital to our flat, but they insisted we take an ambulance anyway.

I've got the whole living room set up, with the expensive bed and all the IVs and medicines. The mothers helped with this. I told them I would call and tell them when to come back. I've got the hospice nurse coming every day.

"As far as I can tell, we're three to five days out," was the way she, the hospice nurse, said it. This I guess she could tell from the bad headaches, the vomiting, the way Haim suddenly can barely move his limbs or his head, the way he can barely swallow. Just like that. Time seems completely beyond you, the traditional divisions (years, months, weeks, days, hours) unmoored from their natural scale inside you, turned into something different, one single period of hourless existence by the side of the hospital bed. It seems like that right up until it doesn't, right up until someone looks at you and says, "three to five days out."

"You think you're such a big perceptive writer-man," Charlie once screamed at me in an argument when we were young. "But you think a person is really just a body. That if you understand my body, then you understand me, then you love me. As if anyone's body is anything more than just an evolutionary mistake. As if the body doesn't persist of its own accord. A person's not a fucking body. A person's a person."

Haim doesn't sleep much, and when he does, he sweats and twitches. He's beyond speech now. His first night home he woke up screaming like someone was electrifying him, and trying to clutch at his head. I rushed to add the morphine to his cocktail of Ativan and Zofran like the hospice nurse said I could if he needed it, and he calmed down some. What's so palliative about this? I thought.

An hour ago one of the nurses from the PICU called and told me that Charlie had just called and left a message with one of the new nurses for her to tell me that she would be landing at Heathrow tomorrow, and would be at the hospital later tomorrow night. The nurse talking to me on the phone said that she was planning on telling Charlie when she got there where I was with Haim, if that was all right with me. The nurse said she'd tried to call Charlie back herself,

would've just told her where to go now, but they hadn't been able to find her number. I thanked her and hung up.

Haim has gotten worse all night. I've been sitting here watching his oxygen levels tick down steadily. I've been on the phone with our hospice nurse, who is across the city dealing with another emergency. I won't call Charlie. I won't tell her to hurry. She has finally won my silence. I have finally learned how not to speak.

At some point I must have dozed off because I wake up to a wet gurgling sound. There is a pale liquid, almost like pancake batter, spilling from Haim's mouth. He is choking on his own vomit, unable to turn his head to the side or sit up. Then I'm standing up and my hands are in his mouth, trying to clear it out, and then I am grabbing him, folding him forward, the vomit spilling onto his lap and there is the sound of his crazed choking for breath, and long tendrils of spit hanging down from his mouth and nose to the mess, and then he is breathing, breathing, collapsing back into a semirecumbent position, and there is the acidic waft of the bile cut with the rotten earthy scent of shit. When I lift up the covers I can see that Haim, in his panic, has soiled himself.

I am standing up, holding him, trying to carry him to the bath, the IV stands tugging along behind us as if being trailed across a wide sea. When I finally get him in the tub and disconnect all the attachments that I need to, I turn on the water and make sure to arrange his head on the lip so that it will be supported. I can see he is having trouble swallowing. He is breathing shallowly, but he will not or cannot open his eyes.

For just a second I straighten up and look back out toward the room, at what Charlie will see tomorrow, if this really is the end. The stained, empty medical bed. The plastic tentacles of the IVs hanging uselessly, disarrayed. The paper wrappers of wound dressing pads

scattered on the floor. She will come back, I know, and see me sitting here, waiting for her. She will walk in that door, and see the empty bed, the useless artifacts of so much medicine and look at me in confusion. She will look at me in those few seconds before she understands as if she is asking me a question, as if to say, *To what end have I brought this great love into the world?* And I will have to look up at her, open my mouth, and answer.

ACKNOWLEDGMENTS

Thank you to the Leah and Robert Hemenway Foundation for Derelict Writers, the Iowa Writers' Workshop, the Truman Capote Literary Trust, the John C. Schupes family, the Sewanee Writers' Conference, the University of Iowa, Baylor University, and the Linda Bruckheimer family. Without their support this book would not have been possible.

Thank you to my teachers, especially Jim McPherson, ZZ Packer, Marilynne Robinson, and Allan Gurganus. Thank you to the poet Bill Patterson for putting the right books in my hand. Thank you to David Platt for taking me around the world, to Alexander Chee for showing me how to trace the line of beauty, and to Kevin Brockmeier for sending me into the next dimension. Thank you to Ethan Canin for being my guide and advocate. Thank you to Dr. David Johnson for helping me find my way home in the storm. Thank you above all to Lan Samantha Chang for giving me chance after chance, for being a tireless reader and dedicated teacher, and for giving so much of herself to her students. Thank you, Sam, for being a patient, kind, and honest mentor, and for being my friend.

Thank you to everyone at Sarabande Books, especially Sarah Gorham, Kristen Radtke, and Kirby Gann. Thank you to Marshall

Rake and Public-Library for their artistic wizardry in helping give this book its cover. Thank you to the editors and magazines who originally published these stories, especially Andrew Feld at *The Seattle Review*, Ronald Spatz at *Alaska Quarterly Review*, Alexis Schaitkin at *Meridian Literary Review*, and Speer Morgan at *The Missouri Review*. Thank you to Deb West, Jan Zenisek, and Connie Brothers at Iowa for all magic seen and unseen. Thank you to Dianna Vitanza and Greg Garrett at Baylor for your continued support.

Thank you to those friends who helped make this book possible for me, in ways both oblique and direct, especially Alan Heathcock, Rebecca Makkai, Rachel Bailin, Quinn Dreasler, Tawny Alvarez, Jodi Johnson, and Jensen Beach. Thank you to each of my classmates at the Iowa Writers' Workshop for their tolerance, help, patience, and kindness.

I wish there were a full enough way to thank Madhuri Vijay and Tara Atkinson, without whose care, love, and faith I (and these stories) would be lost at sea, but this will have to do: with every day of my grateful life, thank you, thank you, thank you.

Thank you to my mom and dad, for believing I could. Thank you to Bluma Hemenway for calling me to the joy of this world.

And finally, thank you to Marissa Hemenway, the love of my life, to whom I owe every word, heart, and hope in this book.

Carmen Maria Machado

Originally from Lexington, Kentucky, Arna Bontemps Hemenway's fiction has appeared in *A Public Space, FiveChapters, Ecotone, Alaska Quarterly Review, The Missouri Review, The Seattle Review, Meridian Literary Review,* and *Bat City Review,* and has been named a Notable/Distinguished Story of the Year in both the *Best American Short Stories* and *Best American Nonrequired Reading* anthologies. He has served as the Peter Taylor Scholar of Fiction Writing at the Sewanee Writers' Conference, and has been the recipient of fellowships from the Truman Capote Literary Trust and the John C. Schupes Foundation. He holds a Certificate of Modern Hebrew from the University of Haifa, Israel, and an MFA from the Iowa Writers' Workshop. Currently Hemenway lives in Waco, Texas, where he serves as Assistant Professor of English in Creative Writing at Baylor University.

Sarabande Books thanks you for the purchase of this book; we do hope you enjoy it! Founded in 1994 as an independent, nonprofit, literary press, Sarabande publishes poetry, short fiction, and literary nonfiction—genres increasingly neglected by commercial publishers. We are committed to producing beautiful, lasting editions that honor exceptional writing, and to keeping those books in print. If you're interested in further reading, take a moment to browse our website, www.sarabandebooks.org. There you'll find information about other titles; opportunities to contribute to the Sarabande mission; and an abundance of supporting materials including audio, video, a lively blog, and our Sarabande in Education program.